JAMES TAPPED H~~...~~
"UM, RAFE?"

Encizo turned and saw the armed men through the front window of the car. "Uh-oh."

Mazouzi was too busy yelling at his informant to realize they were in trouble. The keys were in the ignition so Encizo put the clutch to the floor, started the engine and got them in Reverse. He let out the clutch and took off with a squeal of tires, causing Mazouzi to curse.

"We have company," James snapped as he pulled out his Beretta.

The armed men, four in all, fired semiautomatic handguns, but Encizo had put enough distance between the Peugeot and them. One shot hit the corner of the windshield, though, and spider-webbed across the passenger side, blocking James' view.

As the Peugeot gained speed, James leaned out the window, leveling the pistol in his right hand on the nearest man, and squeezed off a double-tap, taking the intended target in the chest. But the jerky movement of the Peugeot pulled him back inside.

Encizo's face was screwed up in concentration as he maneuvered along the narrow street. At one point, he sideswiped a parked vehicle, leaving behind a large gouge with the echo of scraping fiberglass and metal.

"What are you *doing?*" Mazouzi demanded.

"Saving your ass," James replied. "I think."

DON PENDLETON'S

STONY

AMERICA'S ULTRA-COVERT INTELLIGENCE AGENCY

MAN®

CHOKE POINT

A GOLD EAGLE BOOK FROM

W**O**RLDWIDE®

TORONTO • NEW YORK • LONDON
AMSTERDAM • PARIS • SYDNEY • HAMBURG
STOCKHOLM • ATHENS • TOKYO • MILAN
MADRID • WARSAW • BUDAPEST • AUCKLAND

Recycling programs
for this product may
not exist in your area.

First edition December 2012

ISBN-13: 978-0-373-80436-8

CHOKE POINT

Special thanks and acknowledgment to
Matt Kozar for his contribution to this work.

Copyright © 2012 by Worldwide Library

Printed in U.S.A.

CHOKE POINT

CHAPTER ONE

Maryland

Senator Charlie Maser slowed as he approached the secondary road leading off the scenic byway that ran through Chesapeake country.

The dash clock on his luxury SUV read 2:52 a.m. and with only a sliver of a moon, Maser had almost missed the turn. He couldn't be late…not at this time and this place. He thought of the metal suitcase on the seat behind him—a suitcase that met the specifications he'd been given, down to the last detail—its contents worth a king's ransom.

Or at least the prize for a princess.

Charlie Maser's princess was a thirteen-year-old girl, a girl who may have been through things so horrible Maser couldn't even bring himself to imagine them. They were things the caller had told him *might* happen if Maser didn't cooperate, but he'd also been assured that so far they hadn't happened. Maser wasn't sure if he could believe his ears when he learned that his only daughter had fallen into the hands of a vile, disgusting lot of kidnappers who had been on a rampage for the past two months.

Only wild and vague rumors had reached his ears about this group—a conversation he'd overheard here, a secure email brief there—but Maser hadn't actually believed most of it. Well, he did now and he still couldn't come to terms with the fact that what had happened to Natalie—as what had happened to the young children, boys and girls, of a number of other politicians—probably could have been avoided if he'd been more diligent in finding the truth. There were lots of people he could've reached out to and gotten the full story: other senators, members of the house and even connections inside the FBI and CIA, as apparently there were transnational matters attached to these men.

None of it mattered now, though. All that mattered was getting his beautiful girl back into his arms safe and sound. He'd never let her go again.

Maser had received the ransom call just after a particularly grueling session on the senate floor, one item after another coming across the wire for him to vote yea or nay, more fat pieces of legislation that spent a lot of money and did next to nothing. Maser had considered not running for a second term just eighteen short months ago, but had changed his mind at the urging of his constituents, and the election coffers filled up in no time at all. Mostly they were donations from friends who owned multibillion-dollar companies, or the untapped wealth of special-interest groups from which he had to draw.

But per the kidnappers, the money riding in that metal case had to be his own and untraceable.

In retrospect, Maser didn't give a damn. If he had to cough up twenty million dollars instead of five hundred thousand he would've raided every fund he had and then knocked off a bank for the balance. Not this time, though, and Maser was smart enough to know the kidnappers hadn't asked for a large ransom because they didn't want him to draw any attention.

Maser's wife had thrown a screaming fit when he refused to let her go, trying to explain to her that following the instructions of the men who had their little girl was paramount to getting her back in one piece. That's the advice a friend at the Federal Law Enforcement Training Center—FLETC—had given him after Maser told him he was seeing some possible new legislation and needed the perspective of someone with practical law-enforcement experience. Maser didn't think he'd raised any suspicions with his questions, and politely thanked the guy before hanging up and going straight to the bank.

Their personal financial officer had thought maybe Maser had gone stark-raving mad, wanting to withdraw that sum of money, but Maser had cited a campaign emergency for which he would spend his own money and then expense it back to the campaign later. Luckily, that had seemed to dispel any other questions and quashed further curiosity. The fact he was running in an election at the present had actually proved a saving grace.

Now he had his money and he'd followed the instructions to the letter, making the drive from Washington, D.C., along the northerly route that took him around the bay and back down to Maryland via Interstate 95 to State Road 213 in Maryland, eventually winding up in Chesapeake country. Maser wondered why the scenic route instead of cutting across the Chesapeake Bay Bridge but he hadn't asked. Again, the advice he'd received was to follow instructions to the letter and don't argue with or agitate the kidnappers.

The golden rule: the caller was in charge.

Maser slowed and as he turned on the side road he noticed a fog had started to materialize. He slowed some more, looking at the clock again and sighing to ease the tension. At this rate he'd be right on time by proceeding two and a quarter miles to a green camping sign that marked an access road. Off the road from there and another mile until he reached an old, gray pickup truck. The clock turned to 2:59 a.m. when the pickup truck came into view just ahead through the increasing layer of fog.

Shit, it was like being on an English moor or something.

Maser wondered how much he'd been directed here for the purpose of isolation and how much for dramatic effect. Whatever the reasons, the kidnappers were sending a message that they knew what they were doing. The caller had been explicit as to the consequences if Maser deviated from the prescribed schedule or disobeyed in any manner. Maser had listened carefully, writing down every detail and the times he'd done things, keeping practically an hour-by-hour journal of his every move. He wanted to make sure that if this didn't pan out and he lost his own life, the cops would at least be able to follow his trail.

Maser rolled up on the truck, stopped and flashed his high beams once before killing the engine.

He'd rolled his window down a space to make sure he could hear any verbal instructions he might receive—not that he'd been specifically told to do so but it made good sense. A minute ticked by, two minutes—then five minutes turned into ten minutes. Finally, Maser began to wonder if he'd made some sort of mistake and he could feel the pang of a panic attack in his chest. His breathing started to shorten and he willed his shaking hands to steady.

Had he fucked it up? Had he made a mistake, missed some direction and forfeited the life of his sweet and beloved Natalie?

The shadow falling across the passenger-side window caused him to jump, and he turned to see the outline of a human figure there. Then his driver's-side door opened and he was yanked out of the car and thrown to the ground. The air burst from him on impact, his lungs burning with the sudden exertion. He realized now why he'd been instructed not to wear a seat belt for the entire journey. Maser could remember how he thought that had been kind of dumb because he might've been pulled over, but then he knew that by starting off at night it would've been next to impossible for a police officer to see he wasn't restrained.

Besides, what cop in his right mind would ticket a U.S. senator?

Maser felt the hard, unyielding form of something metal pressed to his head, something that could only have been the muzzle of a gun, and a foot planted on the small of his back.

"Arms out to your side," a muted voice ordered. It sounded like a mask covered the speaker's mouth. "Where's the money?"

"Backseat, like instructed," Maser replied. He probably hadn't really had to add that last part, but he didn't figure pointing out that he'd followed instructions could hurt him any at this point.

He heard the rear door of the SUV open, then some rustling and finally the unmistakable clicks of the latches being disengaged. For a long time he didn't hear anything, but his captor eventually spoke again.

"You think you're smart?" the guy asked.

"What do you mean?"

"Answer the fucking question, asshole!" another voice said, this one also muffled by something.

"I—I guess so," Maser said.

"You guess so?" the first speaker replied in a mocking tone.

Or was it mocking? Hard to tell, with the man's voice being obscured by whatever the man wore over his mouth.

"We got us an indecisive politician," the second voice remarked, and this time Maser could detect just a hint of an accent—something maybe Scottish or British. "That's sad. That's very, *very* sad. A scathing indictment of our leadership today in Washington."

Scathing indictment of leadership in Washington? What the hell kind of kidnappers were these? The first one sounded like a miscreant but the other had a touch of class, as if he'd been educated abroad. That would probably fit with the accent. Maser continued to mark each one of these facts in his memory, bound to write down the details if he walked away from this alive. Being he was lying here in the middle of nowhere on his belly, helpless and unarmed, with no one in law enforcement having any knowledge of where he was or what he was doing, Maser entertained a notion for the first time that he might not walk away from this situation alive.

The thought prompted him to boldness. "Why don't we cut the bullshit? You guys have your money so give me my daughter. We'll walk away and nothing more will be said."

"Shut up!" the first kidnapper sneered. "Just shut up. We give the orders around here, not you."

Maser thought about pressing the point but decided it wouldn't do a bit of good. These two weren't to be reasoned with, and in all likelihood they were just lackeys anyway. Pickup men weren't uncommon in well-organized kidnapping rings, another fact Maser's friend at FLETC had turned him on to, which probably meant there were limits and boundaries. So far, things weren't going well but they weren't exactly going bad.

Best to just play along with the game.

The European-sounding one knelt by him and Maser thought he detected the odor of cigarettes. "My partner asked if you were smart because you've done some really stupid things."

"Like what?" Maser asked.

"Like coming out here by yourself," the man replied

easily. "Like being a good little boy and doing exactly what you were told. You see, the main problem you have is that now we got the money, we have no real incentive to keep you alive."

Now it was going to go badly and Charlie Maser knew he couldn't do a damn thing about it.

"What's more," the man continued, "you didn't get proof of life. We know you called some people, that you got advice. Too bad you listened to your friend in the FLETC because the truth is you got *bad* advice. You should've gotten proof of life before you agreed to pay a ransom."

"Let my little girl go, you bastards!" Maser pleaded, his voice cracking as he whimpered, "I don't give a damn what you do to me, but please let my girl go."

"Shh, don't cry," the man said and then he burst into a fit of laughter. He rose and said, "We're not going to kill pretty little Natalie. She's much, much too valuable alive and well. But we can't really have you running around blabbing this business to anybody."

"Wh-what are you saying?"

"I'm saying you've outlived your usefulness, Senator. It's time for you to step down."

"Yeah," the slimy one interjected. "Time to go visit that big capitol building in the sky."

"You can kill me if you want," Maser said, "but it won't do you any good because someone will be looking for me. And when they find me, they're going to figure out who did it, and then your days of kidnapping will be over."

"I highly doubt it," the one with the accent replied.

And those were the last words Senator Charlie Maser ever heard.

CHAPTER TWO

Stony Man Farm, Virginia

"The murder of a federal official, even a U.S. senator, is typically assigned to a task force within the Justice Department," the President of the United States told Harold Brognola. "Not this time."

"I understand, Mr. President."

"I've instructed the deputy director of the FBI to transit information directly to your office by secure channels. Use that information to find out who's behind the murder of Senator Maser and why."

"And once we know?"

"Do whatever has to be done," the President replied in a tone as cold as Brognola had ever heard him use.

"I understand, sir."

"Good luck, Hal."

"Thank you, Mr. President." The line went dead before Brognola could even wish the President a good evening, which he obviously wasn't going to have no matter what Brognola said.

The Stony Man chief hung up and sighed, barely able to quell the burning in his throat. The twinge from the esophageal spasms, a chronic condition he'd suffered for more years than he could remember, reminded him of the roll of antacids in his desk drawer. He popped three and then made a note in the digital recorder he'd received from his wife for Christmas to buy more.

That task complete, Brognola proceeded from his office to the electric tram in the basement. A hundred yards later, he stepped from the small transporter into the Operations Center of the Annex, a subterranean facility that housed the most modern electronic and human resources ever assembled for one purpose: combating America's enemies. There were hundreds...nay, *thousands* of those who wished to do harm to the United States. Every single day of his life since agreeing to serve as top dog for the special-operations group code-named Stony Man, Brognola had worked tirelessly to protect the liberty and peace of his nation.

Stony Man did one thing and it did it very well, better than probably any other agency of its kind. But Brognola wasn't so deluded to believe it was his consummate leadership skills that had held it together. Not even close. Stony Man worked for three reasons: brilliant and dedicated support staff, the finest and bravest collection of fighting men ever assembled and the ideals born from the devotion and loyalty of the man named Mack Bolan.

It was Bolan's War Everlasting against the scourge of organized crime, and subsequently the forces of terrorism, that spurred the founding of Stony Man. It was Brognola's relationship with Bolan—one that had started as a federal cop in pursuit of the fugitive nut-job calling himself the Executioner—that had led to his appointment as head of Stony Man. Today, Brognola was privileged to call Mack Bolan a lifelong friend. If Brognola had his way, he would have tracked Bolan down at that moment and sought his advice.

Brognola didn't know exactly what the President's intelligence people were sending, but he did have some inkling of where it was going. Maybe it was something that had to be handled by one of the teams, although he couldn't imagine how the murder of one senator could spark a concern for international security. Still, Stony Man served at the pleasure of the Oval Office and whoever happened to occupy it, and Brognola could count on one hand the number of times the subject had been broached about whether it was necessary for their operations to continue. Every time, nixing the program had ultimately been shot down as a way to turn a very good idea into a potentially bad one. To Brognola's knowledge, every President who'd entertained the idea had never come to regret the decision to keep Stony Man going: it was *the* final option.

"Is that coffee fresh?" Brognola asked Barbara Price as he entered the conference room.

"It is," she said. "Would you like a cup?"

"Depends on who made it," he replied. "I'm not sure I could handle any of Kurtzman's rotgut right at the moment."

Price raised one of her beautiful eyebrows. "You're in luck, then. I made it."

Brognola nodded in gratitude and then helped himself to a large cup. "You alerted Able Team?"

"I did," Price said as she returned her attention to the built-in monitor in front of her, one of the many recessed into the massive conference-room table capable of seating a small army. In this case it was actually not an exaggeration. "I told them we'd be in touch as soon as we had some intelligence. And before you ask, Phoenix Force has been upgraded to standby."

Brognola mumbled a thanks as he sat with his cup. He rubbed at his eyes and said, "The President's intelligence reports from Justice should be coming through at any time.

I don't know the details yet, but obviously there's much more to this than a dead politician."

"Well, I thought I'd get a head start and had Bear pull Senator Maser's dossier."

"Items of interest, anything perhaps out of the ordinary?"

Price stared intently as she paged down the electronic file assembled by Stony Man's resident computer expert and cyber-team leader, Aaron Kurtzman. "Unremarkable, to be honest. Maser was born and raised in New Hampshire. Entered his first term in office after working his way from a junior position in sales and marketing, and ending as CEO of the Biddler and Holmes Corporation."

"What does that firm do?"

"What they *did*," Price replied. "Past tense. They went under about three years after Maser left."

"Maybe that's our angle," Brognola said. "It's possible he left them high and dry, and when the company went belly-up somebody went looking for payback."

Price shook her head. "That's what I thought at first but it doesn't fly. Maser left the company in the black, and actually it was extremely profitable. They went out of business due to poor investments and inadequate leadership, according to the financial statements and reports from independent audits conducted after Biddler and Holmes filed for bankruptcy."

She handed one of the data sheets on that particular event to Brognola so he could see for himself. "Okay, so he'd been gone and running for public office long after that so it's not likely anybody would have connected him to the company's demise."

Price nodded and then sat back in her chair and stretched. She continued, "His wife apparently comes

from a wealthy family, and they're the ones who originally backed his bid for a senate seat."

"So you figure whatever happened here has something
to do with the time frame after he entered public office."

"I think it's our best working theory, Hal."

"What about that? Has there been anything extraordi-
nary about his political career?"

"I'd say about average," she said. "He hasn't been particularly supportive of any key legislative issues, at least
none that would be hot topics of debate, so it's likely he
didn't draw the attention of any crazies. I—"

A loud ping echoed through the conference room and
Price turned her attention to her display terminal. She
mumbled something Brognola didn't make out and then
began tapping at the keys with the dexterity of an experienced typist, her unfashionably short fingernails producing
clacking noises. When she'd finished typing, the display
at the end of the conference room lit up to show a report
stamped with "confidential" and bearing the seal of the
U.S. Department of Homeland Security.

"It's the reports from Justice that the President promised."

Brognola squinted at the initial breakdown of the information contained within the file and then referred to a
closer copy available on the terminal screen he raised out
of the table. He perused the table of contents before finally
pointing to one particular item: *Associative Criminal Activities, Nonredacted.*

"There," Brognola said. "Pull up item fourteen, please."

Price did and Brognola began to read in earnest. With
every report of this kind, particularly if it contained sensitive or classified material, two official versions were
typically circulated. To those outside the intelligence communities, there were redacted, abridged or even omitted

pieces of data categorized by the Justice Department and National Security Agency with the remainder being labeled sensitive but classified, or just controlled unclassified information, which was typically reserved for official use only.

The material remaining was then considered either classified, secret or top secret and it was into one of these three categories that the kind of material Brognola now read typically fell. As the Stony Man chief absorbed the information he began to understand why such damning information wouldn't be for dissemination to the public, or even to most individuals who didn't possess a security clearance for it.

"Holy mother of—" Brognola began.

"My sentiments exactly," Price interjected.

"Get Lyons on the phone. Immediately."

WHEN CARL "Ironman" Lyons got the page from Stony Man to be on the alert, he was in the middle of climbing the Grand Tetons.

A particularly long and grueling mission that had taken him and his two compatriots into the heart of Iran, ending in a scrap from which Phoenix Force had come running to bail them out, had left the Able Team leader tired and ready for some vacation. The past three weeks had been a good rest—they'd gone to Florida for the first week, the second week Lyons had gone to northern Minnesota by himself on a fishing trip, and this week he'd reunited with his teammates, Hermann Schwarz and Rosario Blancanales, for a sprightly few days of fun and camping in the Rocky Mountains.

While Grand Teton National Park provided an excellent environment for these activities, Lyons had always been much more of an outdoorsman than his two companions, so they had opted not to join him for this climb. Instead, they stayed at the campsite to drink beers and talk of whatever exploits regarding the female species came to mind, half of them probably fiction.

Lyons had just pulled himself up and over a huge rock, swinging his muscled legs into an anchoring position and getting his angle before negotiating it with the rest of his body. Lyons stopped to mop sweat from his brow with a bandanna he'd secured around his neck and tucked into the neoprene shirt he wore. He surveyed the shimmering horizon, realizing it was just about time to think about going back. He'd promised his friends he'd return before dark and if he didn't make good on it, chances were they would get concerned and come looking for him.

The vibration of his secured satellite data phone, the invention of Kurtzman's electronics team, signaled for his attention. He snatched it from his belt and barked, "Go for Lyons."

"Carl, it's Barb. Are you with the others?"

"Not at present. What's up?"

"We just received an intelligence report compiled from several multijurisdictional investigations conducted into the death of New Hampshire Senator Charlie Maser."

"And?"

"We're sending a chopper to get all three of you now," Price replied. "I'm afraid R and R is canceled."

"That doesn't sound good."

"It's not," Brognola's voice boomed in Lyons's ears. "We'll be able to better brief you on the details once you get here."

"We're coming to the Farm?"

"Yes, although it's entirely too lengthy and difficult to explain now," Price said. "Just get here as soon as you can."

"We're on our way," Lyons said and signed off with the standard catchphrase, "out here."

Lyons returned the phone to his belt, took a deep breath and sighed. He'd hoped for another couple of days to recuperate but he could tell just from the tension in the voices of Price and Brognola that something had gone very wrong. Lyons couldn't even recall having heard the name Charlie Maser before, not that he kept a running tally on every elected official in Wonderland. For sure, there were some who were much more visible than others and needed to get some attention from Stony Man Farm, in Lyons's humble opinion. But it wasn't really in his job description to make those kinds of determinations—he preferred to be pointed at the threat and let loose to deal with it.

The hit-and-git mentality defined the collective psyche of Able Team. They were America's urban commandos, three berserkers trained to bring justice by fire to American streets and keep its citizens safe. This mode of operation was not only the one that Lyons preferred, but also the one in which he felt most comfortable. Lyons wondered if he'd ever live long enough to retire. What the hell would he do with his life when he didn't have something desperate to pursue, some terrorist or crime lord to take down?

He'd only completed about a third of the distance to the camp before he heard the *whip-whap* of chopper blades, spotting the light from the setting sun reflecting in redorange tints off the body of the helicopter before the whole shape came into view. The chopper dipped low and Lyons saw the familiar form of Blancanales as he reached out and gestured to some point nearby, probably a clearing beyond a copse of trees. Lyons waved his understanding and then broke into a jog so they wouldn't have long to wait for him.

Within a few minutes he emerged from the line of evergreen trees to find the chopper waiting for him. It was the dead of summer but even the nighttime air was significantly cool. The rotor wash whipped at Lyons's blond hair, which had started to become increasingly tinged with hints of gray over the years—probably a bit prematurely given the nature of his job—although not anywhere near the blanched white of Rosario Blancanales.

Blancanales, a husky man with muscular forearms and dark eyes, smiled at his friend and offered Lyons a hand. The Able Team leader nodded his thanks as he gripped his friend's hand and hopped aboard a chopper belonging to the U.S. Forest Service. In a moment, the blades increased in pitch and the chopper lifted smoothly from the green-brown terrain of Jackson Hole Valley.

Seated on a bench with his back to the rear wall of the fuselage was the other Able Team member. Hermann Schwarz was not only the team's resident electronics and computer expert, a talent that had earned him the "Gadgets" nickname, but he also possessed a wicked sense of humor. Schwarz was actually one of the most fearless men Lyons had ever met, not reticent to start cutting up even in the middle of a firefight. He was wiry but strong, not scrawny in the least, with wavy brown hair and a thick mustache.

"How was your stroll?" he asked Lyons over the thunderous noise of the chopper.

"I wasn't strolling," Lyons replied. "I was climbing."

"You're one of those mountaineering snobs, aren't you?" Schwarz deadpanned.

"You should try it sometime. It's good exercise."

"I don't mind fresh air. I just prefer the finer things in life."

"Such as?" Blancanales asked, unable to resist bantering with his two friends.

"Swimming pools surrounded by beautiful women sunning themselves in bathing suits."

Lyons shook his head and jerked a thumb at Schwarz. "You believe this guy? Surrounded by all of this natural beauty and he's pining away for a Marriott."

"It's sad," Blancanales said with a mock despondence. "He never wants to rough it."

"Any hotel that doesn't carry your bags in for you is roughing it," Schwarz replied.

"Pathetic," Carl Lyons said. "Simply pathetic."

"WE'VE UNCOVERED a horrific situation," Barbara Price announced.

"Barb's correct," Brognola said. "I don't think we've ever seen anything quite this bad before. Not on our own turf."

"What the hell's going on?" Lyons asked.

"Senator Maser was being extorted for a ransom payment to free his daughter," Price began. "Near as we can gather, his daughter had been kidnapped by parties unknown, who then contacted Maser and demanded a half-million dollars."

Schwarz let go with a whistle. "Holy cripes. So he delivered the money and you think the kidnappers killed him."

"It's not clear what happened since there was really no evidence in the area where Maser's body was found," Brognola replied.

"Local police are convinced Maser was killed somewhere else and dumped in a shallow marsh site near one of the many coves in Chesapeake country," Price continued. "Apparently, a duck hunter spotted his body and called police, who in turn called the FBI when they discovered the deceased was a U.S. senator.

"There isn't much physical evidence but the police eventually found Senator Maser's abandoned vehicle off a secondary road. There were tracks but nothing distinctive enough to allow them to make a positive identification. It's believed the vehicle was a pickup truck and that's where Maser had gone to make the exchange. Rain was apparently the chief culprit in dispersing any other hard physical evidence the police might have collected."

"So what's all the excitement?" Blancanales asked easily.

"We've discovered that Senator Maser isn't the first one to have been the victim of this kind of thing," Brognola said. "Although this is the first death that's resulted from it."

"You mean there have been other politicians whose kids got snapped?"

Price nodded with a frown. "Unfortunately, yes. But apparently authorities were never alerted because the kidnappers always returned the kids unharmed. The kid would get snatched, the kidnappers would call with a ransom, the official would cough up the money and the kid would make it home in one piece."

"Exactly how many kids are we talking here?" Blancanales asked, shifting in his chair uneasily.

Price looked at Brognola, who nodded, and they could see her swallow hard before she exchanged glances in turn with each of them. Finally she replied, "Hundreds."

CHAPTER THREE

"What?" Lyons stiffened in his chair. "How the hell could that be?"

"Easy, Ironman," Blancanales said, putting a friendly but firm hand on his friend's shoulder. "Let's hear this out before we start jumping to conclusions."

Lyons looked hard at Blancanales at first, but then his expression cooled some and he relaxed in his seat.

"Go on, Barb," Blancanales urged.

"There's no question this organization has been operating for some time," Price said. "They've built a reputation as a secret society, dubbed by many of their victims as the Red Brood."

"That's a lovely name," Schwarz said with a snort.

"Do we know any more than that?" Lyons asked.

It was Brognola who replied. "We do. And that's why we've called you back here. We believe there's a better than off chance the group that hit Maser is just part of a larger organization, a slaver outfit that's been kidnapping kids all over the country. Boys, girls, blacks, whites, Hispanics…the list is nearly endless."

"And they've chosen to expose themselves now?"

"It looks like these operators actually ended up stepping outside of the parameters of their original orders," Price said. "We think they got greedy and stole the money. What they didn't count on was that Senator Maser kept a journal of everything he did—the phone calls and the money and the drive they took him on. Local authorities found the journal he left behind in his SUV. They believe, although can't prove, that the location of the vehicle is likely where he was killed."

"So where do we start?" Blancanales asked.

"Charlie Maser had a close friend, Congressman Thomas Acres of Florida," Price replied. "Nine hours ago, Acres got a call at his private residence outside of Georgetown and was told his son had been taken from the private school he attends. They gave Acres instructions to put together a half-million-dollar ransom and told him they would contact him with delivery instructions."

"How did they make the connection?" Schwarz asked.

"The FBI has had a wiretap on Acres for some days," Price said. "Completely coincidental but as soon as they heard this they contacted their highers, who immediately flagged it and in turn routed it to the investigative team assigned to Maser's case."

"Your mission is to follow Acres to the delivery point and attempt to apprehend the kidnappers," Brognola said.

"And if they won't come quietly?"

"Terminate with extreme prejudice."

Lyons nodded. "Now *that* I can understand."

IT TOOK THE THREE MEN of Able Team less than a minute to figure out that Thomas Acres, Republican congressman from the great state of Florida, was being tailed.

According to Stony Man's intelligence, the route the kidnappers gave Acres was identical to the one Maser had driven—a fact that had come straight from the deceased senator's journal—although the destination turned out to be quite different. Instead of turning south once in Maryland and following the Chesapeake Bay route, Acres had been instructed to head straight into the heart of downtown Baltimore.

They were in a late-model Dodge Charger, just one of the many vehicles in the Stony Man fleet, with untraceable Washington plates. Any cops who ran those plates would be politely informed that, while domestic, they belonged to the U.S. Diplomatic Corps and as such the occupants of the vehicle were immune from detainment or search. It wasn't an uncommon thing in this part of the country, especially so close to the nation's capital, and was typically enough to send the police off to look for juicier prey.

The tail on Acres turned out to be a Chevy van with New York plates. Blancanales had suggested contacting Stony Man to run the vehicle registration but Lyons dismissed the idea.

"Better to stay back and see where this goes," Lyons said as he withdrew the Colt Anaconda from shoulder leather and double-checked the load.

While his partners chose semiautomatics, Lyons preferred a wheel gun. He had plenty of experience with semiautos and no problem using them in a pinch, but in the end he felt more at home with the knockdown power of the .44 Magnum loads. John "Cowboy" Kissinger, resident gunsmith for the entire Stony Man arsenal, had once asked Lyons to try a .44 Desert Eagle, the Executioner's preferred heavy-duty pistol, but Lyons ultimately dismissed the idea for his trusted Anaconda. In earlier days Lyons had often carried the .357 Colt Python, but he realized eventually the necessity of an upgrade. It suited him, frankly, and Carl Lyons would never apologize for carrying whatever firearms seemed most comfortable to him. The sleek weapon's stainless finish glinted in the overhead lights of the highway as Lyons holstered his weapon.

Blancanales had opted for a P-239 chambered for .357

Magnum. The SIG-Sauer sported a 7-round detachable box magazine and a muzzle velocity of more than 400 meters per second. In the hands of Rosario Blancanales, the weapon meant death for whatever target he aimed at.

The arsenal was rounded out with a Beretta 92F. Designated the M-9 by the U.S. military when adopted as its official sidearm, the 92F chambered 9 mm Parabellum rounds custom-loaded for the pistol in 158-grain SJHP, the hottest load Kissinger would permit for the weapon. While the pistol had been known to endure up to 185-grain loads without jams or misfeeds, Kissinger had insisted the lower grain was more effective for the semijacketed hollow points. Schwarz would not dispute it, having seen the pistol perform fantastically in the field time and again.

"You realize," Blancanales said as he signaled and changed lanes to maintain flank on the driver's side of the van tailing Acres, "that we have no idea if these are just observers or the actual kidnappers."

"Doesn't really matter," Lyons countered. "The fact is we have orders to either take them alive or take them out."

"I understand that." Blancanales maintained a suave, easy tone, leaving no doubt as to how he'd earned his "Politician" moniker. "All I'm saying is that this could go hard very fast if we jump the gun."

"Understood," Lyons said. "Let's just see where it goes before we start getting jumpy."

"Tell you what I'm getting," Schwarz interjected. "Hungry."

Blancanales's eyes flicked to the backseat. "How you can think of food at a time like this?"

"How you can you not?" Schwarz cracked.

"Heads up," Lyons interjected. "Acres is exiting the highway."

"Here?" Schwarz shook his head and referred to his

phone with a full, secure satellite uplink direct to the Farm's computer network. "This isn't anywhere near the stopping point."

"It's a rest area," Blancanales said as he had to negotiate two lanes of traffic in order to make the exit in time.

"Idiot," Lyons muttered. "The transcript from the wiretap indicated his instructions were not to stop anywhere."

"Maybe he has to take a leak," Schwarz observed.

"And risk his son's life?" Lyons shook his head. "I don't think so. Something's not right."

Acres cleared the exit, followed by the van with the Able Team vehicle bringing up the rear. Blancanales tried to drive as nonchalantly as possible, although he realized that was a bit of a misnomer. How the hell could anybody *drive* nonchalantly? There wasn't anything casual or nonchalant in what was going on here and it was pure stupidity to think for a moment that his driving could somehow make it appear differently.

Acres parked his car in one of the many open spots directly in front of the entrance to the restrooms. He remained in his car as the van rolled past him and swung into one of the spaces three down from Acres's spot.

"Damn, I was hoping they'd park closer," Blancanales said.

"It's going to look weird us pulling in well beyond either of those vehicles."

"I don't think we're going to get the chance," Lyons said.

To the surprise of all three Able Team warriors, Thomas Acres climbed out of his car, closed the door and turned toward the van as he pulled a pistol from a belt holster concealed beneath his suit coat. Muzzle-flashes cast his silhouette to Able Team as Acres fired round after round into the passenger-side window of the van. The glass shat-

tered under the impact of the first two rounds, and the third
rewarded Acres with a bloody spray. He'd hit someone.

"Shit!" Lyons whipped the Colt Anaconda into play.
"Get between them!"

Blancanales stepped on the gas and whipped the nose of
the sedan into a point between the two vehicles, although
much too late to reach Acres in time. The van's side door
slid aside to reveal a pair of tough-looking gunners clutching semiautomatic machine guns. The pair opened up simultaneously and red splotches exploded from Acres's
body in grisly, random patterns. The man jerked and
twisted under the impact and eventually succumbed to
the onslaught as his body collapsed to the dirty pavement.

Blancanales had his window down and extended his
arm, the SIG clutched steadily in his left fist. He squeezed
two rounds and then tromped the accelerator, causing the
sedan to ride onto the shallow curb. The shots weren't
meant to actually hit anything as much as to keep heads
down and buy Blancanales the time he needed to get their
vehicle out of the direct line of fire. The maneuver worked
well enough, taking the gunners by genuine surprise.

As soon as Blancanales reached the pinnacle of the turn,
he put the accelerator to the floor at the same time as he
hammered the brake pedal. The maneuver spun the rear
of the vehicle, churning grass and mud from the finely
manicured area designed to walk pets. As soon as the vehicle came to a stop, Lyons and Schwarz went EVA with
pistols at the ready.

The first of the two gunners appeared at the front of the
van and sprayed his enemy with autofire from his SMG.
Lyons and Schwarz ate dirt and Blancanales ducked to
avoid the rounds that went through the windshield and
caused a massive spiderweb to form across the safety glass.
Lyons, propped at the elbows, leveled the muzzle of the

Anaconda and squeezed the trigger. The weapon boomed twice, undoubtedly causing as much fear as physical damage in its reports. The first 300-grain SJHP connected with the gunner's chest, punched through his right lung and exited his back. The hit spun the man, causing Lyons's second round to graze his neck, but he twisted enough to reveal the gaping hole left in the wake of the first.

Schwarz spotted the second gunman rush toward Acres's sedan. The man whipped open the back door and retrieved a large silver suitcase that Schwarz knew would be filled with cash. Oh, no, that just won't do, Schwarz thought as he lined up his sights on the man and took a deep breath. He let half out, adjusted for lead time and then triggered three successive rounds. The first caught the man at a point just above his left knee and as he pitched forward a second round ripped through the side of his neck. The last passed a bit too high over his head but at enough of an angle it would easily clear any vehicles on the highway and likely come down harmlessly in the field beyond that point.

As Schwarz and Lyons climbed to their feet, the van engine roared to life and the vehicle began to back out of its space. Blancanales thought desperately for a moment before hammering the gearshift downward and tromping the accelerator. More mud and grass flew from under the wheels as the sedan sluiced forward and finally gained purchase on the broad sidewalk. The van was just at the point of stopping when Blancanales tapped the brakes and connected with the right fender. The maneuver spun the nose of the van into a 180-degree arc and smoke rose from the wheels as rubber burned on the asphalt.

Unfortunately for the driver, who could not keep his vehicle under control, the van's rear tires connected with the opposing curb. The impact jarred the van just enough that it listed sideways. Gravity and Archimedes's law of the lever did the rest, flipping the van onto its side and causing it to come to rest on the slight incline of the hill that separated the rest area from the interstate.

Blancanales jumped from the sedan and rushed the incapacitated enemy vehicle, SIG-Sauer held at the ready. The driver had wriggled his way through the open window just as Blancanales reached him. He saw the Able Team warrior's approach and clawed for shoulder leather but not before Blancanales managed to jump up and snatch hold of the back of the man's neck. Blancanales yanked as he came down and then twisted his body with enough strength to flip the man head over heels. The thug landed ass down on the pavement and air audibly whooshed from his lungs.

The gunman started to moan with pain, rolling onto his side and clutching his wounded tailbone with one hand. He froze and a horrified look crossed his face as Lyons and Schwarz arrived and both leveled their pistols at him.

Blancanales smiled at his friends as he holstered his weapon and then dusted his hands. With a flair for the dramatic, he put his hands on his hips. "Well, looks like I managed to keep *one* of them alive."

"Kiss ass," Schwarz replied.

AFTER VERIFYING Congressman Thomas Acres was in fact dead, Able Team got the hell away from the scene before police arrived.

They needed a chance to question their prisoner before turning him over to local authorities and it wouldn't do their timetable a lot of good to hang around and wait for the cops to arrive. And as Lyons had pointed out, he didn't want to have to explain the situation to the boys in blue any more than he wanted to involve Stony Man to clear them if they could avoid it. Instead, it made more sense to take their prize and run.

They took the money with them, as well, intent on making sure it was returned to the Acres family—it probably wouldn't save the life of Acres's son at this point anyway.

Able Team returned to the outskirts of Washington, D.C., and proceeded straight to a safe house the Farm kept in the area for just such occasions. En route to the place, Lyons placed a hurried call to Stony Man and requested Calvin James meet them there.

James had been the successor to Keio Ohara, one of Phoenix Force's original members, and had become a critical part of the field units. A former Navy SEAL and medical corpsman, James had grown up on the mean streets of Chicago and studied police science. He'd been working as a SWAT officer when chosen to join Phoenix Force. He was an expert in underwater operations, and as someone with advanced medical training, he'd become proficient with the chemical interrogation of prisoners.

Many liberals would have considered such techniques inhumane, but Calvin James felt the opposite for a number of reasons. He'd never administered the drug to anyone without a fundamental knowledge of their anatomy—it was critical to ensure the viability of a subject's cardiac and respiratory systems before proceeding with the tactics. Moreover, James considered chemical interrogation significantly more humane than some of those methods employed by CIA and others on the prisoners at Guantanamo Bay, for example. That boiled down to torture even in the most abject sense, but what James did—while most would fault him for it—could be implemented in a controlled environment.

"What are you going to use?" Blancanales asked with interest as he watched James draw five cc's into a syringe followed by ten from a different vial filled with something milky.

"It's a mixture of amobarbital and temazepam," James replied as he pushed the excess air from the syringe. "Either drug by itself isn't really effective in making a patient talk but the two together can be quite persuasive."

"I've heard most people can resist it," Schwarz said.

James smiled. "Introduction of barbiturates into the bloodstream is only part of the interrogation technique. The other two parts are psychological. In essence, you make the subject believe that they will not be able to lie under influence of the drug. Most people, even thugs like this, don't have the first clue about truth serum…other than what they see in the movies."

"You said there was a third part?" Lyons asked.

"Why, yes," James said, setting the syringe down and reaching into his bag of tricks to withdraw an electronic box with a digital display and a nylon cuff attached to it. "We make them think they're also hooked up to this."

"A polygraph?"

James shook his head. "No, actually this is just an automatic blood-pressure machine but we make the subject *think* it's a polygraph."

"Ah," Schwarz said with a nod. "Very crafty."

"I am, aren't I?" James quipped.

He retrieved the syringe, wheeled and went through the door into the adjoining room, where Able Team had secured their prisoner to a chair with plastic riot cuffs. They had also blindfolded him and put gun muffs over his ears to provide a disorienting effect. No point in the guy hearing or seeing anything going on around him. Night had now settled on the city, its lights twinkling in the distance through the one-way windows installed in the safe house that had the added feature of being bullet resistant.

James applied the cuff to the man's arm before ripping away the ear protection and blindfold. He sat on the edge of the table just in front of the chair and assumed the sternest expression he could muster. Actually, these kinds of head games were somewhat amusing and James didn't mind playing whatever role he had to in order to get the intelligence they needed.

"Good evening," he began. "That device attached to your arm is a highly specialized lie detector. In a moment, I'm going to turn it on and begin asking you questions. In addition to the polygraph, I'm also going to administer a drug designed to force you to answer my questions honestly. You would call this truth serum, but I would call it good insurance. You will not be able to resist and you will be forced to comply."

The prisoner had first worn a mask of hatred and defiance, but as James talked the man's expression changed to something much less confrontational. James could tell that he wouldn't have any trouble extracting the truth from the guy even if he didn't end up having to administer the drug. Of course, he'd loaded a very small dosage and he wouldn't administer more unless he perceived the subject wasn't telling the truth.

"Do you have any questions before we begin?"

"I... You mean you ain't going to torture me?"

"We could go that way, if you'd like," Lyons interjected.

James looked like he wanted to counter Lyons but then thought better of it. This was Able Team's show and he'd only been brought in to assist and observe. Lyons was still in charge and James wouldn't contradict his friend and colleague on any point unless it crossed the boundaries of his expertise.

"There's no need to torture you," James replied. "As I've already explained, this device and the pharmacological agents I'm about to administer are the only things required. That is, unless you'd like to skip that altogether and answer my questions without that intervention."

"I'm no squeal, blackie."

"Blackie?" Schwarz said. He looked at Blancanales. "What is this, the 1850s?"

Blancanales shrugged in way of reply.

"Okay," James said as he administered the injection in the man's vein. "Have it your way, asshole."

CHAPTER FOUR

Casablanca, Morocco

As soon as Abbas el Khalidi finished reading the secure message on his computer, he picked a massive paperweight off his desk and heaved it across the room with a disgusted sigh.

The tumult brought two guards and a secretary into the room, all three of whom he ordered to get out. They backed out of the room with conciliatory bows, diligent to close the doors after them. They had worked for Khalidi long enough to know that he wasn't to be meddled with in such a mood as this and would rue the day they ever departed from protocol. Khalidi had never been known as a lenient master—he was even less so when he discovered the Americans were screwing up his plans.

Again! he thought. Those sons of dogs are *always* trying to interfere!

Khalidi didn't need the money, but that was hardly the point. He'd grown up a poor man on the streets of this very city, earning his way from a part-time paper route to the head of a news agency that had become one of the most powerful and influential of its kind throughout the world. Syndicated in nearly seventy countries with more than one billion subscribers, Khalidi had made his mark on the international media.

His notoriety as a newsman who knew no equal—a

status that had earned him his "Prince Story" title—had also been the thing that allowed him to operate in relative privacy and seclusion. These were things Khalidi prized above all else, the power to determine his own destiny and control what information he would release to people while withholding the juiciest tidbits for himself.

Juicy and profitable, he reminded himself.

Still, it had not been about the money as much as the power. This was why his slaving operation in America had grown to such massive proportions, an operation so large that it defied conventional belief. Khalidi had his hand in a very big pie. The teen children of the American dogs were ripe for the harvest and brought a most handsome price on the international trafficking market. None of the so-called white slaves moved in or out of the country without Khalidi knowing about it. Sure, there were a few operations here and there, but they were mostly run by hoodlums and two-bit thugs. These individuals didn't believe in *quality* of their work while Khalidi staked his personal reputation on it. And what had it yielded him in return? Greedy underlings who were so incompetent it bordered on pulp fiction cliché. That kind of mishandling could also expose his newspaper corporation, *Abd-el-Aziz,* to inquiry by the local government as well as international law-enforcement scrutiny.

The half-million-dollar ransom he'd lost, thanks to the pair of bunglers he'd now ordered his American contacts to find and terminate, wasn't any issue. They still had the young girl and boy in question and his network could get them out of the country in the next twenty-four hours. Barring any other foul-ups, Khalidi figured this would blow over in a short time.

And what was the death of a congressman and a senator? The Americans didn't generally like their elected of-

ficials anyway, conspiring to assassinate or expose them
to public ridicule at every turn.

No, Khalidi figured he shouldn't let this bother him
in the least.

He decided to cheer up by having a long lunch at his favorite local establishment, a restaurant that served a fabu-
lous array of traditional Arabic dishes, before taking the
remainder of the afternoon off in favor of a long drive
along the Moroccan coastline. Khalidi navigated the A5
out of Casablanca, top down on his Mercedes Benz SL-
Class convertible, and drove south. He'd decided to change
his usual northern route—one that often ended with a trip
by ferry into the coastal Spanish city of Tarifa—in favor
of a trip to the Doukkala-Abda region capital city of Safi.
While most had a problem entering Spain from Morocco
due to the intense narcotics trafficking out of his country,
the real enterprise behind Khalidi's empire, the newspaper mogul moved with autonomy.

Any customs officials on either side who didn't want
to play ball, and they were few indeed, were usually dealt
with in swift and direct fashion.

Among the pottery markets in Safi, Khalidi would seek
out one of his regular women and lavish her with an evening of new clothes and fine dining. This did wonders in
warming up the young lady lucky enough to be chosen
and then Khalidi would satisfy all of his natural urges.
Unlike some of his less staid brothers, Khalidi maintained
his dedication to the pure faith and neither drank alcohol,
nor participated in the perversion of homosexuality. He
stuck to females and all of them seemed to understand the
relationship was one of convenience.

Abbas el Khalidi never let a woman get too close to
him. He had only ever heard from one woman again. She
had tried to set him up by claiming she was pregnant with

his child. Khalidi had only needed to make a phone call and the girl disappeared, never to be seen again. Khalidi smiled when he thought about that fact. Of course, he had verified with certainty that she was lying before he had disposed of her, since he never would have permitted harm to come to any of his children. However, this girl had been the only one to make such claims and whether by reputation or merely plain good fortune, Khalidi had never been extorted by another. It wasn't really all that surprising since rumors of such things at least got around in close-knit communities like those in Safi.

Lights came visible, twinkling as he rounded the road of the coastline heading into the city. Safi had a population of less than 300,000 people, while the surrounding communities brought the aggregate total to about a million, all told. Khalidi enjoyed this city above so many others in his country because most of it was sparsely populated, thereby setting the stage for a generally poor community that made most of its money from tourism and sales of handcrafted pottery. In fact, Moroccan pottery and rugs from this region were world-famous, although most of the citizens hardly made a dime from their sales.

Mostly, it was the exporters who took the majority of the profits, and they paid a significant kickback to Khalidi. Not only did pottery cross the transnational boundaries, but drugs did, as well. Yes, Khalidi had built his entire fortune on this type of trade. He had a mind for it, he happened to be very good at it, in fact, and he tended to hire others with a mind for it, as well.

It was dark by the time Khalidi reached the downtown area but still early enough that most shops in the marketplace were open, and people coming home from work crammed the streets shopping for food or other items. Tomorrow was Saturday—while most everyone would go to work it tended to be later in the day because of morning prayers and meetings at mosques throughout the entire Doukkala-Abda region. Khalidi roamed the streets for a while until he found a nicer shop filled with a variety of jewelry.

Khalidi stepped into the building and knew immediately the shopkeeper was doing well. The store had full electrical service and also ran an air-conditioning system. Khalidi nodded at the man and perused the shop for about an hour until he found the perfect trinket. He paid cash, adding a little extra when the proprietor moaned about his large family.

He could empathize with the old man, who did not look to be too healthy. After all, Khalidi had been there once—he was a businessman, not a monster.

Khalidi proceeded directly from the shop to the central marketplace, where he eventually found what he'd been searching for: Jasmina. Yes, a most excellent choice for the mood he was in. Not only was she a beautiful young woman, elegant and graceful for a commoner, but she'd also proved very accommodating to just about anything Khalidi suggested. Willing to please, with skin like bronzed gold and dark, sensuous eyes. He'd not seen her in some time but it only took a moment before the flicker of recognition crossed her features.

She greeted him with a warm smile, her dark eyes sparkling. The light reflected back from the rattan shades drawn over the marketplace that were strung between the buildings to provide shade to shoppers in the brutal heat of the day. They were doubly useful by reflecting the firelight in the evening and reducing the demands for electric lighting. In some parts of the city the local government would still cut power to conserve electricity.

"Good evening, Jasmina," Khalidi said.

She inclined her head in a bow of respect and replied, "Good evening, Master el Khalidi."

"Come, come, there is no reason to be so formal."

"If I seem too formal it is only out of respect and not to offend you."

"Are you not glad to see me?"

Jasmina nodded with enthusiasm. "I am most glad to see you, Abbas, but your arrival here and at this time took me unaware."

"Come and have dinner with me," Khalidi said, moving close and tracing the smooth skin of her arm with the back of his hand. "I am most interested to hear of how you have been."

"And perhaps interested in something else?" she asked with a knowing expression.

"Yes," he replied with a smile. "Perhaps, no…definitely more."

"It will be my pleasure to serve you, Abbas."

Khalidi couldn't ignore the sudden swell in his groin. "And mine."

Stony Man Farm, Virginia

"No question about it, lady and gents," Lyons told his colleagues at the Farm. "This is one nasty outfit we're dealing with. The intelligence you got from that Justice contact wasn't exaggerated by any stretch."

"How much information were you actually able to get from the subject Able Team took alive, Cal?" Price asked the Phoenix Force warrior.

"Quite a bit," James said. "It's all in the notes I took."

"Not to mention, most of it shouldn't be too difficult to verify," Blancanales added.

Brognola nodded. "Bear's working on it as we speak. I'd imagine he'll cook up a mess of data in no time at all."

The statement didn't surprise anyone in the War Room. Aaron "Bear" Kurtzman hadn't been defeated by the bullet in his spine that had confined him to a wheelchair. Lesser men would have suffered an irreversible psychological trauma, adopting an attitude of self-pity that would have crushed them for the duration of their lives. Not Kurtzman. The man's spirit was nearly as indomitable as his wrestlerlike upper body, a physique he kept in prime condition through exercise and, as his best friend and confidante Barbara Price had pointed out on more than one occasion, "sheer orneriness."

As soon as they had notified Stony Man of their intelligence gleaned from James's interrogation of the prisoner—intelligence that the outfit they were fighting actually operated on an international scale—Brognola had ordered a full-alert status for the remaining members of Phoenix Force. They now sat around the table, most in various modes of dress indicative of their actions.

Rafael Encizo had been volunteering for diver duties with the D.C. police in search of a missing mother who'd gone out for a jog as she did every night and never returned home. David McCarter and T. J. Hawkins had been at a local gun-club event, participating in a regional shooting match. Gary Manning had actually been the farthest one out, embarked on a hunting trip with some friends in the deep, rugged forests of the southern Smoky Mountains.

"What's the general lay of it, guv?" McCarter asked.

Brognola looked at Price. "Barb?"

Price, the Stony Man mission controller, nodded and began, "This group calls itself the Red Brood. At first we thought it was a kidnapping ring with a radical agenda aimed at internal politics. Now, with the information courtesy of the man Able Team managed to take alive, we're convinced there's a lot more to it than that."

"Isn't there always," Hawkins interjected in his Texan drawl.

"Look on the bright side," Schwarz said. "Job security."

"All right, pipe down and you might learn something," Brognola said.

As if on cue, Kurtzman entered the War Room and proceeded to his reserved spot. He brought up the computer projector—one much older than the modern facilities in the Operations Center of the Annex—beginning with the picture of a very young and handsome Arab in his twenties.

"I've run the gambit on the intelligence you brought back," Kurtzman told the group. "It's mind-boggling."

"That's serious coming from Bear," James said.

"All, I would like you to meet Abbas el Khalidi, head of the world news outfit known as *Abd-el-Aziz* and suspected by Interpol as one of the biggest drug kingpins ever."

"Drugs?" Lyons shook his head. "I thought we were dealing with a white-slaving group."

"We are," Brognola said. "But white slavery's just the tip of the iceberg. And it's plainly obvious the Red Brood is only a front for Abbas el Khalidi's international drug transshipping pipeline. Now that Aaron's identified Khalidi as a player in this, there's no doubt left in my mind that we've stumbled onto the real threat."

"Seems a little crazy that someone as high-profile as Khalidi would dabble in drug and human trafficking," Encizo said. "I don't get the connection."

"There's a big connection," Price said. "And don't assume that Khalidi's a mere dabbler in this thing. Abbas el Khalidi's been on our radar for quite some time, but up until this point we had no reason to think he posed any serious threat to the United States. Mostly he was suspected of trafficking narcotics out of his home country of Morocco and into areas all over Europe.

"Now it's plain to see he's up to much more than that, including using the Red Brood as a way to funnel additional funds to support his main effort."

"And he's decided to target American kids to do it," McCarter said.

His voice edged with quiet anger, Lyons said, "I think I speak for all of us when I say I want a shot at bringing this guy down. Hard."

"Well, you're going to get it," Price said. "Although I'm afraid you may not get a personal meeting. Khalidi is a known recluse and rarely travels outside of Morocco save for the occasional appearance at one of his satellite companies. He's been known to travel to Spain rather often, but in all cases he manages to operate outside the jurisdiction of either U.S. officials or Interpol."

"So he sticks to places where Americans are effectively persona non grata," Hawkins ventured.

"Correct."

"There are a number of allied intelligence organizations who've attempted to assassinate Khalidi," Brognola said, "but they've always somehow managed to miss the target. Mostly because he doesn't stay in one place long enough to establish a pattern, and his travels are typically kept secret until he's actually headed to his destination."

"And as previously indicated," Price said, "he's not posed any direct threat to this country. Now the situation has changed and we're pulling out all of the stops. We have the full cooperation and direction from the Oval Office to handle this in whatever manner we see fit. The assassination of American citizens and kidnapping of their children for the purpose of drug trafficking is unacceptable on any level."

"What's the game plan?" Manning asked, obviously itching to join the fight with the rest of them.

"We're sending Phoenix Force to Morocco. We've secured the cooperation of a local policeman there named Zafar Mazouzi. Officially, Mazouzi's an employee of the police force in Casablanca, headquarters for *Abd-el-Aziz,* but we have reliable intelligence he's been cooperating with Interpol officials to pass whatever information he can on Khalidi's activities. If he's managed to stay alive this long, we're confident he must know quite a bit of Khalidi's movements and should be an excellent liaison. Your mission, David, is to penetrate the country, disrupt Khalidi's pipeline operations between here and Morocco and, if the opportunity presents itself, terminate with extreme prejudice."

McCarter nodded, as did the other members of his team.

Price turned her attention to the trio of Able Team warriors anxious for their own assignment. "As for the three amigos, you'll board a commercial flight for Florida. Your first stop is Daytona Beach, the district in which Congressman Acres maintained his home and headquarters. Acres is our only lead, not to mention the prisoner you took is from that area. The fact they managed to snatch his son means they had him under observation for some time, knew where he lived and where he worked. That's the most logical starting point."

"What are we supposed to do once we find them?" Blancanales asked.

"Yeah, do we get to terminate with extreme prejudice, too?"

"Be careful what you wish for," Brognola said. "Your mission is to run this group to ground, closing the pipeline from this end while Phoenix Force handles the Moroccan angle. A two-headed spear is what we're shooting for."

"And we're not concerned so much about the drug trafficking into Europe," Price said. "That's of a secondary concern. The first is to cut the pipeline off at the knees, which will have the effect of not only securing the safety of the American public, but also of removing a major source of funding for Khalidi's organization. Any questions?"

The men shook their heads nearly in unison.

"Then let's get it done," Brognola said.

As the group broke up, the members of the team saying their respective goodbyes or taking a minute to engage each other in lighter conversation, Lyons took the opportunity to grab McCarter, who had stepped outside for a smoke.

"I know exactly what you're going to say," McCarter said to his friend. "You wish you were going with us."

"That's not exactly what I was going to say, although the sentiment's implied," the Able Team leader replied. "I just wanted to ask a favor."

"Shoot."

"If you get close enough to Khalidi, I mean *really* close, take him apart with your bare hands. Not for me—for these kids."

The fox-faced Briton favored Lyons with a genuine smile of glee. "You can bloody well count on it, mate."

CHAPTER FIVE

Daytona Beach, Florida

Although the light breeze blew across the sweat that furrowed Carl Lyons's brow, it didn't do much to cool him off.

July was one of the hottest and most humid months of the year in Florida, and even being from Los Angeles hadn't given Lyons any more reason to like the humidity. Blancanales, on the other hand, loved this kind of weather.

"Miserable and muggy," Lyons muttered as they stepped out of the air-conditioned airport and waited at the curb for their vehicle.

"I love it," Blancanales replied.

"Did either of you guys consider the fact we were here just a few weeks ago?" Schwarz asked.

"That's right," Blancanales said. "I'd completely forgotten."

"I'm still trying to forget," Lyons said.

None of the three men had completely shaken off their experiences in Tehran. Lyons had gone on record to say he'd thought their mission in the heart of Iran's capital had been one of the toughest Able Team had ever undertaken. The Islamic Republican Guard Corps, in concert with Muslim clerics of the Pasdaran, had attempted to overthrow members within their own government while secretly planning to launch attacks against American soil using a Hezbollah unit they were training in the jungles of South America. While Phoenix Force had been occupied trying to find the Hezbollah-IRGC contingent training camp where hostages of the U.S. Peace Corps were being held, Stony Man had elected, been forced really, to send Able Team to Tehran to extract an Iranian intelligence asset claiming to have information about the plot. It had turned into nothing short of a nightmare, resulting in the deaths of two CIA agents and a twenty-four-hour nightmare for Able Team as IRGC and police units hounded their every step.

Lyons shook it away just thinking about how close they'd really come on that one and said, "Let's leave that behind and talk about the current operation."

His two friends agreed with solemn nods just as their vehicle, a late-model SUV rental, rolled up.

As Schwarz tossed their shoulder bags into the rear compartment, Blancanales climbed behind the wheel with Lyons on shotgun. This tended to be their modus operandi on most missions, born more from habit than much else.

"I miss Black Betty," Blancanales said as he put the SUV in gear and eased from the curb.

"Me, too," Schwarz said.

"Well, unfortunately there wasn't enough time so we're just going to have to make do," Lyons said.

Their remembrance of Able Team's customized van, a vehicle out of which they normally operated, left each man nostalgic for that home away from home. Painted midnight-black with tinted bullet-resistant windows, Black Betty was an armored tactical and communications center that boasted a comprehensive armory and the latest in surveillance-countersurveillance equipment. Unfortunately, it wasn't practical to ship to every location within the U.S. Able Team might operate, and Stony Man therefore reserved it only for unique occasions or at the team's specific request.

"Where to first?" Blancanales asked.

"I'm guessing we need to start with Mrs. Acres," Lyons said. "She's going to be our first, best source of information."

The other two men agreed, reliant on the expertise of Lyons's former law-enforcement experience as an LAPD tactical sergeant. It was his position as a cop that had first brought Carl Lyons together with Mack Bolan, aka the Executioner, although at that time they had technically been on opposite sides of the law. Bolan's war against la Cosa Nostra had just begun and Lyons had been just one of the many cops with mixed feelings about the game. On one hand, he'd secretly enjoyed watching Bolan mix it up with the criminal empire of Julian DiGeorge and the Giordano family; on the other, he'd sworn an oath to uphold the law against anyone choosing to break it.

Only because of Bolan's first taking action to save the life of Lyons's family, and later opting to give Lyons his life back when he could well have snuffed it out in a moment of pitched battle, did Carl Lyons gain a high respect for the man called Mack Bolan. When he'd been offered a permanent position with Able Team as an urban commando against crime and terrorism on the streets of America, Lyons jumped at the opportunity to do something effective, where he could operate outside the official restrictions on law enforcement. Able Team worked because they could operate outside those restrictions while ensuring they didn't risk the safety of good, law-abiding American citizens.

In fact, they were there to protect the American way of life, and they had become legendary in that regard.

Mrs. Annette Acres lived in a two-story brownstone just

off the coastline. While it had a very traditional, almost Georgetown look to it, the decorative side of the heavy metal plates designed to protect the home from hurricanes and the inclement weather of Florida coastal living wasn't wholly indiscreet. Reinforced plating lined the waist-high walls topped with wrought iron and decorative lighting that ran the length of the property line.

Lyons could feel the additional plating beneath the wood steps ascending the massive front porch with vast columns that supported a second-floor balcony, which probably branched off the master bedroom. The death of Thomas Acres had been kept quiet through the vast connections of Stony Man, so the arrival of the trio at their home—carrying forged credentials identifying them as agents with the FBI—signaled not only their initial interrogation, but also the gruesome duty of making a death notification.

Lyons had done it before; hell, they all had at one time or another. That didn't make it any easier and he'd never really become used to it. Frankly, he'd never understood how those in the military could do such a job, their whole existence predicated on traveling around specific regions in the country to deliver the news to some family that their beloved soldier had been killed in action. Now *that* job would suck.

Lyons pressed the doorbell and the singsong chimes echoed from within.

Nearly a minute passed before a short Hispanic woman in a pastel dress with an apron answered. "May I help you?"

Lyons nodded as all three men produced their credentials, immediately getting into their respective roles. They had donned suits before leaving the airport and now stood there with stony expressions behind sunglasses.

"Yes, ma'am," Lyons said. "Agent Irons, Federal Bureau of Investigation. We'd like to speak with Annette Acres."

The young lady looked immediately distressed. "Um, well, of course…is she expecting you?"

"No."

"So you don't have an appointment," she said.

"I just said that," Lyons replied.

Blancanales stepped in at that point, reliably assured his friend's patience wouldn't hold out if the conversation took a worse turn. "Ma'am, we do need to speak with Mrs. Acres on an urgent matter and it's not one we'd like to discuss out in the open. Please let us in."

Blancanales offered a smile that most found utterly irresistible, and the maid returned the smile as she stepped aside to admit them. She closed the door and then led them to a broad, comfortable sitting room decorated in light woods and expensive works of metal. She waved them toward some chairs in the middle of the room and then went to retrieve the mistress of the house, but none of them helped themselves to a seat. They wouldn't be here long.

Annette Acres entered the room with all of the elegance and grace one might have expected of a congressman's wife. She had long blond hair and a petite figure. Her eyes were crystal-blue and while most might have called her expression "pinched," she possessed an obvious cultured beauty within the high cheekbones and thin lips that bore just a hint of lipstick. A pair of tight slacks and an elegant white blouse completed the ensemble.

"Good morning, gentlemen," she said as she entered, and all three Able Team men inclined their heads in recognition. "Please have a seat."

"Thank you, ma'am," Lyons said as he gestured toward a love seat. "But please, after you."

Mrs. Acres nodded and took a seat, and then Lyons

dropped into a wingback chair catercorner to her. Blanca-nales and Schwarz stood close by, hovering above Lyons like a pair of gargoyles over the entrance to a medieval church.

"Mrs. Acres, my name is Special Agent Irons," Lyons began. "These are agents Rose and Black. We're with the FBI."

For the first time since coming into the room, Annette Acres lost her composure a bit and worry immediately etched the otherwise flawless lines of that pretty face. "Oh, dear…this is about Tom, isn't it?"

Blancanales quietly asked, "What makes you think that?"

"What's happened to him?" she asked Lyons, ignoring Blancanales's question.

"Mrs. Acres, there's…well, there's no easy way to say it so I'll just say it. I'm very sorry to inform you that your husband is dead."

Her eyes crinkled at the corners at first and then abruptly she burst into tears and began to wail. The maid came running into the room and immediately put her arms around the grieving widow, attempting to shush her while gripping her shoulders in as comforting an embrace as her tiny arms could manage.

Lyons's heart lurched within him at first, but he stayed rock-steady, pressing his lips together. He wished he could say something more but what the hell would it be?

The men of Able Team fought their impatience and frustration as they waited for Annette Acres to get the majority of the initial shock out of her system. Once she'd calmed, the maid went and retrieved a handkerchief from the drawer of a nearby table and brought it to her mistress. She then nodded as Mrs. Acres told her to bring some tea for them and the number to John Jay's school.

"And John Jay is…" Lyons began.

"Our son."

Lyons nodded although he'd already known that. It had been somewhat of a test, a desire to see how much she actually knew about what had been happening. They had decided not to go into this with any assumptions, especially in believing that Annette Acres might not have had something to do with what was happening. By virtue of the fact she'd wanted to get in touch with her son at his Catholic school it was now apparent she had nothing to do with what had happened.

There was a remote chance she might have been playing it very clever, but Lyons's gut told him no. She hadn't been complicit in his kidnapping.

"Mrs. Acres, you should prepare yourself that your son will not likely be at school," Blancanales said. "In fact, he's been reported missing and his disappearance is related to Congressman Acres's death."

Lyons then went on to tell her the full story, excluding their direct involvement on the scene or anything related to the Red Brood and Abbas el Khalidi's involvement in human trafficking. There wasn't any reason in their minds to reveal more than absolutely necessary on the off chance someone close to the family was involved with the events of the past twenty-four hours. This was basically their only lead and they had agreed the wisest course of action would be to play things as close to the vest as possible until they had a more solid lead.

Frankly, this kind of thing didn't bode well with Lyons or his teammates. They were troubleshooters, after all, not investigators. They preferred to let Stony Man gather the intelligence and then take action on whatever the Farm had found. This time, however, they had to play the game with the hand they'd been dealt. Hell, it wasn't the first time they'd been called upon to improvise and it certainly wouldn't be the last.

"What are you saying?" the widow asked after Lyons had finished. "That my son, my only child, has been kidnapped?"

"Mrs. Acres, please understand we're doing everything we can to find your boy," Schwarz said. "We think the kidnappers killed your husband only with the intent of stealing the money."

"Is there anything you can tell us that could help us find him? Had your husband received any threats like this before? Anybody within his staff here locally, or any situations that come to mind that might clue us in to who's involved in this?"

For the next ten minutes they questioned Annette Acres as gently as possible, getting clarification wherever they needed it. Eventually, the trio silently agreed by an exchange of glances between each other that the most likely suspect was Acres's personal assistant, Genseric Biinadaz.

"I'm ashamed to admit it," Acres confessed. "Tom had hired Genseric about two years ago to show he wasn't prejudiced against Muslims or the Islamic faith. I was hesitant at first, but...I decided early on in our marriage that I would fully support Tom's political career and not attempt to unduly influence his decisions. He was always an excellent congressman. He really cared about his... about our country."

The talk brought back memories too difficult to ignore and the woman broke into a fresh wave of grief. When a few minutes passed, she sniffed and asked, "But you don't think Genseric has anything to do with this. Right?"

"We can't rule out anyone," Lyons said.

"We'll look into it," Blancanales added.

"Can you provide me with *any* information?" Mrs. Acres inquired.

"At present, that's all we really know," Lyons said. He stood as a signal to his teammates it was time to leave. "Someone will be in touch shortly to arrange the transport of your husband's body back to Florida."

Acres didn't rise but her eyes followed Lyons's movements. "Am I in danger, too, Mr. Irons? Please be honest."

"I don't believe so," Lyons said. "You have personal security?"

Acres shrugged. "Usually only when I go out. After Gabrielle Giffords was shot, Tom insisted on it."

"Perhaps it would be best to have them around the house for the next few days," Blancanales suggested. He tried to express as much comfort as he could. "Just to be safe."

"And, Mrs. Acres, I'm going to have to ask that you not discuss any of the details of this case with anyone for now," Lyons said.

"What? Not even our family?"

"Not anyone."

"Please understand, ma'am," Schwarz added. "It could compromise our investigation and potentially pose a danger to your son. If he's still alive, and we believe he is, the kidnappers may kill him if they feel threatened. As tough as it might be not to want to get involved, it's best to let us handle this for right now."

"And if you're contacted by the kidnappers," Lyons said, passing a card to her, "you should call that number immediately. Don't agree to anything, don't ask any questions and for God's sake *don't* tell them we've contacted you."

Annette Acres looked at first like she might argue but then finally tendered a slow, deliberate nod as she took the card, tossed it on the end table and then folded one hand over the other in her lap.

She clutched the handkerchief tighter. "I understand. Gentlemen, you will have my full cooperation. But please... *please* bring my John Jay back safely to me. I don't think I could stand to lose him, as well."

"We won't make promises we don't know we can keep, Mrs. Acres," Blancanales replied easily. "But I assure you we'll do everything in our power to find and return him safely."

Acres managed a smile. "Thank you, Agent Rose."

"We'll show ourselves out," Lyons said.

After expressing their condolences one last time, Able Team beat a hasty retreat from the house and returned to their SUV.

Lyons placed an immediate call to Stony Man as they made their way for Acres's downtown office.

"What do you need?" Price asked.

"Everything you can tell us about one Genseric Bii-nadaz," Lyons replied.

"You'll have it within twenty minutes," she said after a short pause, the clack of computer keys evident in the background. She was obviously messaging Kurtzman to get on it as they spoke. "What about Mrs. Acres? Anything there?"

"Nothing that spoke to us," Lyons said. "We agree she probably doesn't have anything to do with this. She cooperated fully with us and wasn't evasive at all during questioning. We also decided not to reveal more than we absolutely had to in case she lets something slip to the wrong people."

"What about others in the family who might be involved?"

"The maid is the only other one with regular access to

them," Lyons said. "You might want to check on her legal status, just in case, but she seems to be very protective of the family. I have serious doubts she's got anything to do with it."

"Tell them about the personal security," Schwarz reminded him.

"Yeah, that's right," Lyons said with a nod. "Apparently after Congresswoman Giffords was shot in Arizona, Acres decided the family needed to have a personal security team assigned to them whenever they were in public."

"I'm not sure what you're driving at," Price said.

"Well, we're kind of curious to know where that personal security was when John Jay Acres got snatched," Lyons said. "And how come there wasn't someone with Acres at all times in Washington. Seems to me that they'd have a better handle on what was going on if they were a professional team."

"Unless there's something to your theory about Biinadaz being on the Red Brood's payroll," Price replied. "It's not unlikely Acres might have turned selection of the security team over to his personal assistant."

"And so instead of selecting a legit outfit, Biinadaz saw an opportunity to get some of Khalidi's human traffickers inside for this job," Lyons said. "That's a very sharp observation, Barb."

"That's why they pay her the big bucks," Schwarz said close to Lyons's ear.

The Able Team leader feinted swatting his friend. "Would you knock it off?"

"What?" Price said.

"Nothing," Lyons replied. "Just Gadgets up to his usual antics."

"Ah, of course. We'll get the information to you shortly. You boys be careful."

"Yes, mother. Out here." Lyons broke the connection and said, "Okay. Let's go have a cozy little chat with Biinadaz."

CHAPTER SIX

Rabat, Morocco

Abbas el Khalidi studied the rocky cliff face off the shores of the capital city of Rabat. While the country of Morocco technically owned all coastal lands, Khalidi had wielded his influence to convince officials to lease this small area for "commercial purposes," which resulted in some additional revenue for the government. In return, nobody looked too carefully at what he was doing. In fact, the contract allowed for government inspectors to enter the property boundaries at any time and for any purpose, although there wasn't much to see. From this vantage point of the cliff face, which looked predominantly like sheer rock covered with lichen and coral pits, the remnant of volcanic seas long dead, the area appeared practically untouched.

At the base of those cliff faces, however, a much closer inspection would have revealed the three separate hidden entrances spaced approximately fifty yards apart. This area formed a sort of cove, although uninhabitable given the sharp, rocky outcroppings that met immediately with the waves of the Atlantic crashing against them. They formed a natural, inhospitable barrier, and it was for this very reason Khalidi had selected the site as the entrance to the underwater complex.

Natural underwater inlets had been dug into the cliffs, thousands of years of erosion slowly chipping away at their base, leaving behind the basalt and granophyres that formed natural and massive caves. From this infrastructure, Khalidi had hired some of the finest minds in archaeology and marine construction from points all over the world to design and build the infrastructure that supported the complex. Highly pressured iron and steel formed cross frames meshed by thick plates of Plexiglas eight inches thick and heat-sealed against the massive water pressure. Vents to the surface provided natural air movement, and a pair of twin, water-driven underwater turbines generated all of the electrical power needed by the vast complex.

Only one surface entrance existed, its location a secret to no more than the two dozen controllers and a complement of mercenary teams that resided on-site. From this base of operations, Khalidi moved the drugs, transporting them in specially designed flat-bottom launches capable of high speeds that moved the product from the shores to ships already in transit. A quick load of the hulls and in no time the ships were bound for ports throughout Europe and even a few distribution points in Southeast Asia.

On the other side, similar teams would off-load the drugs while still in international waters and the ships would arrive on schedule, if not ahead of time, carrying only the cargo on their manifests. It was this vast system of smuggling that had built wealth upon Khalidi's wealth. Every employee underwent a rigorous screening and once in they all knew there was only one way out besides accepting a generous retirement package: attrition in Abbas el Khalidi's outfit only occurred feetfirst. A few had managed to escape but none had ever been stupid enough to betray Khalidi—such an action would've spelled certain death.

Khalidi wasn't stupid enough to think he hadn't been extremely fortunate up until now. No operation of this nature lasted forever, so Khalidi proceeded under the guise of covert operations supposedly on behalf of the Moroccan government. Since there were officials within the highest halls of power who regularly consorted with Khalidi, some even on his payroll because public service in such a country didn't exactly pay well, most never questioned what they were doing or why. It was an arrangement Khalidi knew he couldn't maintain indefinitely, but to this point he'd operated with considerable autonomy.

When it all fell apart, he would simply pack up operations and move somewhere else.

Whatever happened, Khalidi had arranged things so that nothing could ever come back to him personally. He could continue to be "Prince Story" for his public, a champion and voice of the worldwide Muslim community, while reaping the profits that would keep his empire afloat probably long after he was dead. Khalidi considered that he would soon need to think of siring legitimate offspring, take a wife so that his children could carry on his legacy. The one thing Khalidi wanted more than all else was to secure the freedom of Islam: freedom from the enslavement of those who would use Islam for purely personal gain; freedom from the Westerners and their allies who wanted to destroy them; freedom from the oppression and poverty and hunger they had suffered in such places as Israel and Libya.

This...yes, *this* was the answer to his goals.

Khalidi took a deep breath and then turned and proceeded back to his Mercedes. He gunned the engine, put it in gear and then proceeded to the shore-top entrance accessible by a private road off the coastal highway just north of the city limits. He drove to the entrance, carved out of the living rock, presented his credentials to the guards with the pass-code of the day and then drove into the cavern that descended sharply to the underground parking area. From this point, it was a fifty-yard walk to a single-access lift that dropped nearly one hundred yards to the main area of the complex. The hiss of bubbles audible in the cavernous chamber dribbled toward the surface outside the main observation viewport, visible in the afternoon sun cutting through blue-green waters.

Occasionally, a shark would swim past, its outline faintly visible from the interior. Dolphins, sea porpoises and dozens of other species of marine life would shimmer along the perimeter of the viewport, occasionally stopping to look through the transparent barrier. They were clearly as curious with regard to the inhabitants within as their human counterparts were fascinated in return. The scene was so peaceful and surreal that Khalidi could not help but let it mesmerize him; this one thing had never really become workaday or routine to him.

The drug trafficker stopped to watch a school of remoras before turning and entering an antechamber that led to control center. Standing at one of the several computer terminals was Ebi Sahaf, Khalidi's chief adviser and director of operations within the complex. Sahaf had first come into Khalidi's employ as a technical adviser for *Abd-el-Aziz,* but Khalidi quickly realized the man's potential after seeing him in action. Not only had Sahaf demonstrated his technical competence and ability to command men, but he was also a devout Muslim and faithful ally. Sahaf took to his new assignment like a dog to a bone. He'd proved his worth and loyalty more times than Khalidi could recall, and in this regard had become one of his leader's closest friends and advisers.

"Good day, Abbas," Sahaf said without even turning from the screen.

Although Sahaf spoke flawless Arabic, the British accent was evident in his voice—a clear sign of his upbringing in New Delhi. It was at university in India where he'd learned his technical skills and demonstrated his uncanny skills as both an information systems and structural engineer. It was a rare and unusual combination of skills and Khalidi had always admired Sahaf for his talent.

"How did you know I was here?"

"The guards called ahead, as they are instructed to do whenever you show for a surprise visit."

"I would hardly call my visit a surprise," Khalidi said, raising one eyebrow.

Sahaf turned and smiled. "I merely jest with you, Abbas. Don't be so serious."

"I'm a serious man with serious issues on my mind."

"You speak of the recent incidents in America?"

Khalidi nodded and Sahaf looked around. The staff seemed otherwise preoccupied with their respective duties, but Sahaf, a man with a singularly suspicious nature, gestured for Khalidi to follow him to a location where they could talk privately. They entered a small conference room adjoining the complex and closed the heavy door behind them. They didn't have to worry about being overheard or eavesdropping. A personal team—handpicked from the mercenary force that oversaw security—swept twice a day for surveillance devices, every door in the complex provided a waterproof and practically soundproof seal.

Khalidi took a seat at the conference table while Sahaf proceeded to a nearby coffeepot and prepared two single-size servings of strong Turkish coffee. Once he'd returned to a seat next to Khalidi and served him the cup filled with the dark liquid, he scratched his eyebrow beneath the lens of his bifocals and groaned inwardly.

"I must admit that the news troubled me, as well, when I heard it," Sahaf said.

Khalidi took a sip from the cup before asking, "How did you find out?"

"During my regularly scheduled call with Ibn Sayed."

Khalidi had always found it difficult to understand why Sahaf refused to call Genseric Biinadaz by his given name instead of the more formal Genseric Biinadaz Ibn Sayed. Of course, Sahaf had very traditional views in this regard, but he also saw Biinadaz as somewhat of an outsider given his affiliation with the Taliban party in Afghanistan.

"Were these men he had selected responsible for this debacle?" Khalidi inquired. "The information I've been given was not detailed."

"It took some prodding but he was eventually forthcoming in saying these two men had gone rogue," Sahaf replied with a shrug. "As far as I know, they were men that he cleared. Whether he *knew* about their plans to operate outside of protocols could never be proved by mere inquiry alone. Older, more tried methods would be needed to ascertain the truth."

"It sounds as if you're inferring some impropriety on Genseric's part."

"Not inferring so much as suggesting we not dismiss the possibility," Sahaf said over his cup.

"Do you have any evidence?"

"I don't. This is why I've not made any *direct* accusation. You know me better than this, I think."

"Indeed I do."

Sahaf took another sip and sighed. He stared at the half-empty cup for a time before saying, "I've never made it any secret there is a level of distrust I have for Ibn Sayed."

"Yes," Khalidi replied, "and this is not the first time we've had a discussion like this. What troubles me is that every time we talk about it you never seem to give me reasons why."

"It's because I do not wish to insult you."

"It would take more than mere candor for me to think you were insulting me, old friend."

"Honesty, then."

"I want nothing less," Khalidi said. "I *deserve* nothing less. No?"

"No." Sahaf took a deep breath in an obvious gesture of collecting his thoughts. "To be plain, Abbas, I do not trust him because he has not made his goals known. I don't trust men who won't verbalize their personal or political ambitions. It speaks of a double-minded man who wavers when questioned about his past affiliations. Double-minded men can be very dangerous."

Khalidi didn't want to laugh but he couldn't help himself in the moment.

Sahaf glowered. "Why do you laugh at me?"

"I'm not laughing at you," Khalidi said. "I'm laughing because I seem to recall times when you first worked for me where you held your own ambitions rather close to the heart. I had to practically beat it out of you when looking for someone to oversee the construction of this facility. And now look!"

Khalidi rose and began to pace the small conference room, waving toward the invisible reinforcement beams high above them. "*Look* at what you've accomplished."

"With your guidance, Abbas." Sahaf sat back in the chair and folded his arms. "It was your vision that inspired me. I would have never achieved this on my own."

"Of course not!" Khalidi said. "But that is exactly my point. Don't you understand, Ebi? Don't you see what the completion of this facility means? We are on the precipice of a success for Islam unlike anything ever foretold. Others merely eke out a paltry living while they stand along the side of Allah's path and observe the trail of history.

But we—" he slapped the table for emphasis "—we are *making* history!"

Khalidi took his seat once more. "When we started this project more than three years ago, I know you couldn't ever see it coming to completion. And yet here you have attained an historical success. And yet you did not start off being plainly ambitious. Is it now so difficult to believe that success cannot be won by Genseric Biinadaz just because he is not forthright with alternative plans?"

"You are right, of course," Sahaf said immediately. "I ask your forgiveness for not seeing it."

"Ha! My friend, there is nothing to forgive," Khalidi protested. "And you must know that I have not completely discounted your concerns. I've found you to be insightful and prodigious, single-minded in your goals and utterly ingenious. You are a superb reader of others and I would be an ignorant fool not to heed your advice. Particularly on a matter as important as our operations in America."

"I appreciate your understanding, Abbas."

"So exactly what is it you propose should concern us about Genseric?"

"I have received some disturbing information about our trafficking operations," Sahaf said. "Information that indicates the Americans have agents now investigating the deaths of their officials, and the disappearance of the boy sired by this Congressman Acres."

"Are you saying that Genseric claims not to know the boy's whereabouts?"

"Yes."

"He's told you as much?"

"No, but one of my spies…" Sahaf's voice dropped off and he expressed horror at the slip.

Khalidi studied his friend with a cold, hard expression for a long moment and then slowly he smiled broadly.

"Ah, my dear Sahaf. Do not look so morose. Do you think I didn't know you would have spies among the ranks? I wouldn't doubt you have one or two even among my closest staff at *Abd-el-Aziz*. It's quite okay as long as they are not spying on *me*."

"Never, Abbas," Sahaf said, coming out of his chair. "*Never* would I allow anyone to spy on you. I would tear them apart. I would—"

"Relax, Sahaf," Khalidi said in a quiet but firm voice. "Please sit down."

The scientist took his seat, removed his glasses and mopped his upper lip with a pocket towel.

"Go on," Khalidi prompted.

"There are some indicators that Ibn Sayed has been slowly amassing a private army."

"Private army of what?"

"Islamic jihad fighters," Sahaf said, donning the glasses once more. "Most of them are said to be brothers who fought alongside him during Ibn Sayed's days in Afghanistan, although a few may have already been in America before he arrived."

"And what purpose is this army to serve?"

"That is not something I can know with any certainty yet. My spy has not yet been able to penetrate the inner circle. However, there are rumors that he is training this army at a secret camp somewhere in America. My concern is that he may try to overthrow our operations there, loosen our foothold and take over for himself."

"And why would he do this?" Khalidi replied. "We have been more than generous with him."

"I would completely agree but who knows what motivates the mind of some men. Ibn Sayed is a young man, trained to fight for the Islamic jihad from practically the day he was born. As a young warrior he will think like one. He's brash and impetuous, and these are not traits that have proved themselves to make for particularly stable representatives in the past. He may see it as duty to Allah, or perhaps even as the only way to prove his commitment to the fatwas."

"Bah! The days of Osama bin Laden's reign are now long dead, buried with the old man and his arcane ideas. Surely an intelligent man like Genseric Biinadaz can see there is a new Muslim order worth fighting for. There are too few left who believe in the old ways, and most of them that do are all but impotent."

"Maybe the old ways are dead but not necessarily in the minds of men like this one. Ibn Sayed is unpredictable, my friend—of this much I am certain. Whatever he plans to do with this army, if he *has* an army—"

"And you believe he does."

"Yes…I believe he does."

"You've given me a lot to consider, Sahaf." Khalidi paused to think about this new turn of developments.

Khalidi had no doubts that someone like Biinadaz, a man with such experience and talents, could build a private army and use it to steal Khalidi's operations. What didn't make sense was the motive. An Islamic jihadist swore an oath as a warrior to promote only Islam and the laws of Allah—there had never been room in that oath for personal gain. If Biinadaz had no intention of taking over the human-trafficking ring Khalidi had established in America, that could only mean he had other plans that would ultimately divert his attention from those operations.

In either case, the amassing of such an army would doubtless prove a distraction and put Khalidi to considerable inconvenience, not to mention the effect on their timetable. They were ready to begin peak transshipment operations to all of their locations in Europe. There had

never been a higher demand for the product Khalidi produced, neither in quantity nor in frequency of deliveries.
With that increase would come more profit and that could
only further the cause of the new Islamic regime Khalidi
envisioned for the world.

"I must admit, Sahaf, that you have now solicited my
complete attention," Khalidi said. "I would appreciate you
looking further into this matter and keeping me informed.
If Biinadaz is building his own fighting force then he has
done so without my permission. Such an activity could
threaten our plans on a number of levels, in spite of whatever his intentions may be."

"So I am to assume you're giving me a free hand in
this matter?"

Khalidi raised a hand of caution. "Only insofar as acquiring more proof of these allegations. When you've provided it, and only then, shall I decide what course of action
may be necessary. Nothing can interfere with our plans.
Nothing. Do I make myself clear?"

"Of course, Abbas."

"Excellent." Khalidi rose from his seat and Sahaf followed suit. "And now, if it is convenient, I'd like to accompany you on a tour of the remainder of the complex,
to see the areas that were not fully complete on my last
visit. And then, perhaps, a few days' leave on the surface.
Allah knows you have earned that much."

"With pleasure, Abbas," Ebi Sahaf replied.

CHAPTER SEVEN

Daytona Beach, Florida

Everything is proceeding on schedule, Genseric Biinadaz thought. We grow stronger each day and soon we'll be ready for phase two.

The thought brought a smile to his lips—the first time he could remember smiling in some time. Managing Abbas el Khalidi's entire human-trafficking location from this part of the country had been a greater task than Biinadaz anticipated when he'd first agreed to undertake it, but what he now heard was proof that his hard work had paid off.

Not that this was the moment to become overconfident.

Rumblings among the ring's network indicated that Khalidi could quite well be aware of Biinadaz's extracurricular activities with regards to the Red Brood. What a farce that was! It sounded more like a Communist organization than a front for one of the largest human-trafficking networks in the world. And right under the Americans' noses, which was why Biinadaz had opted to exploit it for his own purposes. Maybe Khalidi would have agreed with his idea and maybe not, but that didn't really matter now. Biinadaz had sunk too much time and was too deep into it to give it all up now.

He would *not* give up his efforts without a fight and whether the great Abbas el Khalidi thought so or not, Biinadaz had now procured an army large enough and well equipped enough to hold that position indefinitely. There were many additional supporters who were not Islamic jihad fighters or trained combatants, but they had thrown other resources into the mix that only strengthened Biinadaz's hold in America. This pooling of resources had proved beyond any doubt that Biinadaz's war against the Great Satan could and would be won—it was only a matter of time.

Of course, he would need to keep Abbas el Khalidi's hounds at bay until his plans came to fruition. Already there were rumors that Khalidi had more than one spy within the ranks, someone actually reporting to that incompetent waste of a Muslim, Ebi Sahaf. The guy was a lecher, a spineless automaton in Khalidi's employ who could do little more than criticize Biinadaz and speak out of turn on subjects that didn't concern him. At one point in their most recent conversation, Biinadaz had suggested that perhaps if Sahaf thought he could do better he should come to America and oversee these operations himself. That had brought about a bit of mad sputtering coupled with some lewd remarks, but nothing of substance to Biinadaz's satisfaction.

That was fine—he would deal with the likes of Sahaf soon enough once he had full control of the situation here.

Biinadaz checked his watch as he exited the highway and entered the city limits. He'd been impressed following his inspection of the small training camp set up in some privatized wetlands bordering a private wildlife park. The undeveloped area, protected by law, had been the result of legislation Biinadaz had encouraged Acres to get passed through his state connections. In so doing, Acres had facilitated the creation of a training site in an area marked as restricted for development or industrialization, putting it under protection of state and federal conservationists backed by government funds. This had become the training ground for a small pocket of personal enforcers under Biinadaz's command, while the remaining contingent was spread in small units throughout the greater Seattle area.

The concept proved doubly useful to Biinadaz's plans since these men also worked as protection of Khalidi's trafficking ring, code-named the Red Brood by certain officials within U.S. law enforcement. Biinadaz sneered at the very name. It sounded like a Communist group politicking liberal and progressive aims in Washington, D.C., and not like a trafficking ring. All it had done was draw attention to Khalidi's operation, demonstrating once more that the newspaper mogul didn't have the first clue how to build or train a proper fighting force.

Biinadaz arrived at his office nearly forty-five minutes late from lunch, although he had little to worry about. Acres was dead, which wasn't something Biinadaz had really hoped to happen this soon, but there wasn't much he could do about it now. The man's demise meant Biinadaz would have to push his plans forward by about a week. It wasn't an ideal situation but Biinadaz didn't see any reason to worry about it. A commander had to be ready to alter a battle plan at a moment's notice, something he'd learned well fighting the American military in his home of Afghanistan.

However, he had difficulty covering his surprise when he stopped at the desk of his receptionist and turned to see a muscular blond man in a suit waiting for him.

CARL LYONS SPOTTED Biinadaz as soon as the Afghan immigrant stepped off the elevator. He was tall—Lyons put him at about six feet—with dark eyes and close-shaven brown hair. Biinadaz had olive skin and eyes so dark they looked black. Even through the suit, Lyons could see the man moved with the ease of a practiced combatant, which came as no surprise given the history Kurtzman had sent Able Team on the man. Biinadaz was a refugee of the Afghan-U.S. war and, although he denied his involvement, Lyons knew much better. He knew a soldier with one look and while Biinadaz might have been comfortable in this role, he wasn't going to fool an experienced vet like Carl Lyons.

"Mr. Irons, is it?" Biinadaz said.

Lyons dropped the magazine on a low circular table, got to his feet and met the guy halfway between the couch and reception desk. He reached in his coat and withdrew the forged FBI credentials. "Actually, it's *Special Agent* Irons. FBI. I'd like to speak with you."

"Do you have a warrant, sir?"

"No." Lyons returned his credentials that Biinadaz had barely seemed to notice. "I wasn't aware I needed one to talk to you. We are, after all, on federal property and I'm a federal law officer."

"Quite. But you would at least need a letter of permission from Congressman Acres, which, of course, we both know will now be relatively impossible to attain."

Lyons didn't miss a beat. "Yes, sadly. My condolences."

"Of course," Biinadaz said. "I would suppose that's why you're here. Please…" He gestured toward the door to his office.

Biinadaz offered Lyons a drink after closing the door behind them but Lyons declined. Once they were comfortably seated, Biinadaz said, "I must ask you to forgive my forwardness, Agent Irons, but the congressman was very sensitive on such matters of legality and proper etiquette. I'm afraid maybe a little too much of that has rubbed off on me. I have, shall we say, attempted to be as fine a personal aide to Thomas Acres as possible."

"I understand," Lyons said. "But surely you're not surprised by the fact I'm here, Mr. Biinadaz. We're investigating the congressman's death, yes, but we're also very concerned about his son."

"To be sure, to be sure," Biinadaz said. "Do you believe he may yet be alive?"

"There's always hope."

"Of course. It's just that, well...after the kidnappers killed him in cold blood like that I'm very concerned they will have no further use for his John Jay and, ah, dispose of him in some horrible way."

"It's too early to jump to conclusions," Lyons said. "And as we pointed out to Mrs. Acres, with whom you've probably spoken by now, there's a chance that John Jay is much more valuable to them alive as long as there's a ransom that can be paid."

"What makes you think that I've spoken to Mrs. Acres yet?"

"Just an assumption."

"Aren't you trained never to assume anything?"

Lyons remained impassive.

"So I take it from what you've told me that the kidnappers didn't receive the money originally demanded."

Lyons shook his head. "Agents managed to recover it before that could happen. And we're now investigating a strong lead. We may even be on the doorstep of the perpetrators, which means there's still a chance to bring the boy back alive."

"Of course," Biinadaz said. He sat back in his chair and folded his arms. "How can I assist you?"

"Can you think of anyone who might have had the resources to carry this out? Someone who had recently threatened your boss? Maybe even someone on the inside, which is one possibility we've considered."

"And why have you considered that?"

"There was a security force hired to protect the congressman when he was in public, as well as his wife and son. I understand *you* were the one charged with securing these services."

"You would need to ask them those questions."

"Well, then, maybe you can tell me where this outfit was when it all went down? Why weren't they protecting Acres when he went to deliver the ransom? Why weren't they watching John Jay at school?"

"Again, I'm certain you would have to ask them."

"I think I will," Lyons said. "You got the name of this security firm?"

"You can obtain that information from my secretary," Biinadaz said. "I do not immediately recall the exact name of the firm."

"So is this a situation where you can't tell me what happened…or you won't?"

"I'm afraid I don't follow you, Agent Irons."

"You don't follow? Okay, follow this. It seems to me like a professional protection firm would be a bit more diligent in executing their duties. They're supposedly on the job and yet they've let their primary get killed and nearly robbed of a half-million dollars, not to mention the man's son is now in the hands of a dangerous trafficking ring."

"Trafficking ring? You mean like…*human* trafficking?"

"Yeah, a child-slavery outfit nicknamed the Red Brood. You heard of them?"

Biinadaz shook his head. "No, and I am certainly glad I have not. These sound like very dangerous and evil people."

Lyons narrowed his eyes a bit. When the hell was this miscreant going to come off the wide-eyed-horror routine? Biinadaz had been raised until his teen years in one of the most violent and unstable regions of the Middle East. Could he really be so egotistical to think that Lyons would believe that he was a cultured and refined moderate? This act only demonstrated Biinadaz was far more than he appeared. In addition to his radical views as an Islamic jihadist, Biinadaz had proved beyond any doubt his direct involvement in what had happened to Maser and Acres.

Lyons decided to play a hunch.

"Are you by any chance a Muslim, Mr. Biinadaz?"

"I am," Biinadaz said. "Why do you ask?"

"Just curious."

"If it weren't for our present circumstances, sir, I might find that question rather offensive. Are you profiling me, Agent Irons? Do you have some reason to suspect me? If so, then perhaps we should terminate this interview and I will contact my attorney. As well as your deputy director. I do believe we have his number in our records."

Lyons put up one hand and rose. "That's okay, no offense. I think we're done here. I was hoping you could provide me with some useful information but it's apparent you're as much in the dark as the rest of us."

"I hope you find and punish these animals," Biinadaz said as Lyons opened the door to leave.

The Able Team warrior turned back and looked Biinadaz in the eyes. With a frosty smile he replied, "You can rest assured I will, pal."

"So BIINADAZ already knew Acres was dead?" Schwarz asked.

Lyons nodded but didn't reply until the waitress in the luncheonette across from the federal office building finished pouring the coffee. A tall stack of half-eaten pancakes swimming in syrup sat on the plate in front of Lyons. Schwarz had already finished his food, but Blancanales was still busy mopping up ketchup with what remained of his bacon double cheeseburger. The lunch crowd had long been gone, leaving the three Able Team warriors to talk in peace.

"Yeah," Lyons continued when the waitress left. "*And* he knew about John Jay's kidnapping, the ransom. All of it."

"So he's in on it," Schwarz replied.

"Definitely."

"No chance Annette Acres told him?" Blancanales said around a mouthful of burger.

"No." Lyons shoved a heap of pancakes into his mouth, chewing furiously before saying, "In fact, he flat out denied he'd spoken with her."

"Seems like kind of a stupid move on this guy's part," Schwarz said.

"What do you mean?"

"Well, it just seems to me an experienced operator like Biinadaz would've been well in front of this whole thing. I mean, surely he knows Acres's death hasn't been publicized yet, not to mention that you let it slip we'd already spoken to his wife."

Lyons smiled. "I did that on purpose. It gave me an opening."

"So you think he's behind the kidnapping."

Lyons took a slug of the coffee to wash down the pancakes. "No, I think Biinadaz has a different game. I think Biinadaz could be running the whole show for Khalidi here."

"That would make sense," Blancanales interjected. "According to the Farm, Biinadaz wasn't exactly a saint. CIA and NSA both have case files on the guy. He's a known former jihad fighter for the Taliban. His father was a high-ranker inside the organization, in fact. He supposedly bought the farm while working with one Colonel Umar Abdalrahman."

"Why do I know that name?" Lyons inquired.

"Maybe because Abdalrahman headed up a splinter cell of members from the New Islamic Front. Mack went up against him sometime back after they tried to steal the Carnivore technology."

Lyons recalled that now. The NIF had teamed up with members of organized crime in the United States to seize control of the FBI's packet sniffer, a technology created for the sole purpose of spying on email communications between terror groups operating within the country and receiving assistance from outside forces. Bolan had blitzed the terrorists, NIF and Mafia alike, and brought the plotters to their knees. The operation had gone into the annals of Stony Man as one more example of Mack "the Bastard" Bolan's talents for waging war against the worst of the worst.

"So like father, like son, is what you're saying," Lyons said.

"Precisely."

"So why don't we just hit Biinadaz hard and fast," Schwarz asked, "instead of sitting here on our hands?"

"It's too soon to make a move, Gadgets," Lyons replied. "We go in there now, there's a good chance John Jay Acres won't survive. Not to mention I think Biinadaz is really just a small fish in a big pond."

"I think you're right, Ironman," Blancanales said after swallowing his last bite and wiping his greasy fingers on a napkin. "If Phoenix can get inside and do the job they were sent to do, that will cut off Biinadaz from resources he might otherwise have available."

"I don't know," Schwarz said. "I'm not so sure it's good us just waiting around here for something to happen."

"We're not going to sit around and wait for something to happen."

"Uh-oh," Blancanales said. He looked at Schwarz. "I've seen that look on him before."

"Yeah, ditto." Schwarz splayed his hands and told Lyons, "But you just got done saying that we have to wait to hit him."

"We do," Lyons said. He reached into his breast pocket and retrieved a business card. He slid it across the table so they could see it. "I got that from Biinadaz's secretary on my way out. It's the security firm he hired to protect Acres and his family."

Blancanales looked up from the card sharply. "He gave it to you voluntarily? You realize if we go knocking on their doors that Biinadaz might well be setting a trap for us."

Lyons nodded with a cheesy grin. "I sure hope so."

As soon as Irons left the office, Biinadaz attached an electronic countersurveillance jammer to the receiver of his phone. It would scramble any bugs or taps on the phone, whether in the room or directly on the lines, and prevent his conversation from being monitored. It was one significant contribution, the only one really, that Ebi Sahaf had made to their operations and Biinadaz had to admit it.

Biinadaz let it ring three times and then hung up. He checked his clock, waited forty-five seconds and then called back. A man with a gruff voice picked it up on the second ring, sounding as if he'd been half-asleep.

"Yes?"

"I was just paid a visit by an agent with the FBI," Biinadaz said. "He was asking questions about the security we provided for Acres."

"Who has he been talking to?"

"The congressman's wife, from what he told me."

"I warned you she was going to become a problem if Acres didn't survive," the man replied.

"You aren't to worry about the logistics," Biinadaz said. "I have direct access. Leave her to me. I was calling to advise you this agent will probably show up at your place of business soon."

"We'll deal with him," the man said. "What about the remainder of the details? Are you satisfied?"

Biinadaz thought about it only a moment before reclining in his chair and smiling. "Yes. In fact I'm quite pleased with the progress of my men."

"These are *our* men. You seem to forget sometimes that we are partners."

"If we're partners, then you should have listened to me and not hired those idiots to arrange for pick up of the ransom. The use of locals is never a good idea. I recall telling you that and you dismissing my ideas."

"Just as you dismissed my idea about the Acres bitch?"

Biinadaz sighed. "Perhaps we are both guilty of not being more cooperative and open-minded, my friend."

A long silence ensued. "Perhaps you are right. We are brothers in blood and Allah sets higher standards for his warriors."

"Indeed he does." Biinadaz returned his attention to the matter at hand. "I will take care of the Acres woman. Get her son into the pipeline as quickly as possible. Use the alternate routes. We do *not* want to risk him being spotted by someone who knows him."

"Understood."

"And what of this FBI agent?"

"You say he was alone?"

"Yes."

"I'm not sure he was with the FBI, then," the man said. "Sounds more like a freelancer, perhaps with one of their special-operations units. Delta Force, perhaps. He poses no real threat, I assure you. He will be dealt with in a most expeditious manner."

"Good." Genseric Biinadaz hung up with a faint smile. "Very good."

CHAPTER EIGHT

The office of Executive Security Services, Inc.—known by most throughout the greater Daytona Beach region as ESSI—turned out to be a single-story office building in the uptown area. Built less than two blocks off the beach and surrounded by mostly industrial or commercial structures, the place was neither large nor particularly fancy. Only a sign above a heavy metal door marked its brick facade and confirmed to Able Team that they had the right place.

"This is it," Blancanales said as he pulled to the curb of the drive directly across from the practically empty lot. "How do you want to handle this?"

"I prefer the direct approach," Lyons replied.

"Agreed," Schwarz added.

As Lyons climbed from the passenger side of the SUV a single round burned past his head, close enough that he could feel the heat of its passing. Even as he cursed and went flat to the pavement, it occurred to Lyons he would have never heard the whip-crack report from the high-powered rifle if the bullet had found its mark. Lyons snaked the Colt Anaconda from his shoulder rigging and swept the muzzle along the parapet of the building. He stopped when a protrusion of a human shape appeared atop the front sight post and squeezed the trigger twice.

The weapon boomed in the open air as the .44 Magnum rounds rocketed toward the target. The enemy had the advantage of high ground and Lyons's chances of hitting

anything were slim, but at least he could buy his compatriots time to go EVA and minimize the chance the sniper
might hit one of them.

Blancanales and Schwarz didn't need coaxing. The
pair bailed and drew their pistols simultaneously, Schwarz
going out the rear passenger door while Blancanales had
to navigate the slower route over the center console and
tumble out headfirst through Lyons's still-open door.

"I guess we're expected," Schwarz quipped.

Lyons flashed a deadpan expression. "You think?"

They all had pistols drawn and checked for additional
threats, which appeared in the form of a half-dozen Arab
types bearing weapons—most held only pistols but a couple toted SMGs.

Blancanales took one of them with a clean head shot,
his marksmanship the product of many years of experience coupled with training. The 185-grain .357 Magnum
slug from his SIG-Sauer P-239 hit the gunner square in
the forehead at an upward angle and blew off the top of his
skull. The man tumbled backward as his SMG flew from
lifeless fingers and clattered to the pavement.

The enemy opened up simultaneously in response,
flooding their position with a hailstorm of hot lead.
Schwarz fired off two shots and then duck-walked to the
back of the SUV. It was time to meet fire with fire. He
opened the rear hatch, keeping his head below the level
of the glass, and changed positions just in time to avoid
a sniper round that whizzed past and thwacked into the
building behind him. Dust and stone erupted from the impact but Schwarz didn't let it faze him—to freeze up now
would spell doom not only for him, but also for his friends.

Schwarz reached into the interior, wrapped his hands
around the carrying handle of an M-16A4/M-203 and came
away with the first of several assault rifles they'd prepared

prior to arrival. Lyons had guessed that in the likely event
Biinadaz happened to be in bed with Islamic terrorists
operating ESSI as a front company for their activities, he
would alert them to Lyons's inevitable arrival. What the
terrorists hadn't counted on was Able Team showing up
in full force and armed to the teeth.

Schwarz quickly checked the M-16A4 assault-rifle action before whistling at Blancanales. His friend turned and
reached one hand out to catch the rifle Schwarz tossed at
him. Blancanales took cover behind the fender of the SUV
and opened the front-loading breech of the M-203 grenade launcher even as Schwarz followed that throw with
the sliding of a satchel filled with 40 mm high-explosive
grenades. Blancanales reached into the satchel, slipped a
grenade into the muzzle and slammed the breech closed.

Cocked and locked, Blancanales waited for a lull in the
firing and then whirled to acquire a picture through the
leaf sight on the sniper above. Blancanales steadied the
stock against his shoulder and squeezed the trigger. The
weapon report equaled that of a 12-gauge shotgun as did
its kick. The grenade performed a shallow arc and struck
the parapet just forward of the sniper's last known position. Amidst the superheated gas and orange flame, Blancanales saw limbs blow in every direction.

"Scratch one sniper!" Blancanales reported.

Lyons already had the next weapon Schwarz passed
out, an SA80. The effort of the now dissolved Royal Small
Arms Factory in Great Britain, the SA80—also designated
as the Enfield L-85A1—chambered 5.56 × 45 mm NATO
rounds and boasted a muzzle velocity of nearly one thousand meters per second. While its early implementations
had been disastrous, this carbine version of the weapon
officially adopted by British forces in 1994 had proved re-

liable under the rigorous testing of John "Cowboy" Kissinger, Stony Man's resident armorer.

Lyons leveled the muzzle at the cluster of troops that had dispersed and tried to find cover in the open lot when they saw the effects of Blancanales's explosive handiwork. They had foolishly underestimated their opponents, figuring to have Able Team outgunned and outnumbered at least three to one, and in no way expecting the enemy to respond with combat weaponry of this order. Lyons made short work of them, pegging two with sustained but controlled bursts from the British assault rifle.

Schwarz joined Lyons's efforts a moment later, adding to the concert of destruction with an H&K ACR. Known as a caseless rifle, the ACR firing principle allowed Schwarz to deliver three rounds at a time without experiencing any recoil or rise in the muzzle. This increased hit probability threefold as well as increased the cyclic rate of fire to approximately 2,200 rounds per minute. Though the weapon was no longer in production, Stony Man had managed to acquire some of the unsold stock before H&K had fallen into receivership and been bought by British Aerospace. Kissinger had been acquiring the specially designed rounds from a defense contractor to the British government.

Schwarz dropped the remaining several fighters with steady 3-shot bursts from the highly accurate rifle. One took all three rounds to the abdomen, the 4.7 × 33 mm DE11 shells pumping through his belly and shredding his guts. Another fell with triple hits to the chest, and his partner tumbled to the pavement next to him a moment later as one round drilled through his shoulder and two more through the side of his neck while he raced for cover behind a vehicle.

The echo of gunfire eventually abated and left only the

sound of death in its wake. The ears of the three Able Team warriors rang as they waited for more enemies to appear but none greeted them. Blancanales watched the roof of the ESSI building for additional snipers while Lyons and Schwarz moved from cover and crossed the street in cover-and-maneuver formation, eventually setting up a perimeter security so Blancanales could join them.

When all three were up against the building, backs to the wall, they paused to discuss their options.

"Doesn't look like any more trouble," Schwarz said.

"For now," Blancanales said. "There could still be a contingent waiting inside."

"You think they could be holding any of the kids here?"

"It's possible," Lyons replied.

"Either way, we're going to have to check it out," Blancanales said.

"Then let's nut up and do it."

Lyons had the carbine so he opted to take point. Blancanales held position while Schwarz advanced on the door and opened it. Lyons snaked through the open doorway and into the dark, cool interior in a combat crouch. He took up position and cleared both ends of the hallway before gesturing his friends inside. They moved up the long corridor that lined the exterior wall of the building, their only illumination provided by sunlight streaming through small square windows near the high ceiling.

The corridor terminated at a bend. Lyons stopped and raised a hand for his friends to stop, checking to ensure they hadn't bunched up on his position. True to form, they were at least fifteen yards from each other and him, keeping spread so that any enemy contact in the narrow confines wouldn't likely result in an instantaneous slaughter. Lyons nodded in quick affirmation, grateful for teammates who were hard-core professionals.

Lyons peered around the corner and stopped, letting his eyes adjust to the gloom and reaching out with every combat sense. The tinnitus had finally subsided so he could hear only the stillness ahead—a little *too* still to suit Lyons, but he didn't see much choice. They had to search the rest of the building for additional terrorists, as well as collect any intelligence. It also occurred to him the cops would arrive before too long, a fact of which he was reminded at the faint sound of police sirens.

"Not much time," Blancanales whispered. "Boys in blue will be here soon."

"We can't leave without clearing the place," Lyons said. "Cops might wind up getting shot in the back if we split now."

"Not to mention us," Schwarz joked. "Rather not get killed today if you don't mind."

"Why?" Lyons inquired in a rare moment of levity. "Got a hot date or something?"

"Well, that waitress was kind of—"

"Shh!" Lyons held a finger to his lips.

At first, neither Blancanales nor Schwarz appeared to hear anything but soon enough they detected what their friend and leader had: footfalls that sounded as if they were closing rapidly. Lyons risked another glance around the corner and, in spite of himself, jumped as double doors at the end of the corridor burst open. Two teenagers, a boy and a girl, dashed up the hallway in his direction.

Lyons stepped into the open and the teenagers stopped short, the boy grabbing the girl's hand as they slid to halt on the linoleum. Both wore socks but no shoes, and their clothes were dirty and torn in multiple places. The girl let out a screech of sorts as they turned and started in the direction from which they'd come.

"Hold it!" Lyons shouted. "FBI!"

The kids continued running but they didn't seem to be moving quite as fast now.

"Really," Lyons exclaimed as he took off in pursuit, "we're the good guys! You're okay now! John Jay Acres? Natalie Maser?"

At the sounds of their names the two young people skidded to a halt again and turned to face Lyons. Their faces showed a mix of shock and mistrust and Lyons slung his weapon as he got closer before raising both arms. "It's okay. I won't hurt you. I'll just stand right here."

They looked a little more at ease as Lyons stopped a fair distance from them and smiled.

Blancanales and Schwarz followed close behind. The kids were unkempt, their faces dirty and tear-streaked; they were visibly shaken, their knees quivering and teeth chattering as the stress of the past few days began to wear off. They still didn't look relaxed, apparently ready to bolt at one wrong move from the three men, but Blancanales stepped a little closer and transformed into his Politician role.

"It's not a trick," he said in a gentle voice. He extended one hand slowly to John Jay, who had sort of stepped in front of his frightened female companion. "My name is Agent Rose. We've been looking for you two."

John Jay finally extended a hand and gave Blancanales a surprisingly firm shake.

"Quite the grip you got there, fella."

"Where's my dad? I want to see my mom and dad."

That wasn't exactly what any of the Able Team warriors had hoped to hear, but they knew now wasn't the time to broach the subject. There would be plenty of time to break the bad news later—better to deflect answering such questions for a more appropriate time. And they still hadn't cleared the entire building yet, which was only complicated by the fact the approaching sirens were now comparatively louder.

"We'll get you to your folks soon enough," Blancanales said. "Right now, we need to get you away from here and safe."

"Do you know if there are any more bad guys in the building?" Lyons asked.

They shook their heads but it was John Jay who said, "I don't think so."

"There were eight of them," Natalie Maser reported. "I've been here for a long time and I counted. I never saw more than eight and they were always the same men."

Schwarz did a quick mental count. "Six out front and one on the roof. That leaves a straggler."

"Who was the last one to leave you?" Blancanales asked.

"I think he was in charge," John Jay replied.

"Pol, get these two outside and turn them over to the cops," Lyons said. "We'll take care of sweeping the rest of the building. And for crap's sake, tell the cops we're in here so they don't blow us away on sight."

Blancanales nodded as he put a guiding arm around the shoulders of the two teens and steered them back up the hallway.

Once they were safely out of earshot, Lyons told Schwarz, "Okay, Gadgets. Let's go hunt us a rat."

IN SPITE OF A DILIGENT search, Lyons and Schwarz didn't turn up the missing terrorist.

After making a quick perusal of the computer system within the building and some wizardry by Schwarz getting all of the system data uploaded to Kurtzman for dissemination, the men of Able Team gave their report, albeit a somewhat abridged version, to the cops. They opted to go with intelligence that suggested the two kidnapped children might be at this location, which, as it turned out, was the case. However, telling such a story now meant there would no longer be any way of keeping the kidnappings or the deaths of the two congressional officials a secret.

Within a few hours the story would break across every news channel in the country.

"Oh, well," Brognola told the trio later. "There was no way we could keep it a secret forever."

The Able Team warriors had checked into a hotel near Daytona Beach International for a short respite. They had already cleaned up, performed maintenance on their weapons and were now in conference with Brognola and Price via a secure satellite uplink through a computer laptop. Lyons sat at the desk directly in front of the laptop and his two friends had taken up positions nearby so they could see the screen, as well.

"At least it confirms our theory Biinadaz is definitely a player in this," Lyons said.

"Did you go back to his office?" Price asked.

"Yeah," Lyons replied. "He was long gone."

"We think he probably split to rendezvous with whatever remains of his forces here," Blancanales added.

"What we can't figure out is how he did it," Schwarz remarked. "How the heck did this guy manage to get a fighting force of Islamic terrorists into Florida without someone taking notice?"

"We've got a theory about that," Price said. "We think Biinadaz has been using Khalidi's trafficking efforts to get Islamic extremists into the country, as well as kidnapped teenagers out."

"Well, that'd put him over good with the boss," Lyons said.

"We don't know if Khalidi knows about it or not."

"But if he does," Brognola added, "then it's safe to assume either he just learned of it or he's chosen to turn a blind eye."

"Either way, it's troubling because it means that Genseric Biinadaz has something else in mind," Price continued. "The Red Brood would be, for all intents and purposes, a means to a greater end. What has us worried is we don't know exactly what that end might be."

"It sounds as if Biinadaz could be planning a large-scale terrorist attack," Schwarz said.

"Okay, but where?" Blancanales asked. The veteran slid off the edge of the table on which he'd been perched and began to pace. "Let's suppose we're right and Biinadaz has some sort of army of Muslim fanatics. First, he'd find some place to train them without drawing attention. He'd need to feed them and equip them, and he'd need to be able to supply them with arms."

"Some of those resources might have come from Khalidi," Price suggested.

"Okay, sure." Blancanales crouched next to Lyons so he could talk face-to-face with Price. "But let's suppose that the whole reason for these last couple of kidnapping jobs was so that he could acquire the money he needed to keep operations going."

"You're suggesting he was running low on cash," Lyons interjected.

Blancanales nodded. "Right. So he goes out on his own and tries to grab up a little something extra."

"I still don't see how that's going to help us determine what he's up to," Brognola said.

"It doesn't necessarily tell us what he's up to, but it does tell us he plans to do it."

"And soon," Schwarz added.

Price said, "I think I'm beginning to see where you're

going with this. Biinadaz probably wasn't planning for any of this to happen the way it has. Twice he tried for some easy money and twice it blew up in his face. These events have probably forced him to step up his efforts, maybe even go forward with his plans sooner than he'd like."

"Right," Blancanales said. "But what this also tells us is that up until recently, Biinadaz had been able to support the operations on his own. Sure, he could use some of Khalidi's money and resources, but it couldn't have been his sole source of financial support. Those terrorists we went up against were well trained and prepared. The element of surprise was the *only* thing on our side today."

"Hear, hear," Lyons said. "If Lady Fortune hadn't been shining a bit of her luck on us, we could well have been outmatched."

"Not to mention those couldn't have been all there are to Biinadaz's forces here," Schwarz added.

"So my point is simply that Biinadaz would need considerable resources to train, feed and house a force of any significant size," Blancanales continued. "My guess is that money was being funneled to him through Acres's office. I'd like to suggest you start digging deep into his official records and see what you can come up with. A front organization, paper company, anything that might provide Biinadaz with a way to hide or even embezzle funds to support his organization."

"It's a great suggestion, Pol," Price said. "I can't believe we didn't think of it."

"Well, perhaps you'll remember that when it comes time for our raises," Schwarz cracked.

"Not likely," came Brognola's rebuttal.

"We'll start checking this out and get back to you as soon as we find something worthwhile," Price said. "In the meantime, you guys get a little rest."

"Your wish is our command, m'lady," Lyons said.

After they'd signed off, Schwarz remarked, "I'm hungry."

"You're always hungry," Rosario Blancanales replied.

"I'm a growing boy."

Lyons rubbed his eyes and groaned. "I need to find me some new friends."

CHAPTER NINE

Casablanca, Morocco

As the sun rose, a cool breeze swept the tarmac of Casablanca-Anfa Airport as the hydraulics of the cargo plane's rear hatch whined.

The ramp lowered to reveal the five warriors of Phoenix Force, all dressed in the cargo uniforms of Royal Air Maroc. Their trip had been anything but pleasant with Jack Grimaldi indisposed on a mission with Mack Bolan, and Charlie Mott presently unavailable due to previous commitments. Their only way in had been through civilian transport, as they'd posed as cargo handlers for RAM, the flag carrier airline of Morocco. The transportation had been arranged through Stony Man's contacts, but that hadn't done much to improve David McCarter's mood.

It was times like these when he realized how much he took for granted traveling in the style and comfort of the "corporate jet" with Grimaldi at the stick.

As if reading McCarter's thoughts, T. J. Hawkins stretched and groaned. "I think the knots on my muscles have knots."

"Yeah, that trip sucked," Manning added.

"Shape it up, mates," McCarter said. "I think that's our man."

He inclined his head toward a tall man with graying hair. He had a thin nose, deep inset eyes of brown and a dark complexion. While he was clearly a Moroccan native, he was unusually built, with broad shoulders and a slight paunch. In some respects, he reminded McCarter of Rosario Blancanales, although the build was where the similarities ended. Beyond that, something deep and intensely dark seemed to occupy those stony features, a grimness that bore out a rough history of experiences.

As soon as the group got close, the man stepped forward and extended a hand to McCarter. "Mr. Brown, I presume?"

McCarter nodded and accepted the man's hand. He had a firm grip. "You're Mazouzi?"

"Yes, Zafar Mazouzi."

Mazouzi wore gray pleated slacks, a white shirt and a pinstripe gray tie with a black leather overcoat that stopped short of his knees. Not exactly the most standard dress but not completely unusual, either. McCarter didn't know much about the Moroccan police outside of what he'd learned from Mazouzi's file. Sometimes known as the Maroc Cops, the police in Casablanca had a reputation for being tough and resourceful—a reputation well earned if there were any truth to the rumors. On occasion, they were known to be downright brutal and Mazouzi's career had seen its share of complaints and reprimands.

Not that it mattered all that much. Most times the reprimands only stayed on record for sixty or ninety days, a year at the outset, and then were conveniently "lost" in the shuffle of bureaucratic red tape. Graft was also an issue, many cops looking the other way for everything from money to sexual favors, although Mazouzi had never been accused of participation. In Zafar Mazouzi's world, McCarter knew that spoke volumes for a cop to stand outside of such activities, a fact that had probably been the reason Interpol approached him on the sly.

"Your men look tired," Mazouzi said. "We have a place prepared for you. You can clean up there."

"Much obliged," Hawkins said.

Mazouzi led them off the tarmac and through a small building that emerged onto a narrow lane logjammed with cars. While Casablanca-Anfa saw nowhere near the traffic of Casablanca's other airport, Mohammed V International, it still did its fair share of business. Mostly it had been closed to commercial traffic and catered more to cargo and local air passenger flights. Apparently, the Casablanca police had made special arrangements because nobody detained them and there were no customs officers in sight. Mazouzi stopped at two sedans parked against the curb.

"I apologize but we did not have a vehicle large enough for all of you and your equipment." Mazouzi pointed to a short, bald man about his own age standing near a Citroën Visa. "This is Trebba, a friend. He can be trusted."

"No problem," Encizo said.

The Cuban immediately tossed his bag in the open trunk of the vehicle next to Trebba and then climbed into the backseat. Hawkins followed suit and Manning took shotgun. That left McCarter and James to ride with Mazouzi in the other vehicle, a later model Peugeot. Once they'd stowed their gear, Mazouzi maneuvered from the airport terminal and proceeded northwest on Omar al Khiam Boulevard.

"This will lead us to the N1, a highway that leads into the city. We've arranged quarters."

"Much obliged, chap," McCarter said. "When do we get into the details of why we're here?"

"You have questions…I understand this." Mazouzi risked taking his eyes from the crowded road and said, "You must be patient. Abbas el Khalidi isn't going anywhere, I can assure you."

"You have him under surveillance, then?" James asked.

"Not exactly."

"Well, what exactly do you have going on?" McCarter asked, trying to keep his tone as light as possible.

"It is difficult to observe this man. He is very powerful in most circles and no judge will give us a writ to follow him. We also do not have the resources so we can only document his activities in our spare time, which isn't much. My superiors at Interpol are also growing impatient. Twice they have attempted to hit him when I reported he was out of the country. Twice they fucked it up, you see?"

"When were you first contacted by Interpol?" McCarter asked.

Mazouzi shrugged. "I would say…well, approximately twenty months ago."

James couldn't suppress a whistle. "You've been at this awhile."

"It is as I say, it has taken a long time." Mazouzi glanced at James in the rearview mirror before continuing. "Khalidi is a powerful man with many friends throughout Morocco. He is also a public figure so it is difficult to be discreet with so many people around him."

"Yet somehow he manages to run a major narcotics-trafficking ring into the better part of Europe and has a full-blown kidnapping network operating in America," McCarter said. "Now, I don't know what exactly you've been told about us, but one thing we should get straight is we're not here to observe or take notes. Our mission is simple. Find Khalidi's base of operations here and shut it down. Permanently."

"And I would assume that means you also intend to kill him?" Mazouzi said.

"If an opportunity presents itself? Yeah," McCarter replied.

"Our mission," James interjected, "is just as Mr. Brown told you. Officially, we have only one main goal and it *doesn't* include sitting on our hands and waiting to see what shakes out."

Mazouzi produced a chuckle. "Please understand, gentlemen, that I have no agenda but to help you. I have been after Khalidi for much of my career. He has brought down many of our citizens into misery, oppressed those who don't strictly adhere to the Islamic faith."

"You mean to say he's a Muslim zealot, too?" James inquired.

Mazouzi replied with a curt nod.

"So that would explain why he's got ties with terrorist connections," McCarter said. "His operations are probably helping to finance them, as well."

"His influence is wide-reaching," Mazouzi said. "He is well-known and respected in many countries where there are large bodies of Islamic faithful. I myself have witnessed the control and command of the Muslim hearts this man wields. And yet I despise him because he stands against everything that a true Muslim believes."

"And what exactly is that?"

"I'm not here to debate religion with any of you," Mazouzi said. "My faith is a private matter to me. I can swear this, that I have no quarrel with those of other faiths or no faith, and I have no quarrel with you. If you will be honest with me, I will be honest with you. Together I think we can find and destroy him once and for all. Is this acceptable?"

"Fair enough," McCarter said. "So where do we start?"

"You should get rest and change clothes," Mazouzi said. "You will draw too much attention in those uniforms, and that we cannot have. Once we've dropped you at your temporary quarters and you've had time to change and eat, I will lay out the plan for you."

"We actually prefer to make our own plans," James remarked.

"My orders are to cooperate with you," Mazouzi replied. "But the fact is that I know these streets like few others, as does Trebba. We've worked and lived here our entire lives, and we know how to get information. We will have to do work you might consider not, um, how would you say…?"

"Ethical?"

Mazouzi shook his head and let out a loud laugh. "There is no such thing in Casablanca, Mr. White. Let us simply say that whenever people won't cooperate with us we are not afraid to get rough."

"That's just the way we like it, mate," McCarter replied.

McCARTER HAD TO ADMIT that a shower and change of clothes did much to improve the disposition of the entire team and he verbally commended Mazouzi for the thought.

The cop barely acknowledged it. Mazouzi had the air of a serious man in many ways—some of the Phoenix Force warriors had even remarked he seemed brooding—with what didn't seem to be much of a sense of humor. But he hadn't been lying when he said he knew the streets of Casablanca. According to his personnel file, Mazouzi had been a Maroc policeman for nearly thirty years, really since he'd turned old enough to join the force, and he'd seen a hell of a lot in that time. While Casablanca was a city open to tourism there were often many protests by students and other demonstrators against the government handling of the economy.

"It has been this way for as long as I can remember," Mazouzi had said. "But there is plenty of information out there if you know where to look and how to ask the right questions."

"And maybe crack a few heads along the way?" Hawkins said with a wink.

"Only when necessary," Mazouzi replied.

They were gathered around a small table in the kitchenette. Their quarters weren't exactly roomy but they were clean and comfortable. One room had been set up with three twin beds and a smaller one contained a hideaway and floor mattress. None of the Phoenix Force warriors minded, however, since they didn't figure they'd be spending much time there. Mazouzi had pointed out that every minute they were in the country increased the chances someone would report back to Khalidi.

"That is why we brought you here instead of to a hotel," Trebba said.

"We use this place to hide witnesses," Mazouzi continued. "But we also lease it out to Royal Air Maroc employees, so dropping you here would not appear out of the ordinary to most anyone who saw you."

Mazouzi pointed to a map of the city he'd spread on the table. "Some of the places we will go you will definitely be out of place. It will be important that we get in, ask our questions and get out as soon as possible. I think it would be best if we only took one or two of you."

"How about we split up?" Manning suggested to the Phoenix Force leader. "It could save us time."

Mazouzi shook his head. "People are used to seeing the police everywhere but they will mark you instantly as outsiders."

"There are still some angles we need to check out on our own," McCarter said. "I think Mr. Gray's correct, and it would be a good idea to split up and let them do their thing while we go with you."

"It would be best if I take Mr. Gold and Mr. White," Mazouzi said.

"Why them?" Hawkins asked.

"It is nothing personal but they are dark-skinned and will not draw as much attention."

"Fine with me," McCarter said. He looked at Encizo and James. "But Mazouzi's got the lead, mates. You follow his cues and come back with your hides in one piece."

"We'll start here," Mazouzi said, pointing to a small block just south of the central downtown area. "Khalidi does not just run drugs into Europe, he also supplies many of the local regions. There is a man who has worked for him for many years. Khalidi made a big show of firing the man and publicly humiliating him for using drugs. In fact, though, we believe it was a ruse so that Khalidi could maintain his hold on the drug trade throughout all of Morocco."

"What makes you think so?" McCarter asked.

"I don't think anything—I *know* it. Khalidi may have many connections outside of Morocco but he could not possibly hope to operate in such a clandestine fashion within the country unless he had cooperation from the local thugs. It's Khalidi's pipeline but the product supplied to him belongs to the manufacturers. Khalidi would need to establish and maintain significant ties if he wanted their cooperation. After all, he must pay the producers their respective cuts."

"So you're figuring the best way to Khalidi is to lean on the local help," Manning concluded.

Mazouzi nodded and then looked at his watch. "We don't have much time. We need to go now if we want to make time to hit all of the places I've lined up."

"Is there anything the B team can do to help?" McCarter asked.

Mazouzi considered this and then nodded. "There are some clubs that cater to nonnationals." He pointed to a section on the map. "This area is frequented by tourists so your team would not look out of place here. But I warn you that you must be very discreet. If you have any encounters with uniformed or undercover officers, I may not be able to help you. In fact, I would most likely disavow any knowledge of your identities or presence in this country."

McCarter gave a short nod. "Understood, mate."

"I will have Trebba show you to the general area," Mazouzi said. "From there you are on your own. We should meet here no later than two hours from now."

They all nodded in understanding and then Mazouzi led Encizo and James out of the house. Trebba gestured for the remaining team members to accompany him to the Citroën Visa. They piled into the cramped vehicle, McCarter on shotgun with Manning and Hawkins in the back. All of them were armed with pistols in shoulder leather beneath loose-fitting shirts. McCarter had opted for his trusted 9 mm Browning Hi-Power while the two in back carried matched H&K P9Ss chambered for .45 ACP.

As Trebba pulled from the curb, McCarter said, "Where do we start?"

"As Zafar said, there is a large tourist area near Boulevard Abderrahim Bouabid. This is not far from the American Academy Casablanca, in fact. It is also close to the police headquarters."

"Lovely," Manning remarked. "At least trouble won't be far."

Trebba chuckled. "I wouldn't let this worry you, gentlemen. Our kind is too busy putting down rioters and muggers to be worried about tourists. At least not too much. And that is how you must look and act."

"We'll have you along."

Trebba shook his head emphatically. "No. This cannot be. It won't do for a local to be seen with Americans. There are too many in the area who know me as police. You will be on your own."

"How do we get information?"

"Do any of you speak French?"

McCarter gestured a thumb at Manning. "He speaks it fluently and I know enough to get by."

"Then you should be fine," Trebba replied. "It would be best if all of you could pretend to be French rather than Americans."

"I don't speak any French," Hawkins pointed out.

"Then it is best you not speak at all."

True to his word, Trebba dropped the trio at the corner of Rue Imam Mouslim and some unknown street. "Straight ahead you will see that club?"

They nodded collectively.

"Inside you will find a waitress, short and ugly this woman," he continued. "But she is trustworthy and can point you in the right direction. You will want to make contact with a man known as Sahib and she can arrange this meeting. She won't ask questions but money, if you have any, would make her more agreeable."

"Who is this Sahib?" McCarter asked.

"A local dealer who has contacts with a number of the same suppliers as Abbas el Khalidi. I would suggest you make contact with him, ask whatever questions you may need to and then leave as soon as possible. You will find me in a different auto three blocks north of here in the lot of a club called Enfa. It will be a red Fiat Uno."

"Don't you think it would be better if you were with us?" McCarter asked.

"As I have told you already, Mr. Brown, it would be bad to be seen with me. All cops of the Maroc get known after a while and my presence would only impede you. Good luck. I will see you in one half hour."

McCarter shrugged, checked the action on his pistol and then when Manning and Hawkins had done the same, the three went EVA. They walked the half block to a street and then turned and spotted the club with a large sign above it that read Nephdat Club.

As they approached the entrance, Hawkins asked, "What was that he was saying about us being near an American academy or something?"

Manning replied, "I think it's some kind of preparatory school. It hasn't been around that long, I believe. There are countries all over where similar schools are set up. They prepare students to enter universities all over the world. They're part of a larger nonprofit corporation."

"Huh. Didn't even know such things existed."

Manning didn't bother to reply but instead turned his attention to the task ahead. McCarter signaled for the men to be on their game as they passed through the doors and into the smoky, dark interior of one of the many night-life establishments littered throughout the greater metropolitan area. Casablanca served as an example of what the combined conditions of overcrowding and widespread poverty—coupled with drugs, alcohol and sex—could do. While there were many nice areas of the city, it didn't appear to the three Phoenix Force members that the club catered to the clientele of those areas.

And as they ventured deeper into the bowels of the club, David McCarter couldn't help feeling as if they could well be walking into a trap.

CHAPTER TEN

Zafar Mazouzi took both Encizo and James by surprise when he suddenly jammed on the brakes of the Peugeot, threw it into Park and leaped from the car.

He moved across the dimly lit street and waded into a crowd of onlookers, who moved out of the way like parting waters. Within the innermost circle, the Phoenix Force pair spotted Mazouzi's intended target: he had dark, greasy long hair done in a harried array of dreadlocks and large beaded tufts. A brightly colored cap kept the mess in place but did nothing for the beard that bore out an equal mismatch of styles.

Encizo and James barely reached the curb of the sidewalk before Mazouzi reached out, snatched the man by the collar and hauled him away from the crowd. The pair were about to reach for their pistols until they realized that while there were shouts from the protestors nobody appeared to dare interfere with the Maroc cop. They did an about-face and followed Mazouzi, who half dragged the Moroccan native across the street, opened the back door and shoved him inside.

Encizo and James got in the front, Encizo behind the wheel, and turned to observe Mazouzi's nearly masterful technique firsthand.

They couldn't understand the furious stream of Arabic that Mazouzi directed toward the man but they could understand the occasional slap across the back of the man's head. Through a smattering of interpretation Mazouzi directed toward them during the impromptu interrogation, they learned the man's name was Osama Ubuntu and that he was actually a former resident of Nigeria until a few years ago.

"Since he's been in Morocco, he's been a pain in our ass," Mazouzi explained. He looked at Ubuntu and added, "But he's also been a good source of information. Haven't you?"

Mazouzi delivered another whack and Encizo bit back commenting. McCarter had told them to follow Mazouzi's lead but if the cop was just going to run about the city, dragging them along with him and smacking no-name drug pushers it wasn't going to do Phoenix Force much good…or get them any closer to accomplishing mission objectives. Encizo would admit that he wasn't any sort of an expert on such matters, at least not in this country, but he wanted his crack at Khalidi and he couldn't see how this would help to achieve that end.

"Um, Rafe?" James interjected, tapping his friend's shoulder and jerking a thumb through the front window.

Encizo turned and, on seeing the approaching band of armed men, said, "Uh-oh."

Mazouzi was too busy yelling at Ubuntu to realize that trouble had materialized. Encizo looked at the steering console and saw Mazouzi had left the keys in the ignition. He immediately put the clutch to the floor, started the engine and engaged the stick into Reverse. As he let out the clutch and revved the engine, withdrawing from the approaching group with a squeal of tires, Mazouzi began to shout and curse at him.

"We have company," James snapped as he withdrew his Beretta 92.

The armed men, four in all, began to rush the vehi-

cle and raise various models of semiautomatic handguns.
They fired several shots but Encizo had put enough distance between their enemies and the Peugeot that none of
the rounds found human flesh. One hit the corner of the
windshield and spiderwebbed across the passenger side,
effectively blocking James's view. As the Peugeot gained
speed, James worked the power window and leaned outside with the pistol held steady in his right hand.

James leveled the muzzle on the nearest man and
squeezed off a double-tap. Twin 9×19 mm Parabellum
slugs rocketed across the gap and struck home, taking
James's intended target in the chest and dumping the man
on his back. James fired another round, but with the herky-
jerky movements of the Peugeot, he held off firing, more
for concern of missing and taking out an innocent civilian target.

James retreated to the interior of the vehicle. He glanced
at Encizo, whose face had screwed up in intense concentration as the Cuban maneuvered the vehicle as best he
could along the narrow street, negotiating the obstacles
of cars parked on either side of the roadway. At one point,
he sideswiped one of the vehicles and left a large gouge
in the body with the echo of scraping fiberglass, metal
and plastic.

"What are you doing?" Mazouzi demanded.

"Saving your ass, I think," James replied.

Before they could engage in a further exchange, Encizo jammed on the brakes and executed a hard jerk of the
wheel. The nose of the Peugeot came around smoothly in
Encizo's J-turn, one of the most difficult vehicle maneu-
vers to perform, and with a hammering of the gearshift
into second and a pop of the clutch, the car lurched down
the street and quickly left the trio of remaining shooters

behind. The men continued popping off rounds but they were too distant to bear any real effect.

"This is one-way, you idiot!" Mazouzi exclaimed.

"I'm only going one way," Encizo quipped.

James gazed levelly at Mazouzi and in an even rhythm said, "Lose the attitude."

As Encizo reached an intersection a vehicle off the side road began to turn toward them. Encizo whipped the wheel to the left, vaulted the curb and then steered onto the road again. He proceeded another block up before turning right at Mazouzi's direction and making for the N1. They had nearly reached the interstate when a new batch of trouble emerged. A dark late-model sedan came abreast of them on the two-lane Boulevard Ghandi headed south and tried to run them off the road twice. Their ramming added to the deep gouge already left as evidence of their narrow escape.

"Now, who the hell is this?" James asked.

"Khalidi's men," Mazouzi said.

The cop began to shout more gibberish at Ubuntu, but the Phoenix Force warriors were too worried about this new threat to even care what he might be asking the drug peddler. This time, Encizo reached beneath his coat and retrieved his own pistol. He leveled the Glock 21 at their shadowy pursuers and squeezed off two rounds of .45-caliber SJHPs. The rounds seemed to spark off the metal body and Encizo cast an aghast look at his friend.

"It's armored!"

James now looked equally concerned. Whatever else might be going on, they had walked into something much bigger than the simple inquisition of a drug-peddling street guy. This went *much* deeper and both men figured Khalidi had to be at the center of it. Somehow the criminal mastermind had learned of Phoenix Force's arrival in the country and had already sent teams of his cronies to dispatch the threat before they could get too close.

There couldn't be any other explanation.

"Get onto the highway," Mazouzi said. "I know a place we can lose them."

The wail of a siren greeted their ears and now they saw the blue lights of two police cars fast approaching the pair of vehicles speeding haphazardly up the road and steering onto the entry ramp for the N1. While it could hardly qualify as a highway in cities like Los Angeles or New York, here it was practically a superinterstate that ran a torturous northwest-to-southeast course through Casablanca. Neither Encizo nor James could see how taking the highway would make it easier to lose their pursuers or help them evade the two new police cruisers that had joined the chase, but they weren't going to argue.

"Yes'm, Miss Daisy," James replied.

Encizo forced back a smile and hoped their companions were having a better time of it.

RIGHT AT THAT MOMENT, the other three men of Phoenix Force were embroiled in a mess of their own, although it wasn't immediately obvious. Gary Manning had sensed something wasn't right the moment they'd entered the nightclub, a feeling reinforced when McCarter leaned toward him and voiced a similar sentiment. After paying a twenty-dollar cover charge each to a mean-looking thug at the door, the three "Frenchmen" stepped into the smoke-shrouded interior. Lights flashed in beat to the Arabic-style rock and there was an odor of liquor mixed with cigarette smoke, tinged by the occasional waft of hashish.

By mutual agreement, they had decided to let Manning take point on this one. When Manning rendered a discreet gesture to his companions, the remaining pair spread out in order to cover his back. This wasn't the first time they'd done this—protocol and training took over in these kinds of situations. Three men, even three French foreigners, would not cluster in a nightclub unless they were gay. The better bet would be to act like three eligible bachelors on the prowl for the female persuasion, all the while moving into strategic positions.

In spite of the gut instinct telling Manning and his friends they were being set up, it didn't prove difficult to identify the woman Trebba had described. She seemed to appear at his side unbidden, short and squat in a uniform too tight and wearing too much makeup. The mascara on the false eyelashes and gaudy earrings made her look more like a Gypsy than a Moroccan native.

"Can I help you?" she asked in flawless French.

"You speak French," Manning replied with mock surprise.

"You haven't been here before," she said. "Otherwise this wouldn't be strange to you."

Manning nodded and thought, good. "I was told if I wanted to have a good time that you would be able to point me to Sahib."

The woman expressed guarded curiosity. She set a napkin down on the tall, narrow table Manning leaned against and said, "Why would you want to speak to Sahib?"

"I was told he could help me locate some, uh, let's just say I hear he can make a party a *real* party."

"You're not from here, are you?"

"Why do you say that?"

"Because you would know that nobody speaks with Sahib directly," she replied. "You will have to deal with one of his men."

"No, I don't think so," Manning said with a hard smile. "Let me put it another way. It's very important I speak to only Sahib. Now, if you have a line to Sahib then you take that message. Otherwise point him out to me and I'll take the message myself."

For a measure of time that seemed to go on longer than it did, the woman stared at Manning; the big Canadian remained impassive. He thought of his pistol and prepared to draw it if any trouble materialized, but he didn't take his eyes from those of the waitress. He wouldn't hesitate to take her if she made the wrong move—they still didn't have a handle on the game here. Trebba hadn't been much help in that regard and while McCarter didn't trust what they had walked into, Manning hadn't trusted Trebba through it all. There was something about that guy that just didn't feel right and Manning had learned to rely on his instincts because they had saved him before.

"Wait here," the woman said and she faded into the darkness and the crowd.

Manning tried for nonchalance although he didn't feel right about it; the Phoenix Force warrior dismissed the doubts since he knew that couldn't help him. It always seemed worse to the subject operating undercover than everyone else, since the average observer wouldn't notice anything unusual about him. In fact, Manning observed a large number of non-Moroccans in the nightclub and so on that count Trebba had been correct—they could fit in without drawing much attention. What had taken Manning more by surprise had been that the woman had approached him, instead of him having to search her out. He looked around and saw the other waitresses moving throughout the club. Had he given something away or had the woman been warned in advance? She sure as hell hadn't batted an eyelash when Manning asked to see Sahib.

A minute passed and then another. Manning was about to leave when the woman returned from the darkness and delivered his drink. As she set it down atop a napkin, she said, "Five minutes, through that door."

Manning looked in the direction she jerked her head and he nodded. Once she turned her back, he looked toward McCarter and Hawkins and then let his eyes hit the door. It was a risk, yeah, but if they were under observation it would be less risky to move into position ahead of time. Manning tried not to look at them as they moved, first Hawkins and then McCarter, toward the door. There weren't any tables close to the door so they couldn't get real close but they could cover his position well enough.

Manning took only two sips from the gin and tonic in the span of five minutes. He dropped enough cash on the table to cover the drink and then some, and then sidled his way through the twisting path of people and tables to the door. He didn't look at either of his partners as he rapped on the door, but he did check his flanks before pushing through it. He entered without hesitation and found a long corridor lit by recessed red lights. Some sort of omen or statement Sahib was trying to make? Maybe, although Manning had to admit against the black walls the red lighting gave the corridor an ominous appearance.

Manning proceeded down the hallway without hesitation. Before he got halfway to the door at the far end, two bruisers appeared at either side and grabbed his arms. They were too busy frisking him and imposing rough intimidation to realize that Manning had left the door ajar before walking down the corridor, a door that would otherwise have locked automatically. They barely had the pistol cleared from his shoulder holster when McCarter and Hawkins joined the party. Hawkins delivered a strong, straight punch to the bony protuberance behind the right ear of one of the goons, jarring that part of the senses that controlled balance. The man crumpled to the carpeted hall in a heap.

McCarter took the other one with a kick to the back of the leg while yanking on the back of his opponent's collar. He slammed the side of the man's head into the polished wooden stud of the corridor wall. The thug's eyes rolled into his head as he slid to the carpet next to his comrade. McCarter reached to the man's hand, retrieved Manning's pistol and handed it back.

"Thanks," Manning said with a nod.

Hawkins looked toward the door. "That our objective?"

Manning glanced over his shoulder as he holstered his weapon and said, "Yeah, I'm guessing that's the place."

"Well, then," McCarter said, "let's go see what's what."

The trio approached the door with some distance between each other, intent not to have their number reduced to nil in a cross fire. Manning reached the door and tested it. It opened with a click and Manning went through it with Hawkins next and McCarter bringing up the rear guard. The room opened up into a wide, trapezoidal shape. Fine art adorned the walls and the interior had been done in dark woods and ornate tapestries. Behind a large desk sat a man with slicked hair and a full beard. He wore a jacket in the same razzle-dazzle, Persian design as the many tapestries on the walls surrounding him. He clutched a big fat cigar in his left hand.

Sahib, Manning thought. Has to be.

The man jabbered something in Arabic and three goons emerged from a sliding door over his right shoulder, AKS-74 machine pistols in their grips. The three Phoenix Force warriors scattered for cover just as the gunners leveled their machine pistols and opened up. A barrage of 7.62 mm hot lead buzzed the air above their heads, punching holes in the wall to their backs that, fortunately, wasn't decorated with anything of value like the rest of the room. It didn't occur to any of them right at that moment this was probably by design—they were too busy responding to their enemies in similar fashion.

Manning shoulder-rolled to the cover of a thick, leather chair, found purchase on one knee, leveled his weapon and squeezed the trigger. A 155-grain SJHP punched through his target's chest, lifting the guy off his feet and slamming him into a pedestal with an antique crystal vase perched on it. The heavy vase slammed against the back wall and shattered in several pieces that hit the carpeted floor about the same time as the body of the man who had upset it.

McCarter got the next one with a double-tap from the Hi-Power, the first of his two 9 mm rounds blowing away the fleshy part of a gunner's shoulder while the other cut a vicious gash through the right side of his neck. Blood, bright red and hot, spurted from the wound and the man dropped his AKS-74 and clutched at the neck wound. His eyes rolled into his head as he began to lose consciousness from the sudden lack of blood to his head; he collapsed to his knees and McCarter ended his life with a mercy shot to the forehead.

Hawkins gritted his teeth as one of the probing rounds managed to take a bite from his thigh, although it only grazed him. It distracted him long enough that Hawkins realized rolling behind another chair would be the only thing to save him. The bullets traced the path of his roll but eventually they impacted the chair and Hawkins managed to evade being hit a second time. The big Texan shouted in anger at getting winged as he switched his pistol to his left hand and grabbed the back leg of the chair with his right. He flipped it up and over, using the tall back as a lever to propel the chair toward his enemy. It didn't act as a weapon but it proved more than adequate as a dis-

traction, something for which Hawkins had hoped. The
gunner's eyes swung toward the chair propelled at him,
a delay that bought Hawkins the couple extra seconds—
those seconds were precious in a situation like this one
and the Phoenix Force warrior made good use of them.
Hawkins caught his target with four rounds, two that cut
through his belly, one in the heart and the last in the chin.
The man stumbled back with the impact and eventually
Sahib's desk stopped his motion.

As Hawkins's opponent twitched in the throes of death,
Sahib reached into his desk drawer and came up with a
small pistol. It looked like a Walther PPK but McCarter
didn't wait for confirmation. A champion marksman, the
Briton snap-aimed and shot the pistol clean from Sahib's
hand. The drug pimp screamed and dropped his cigar to
grasp his wounded hand.

Manning was on the man in moments. He came around
the desk, grabbed Sahib by the collar of his gaudy silk de-
signer jacket and hauled him out of the chair. He stuck the
barrel of the still-warm muzzle under Sahib's chin.

"Parlez-vous français?" he asked the man.

"He probably speaks English," McCarter said as he
moved toward Hawkins.

"What about that?" Manning asked.

"Yes," Sahib said with a heavy Arabic accent. "I speak
English. But you are not French."

"Never mind that," Manning said in a frosty tone.
"We're here to ask questions. You're going to answer
them."

"I will tell you nothing."

McCarter was busy examining Hawkins's bullet wound
with a practiced eye. It had torn a neat little furrow in the
meaty part of his friend's thigh but it wasn't serious. Mc-
Carter ripped off the sleeve of one of the dead gunner's

jackets, cutting it away at the shoulder with a pocketknife. He used the sleeve to bind the wound and tie it off with a bulky knot at the deepest point.

"We'll have James give you a tetanus shot and antibiotics when we get back."

The Briton stood and approached Sahib, who now stood with his eyes wide. He watched McCarter's approach with a mixture of terror and curiosity.

"You probably think we're going to kill you," McCarter said. "But that's not our plan at all. You're much too valuable to us."

"What do you want?"

"Like my friend says, we have some questions."

"I will not tell you anything."

McCarter smiled. "Oh, you'll tell us *everything,* you bloody piece of shit. But first, there has to be a back way out of this dump."

When Sahib nodded, Manning said, "Show us."

Just as the drug dealer turned to lead the Phoenix Force trio out the secret exit, there was a commotion in the hallway through which they had entered Sahib's inner sanctum.

"Freeze!" ordered a heavily accented voice, and a handful of Moroccan police burst in.

Sahib's sly smile froze in place as one of the cops thrust a pistol in the drug dealer's face. "You're coming with us, too," he ordered.

CHAPTER ELEVEN

"We're going to get killed if we stay out here much longer," James said.

Rafael Encizo swerved to the right to avoid another bone-jarring impact from the pursuing sedan before replying, "Wouldn't want that."

"That exit...there!" Mazouzi said. "Take that next exit."

Encizo nodded and merged into the left lane, keeping the Peugeot just ahead of the enemy car. In the rear distance through his mirrors, he could still make out the flashing blue lights of the police vehicles. The authorities had obviously not determined yet they were not the aggressors in this situation. James had inquired why the Moroccan couldn't contact them by radio or cell phone and let them know what was going on, but he reminded them that officially he wasn't on any surveillance for Abbas el Khalidi and neither could he acknowledge the presence of the Phoenix Force warriors.

"You must be able to do something," James said.

"If I do, it will mean I go to prison and you will be immediately deported," Mazouzi said. "That's if they don't shoot you both on sight."

"Great," Encizo said through clenched teeth as he whipped across two lanes and took the exit.

The sedan attempted to keep pace but Encizo had managed to jam it up with cars and the vehicle didn't quite make the exit, instead crashing through a low guardrail and sidesweeping a concrete barrier. Sparks flew from the body of the sedan as it ground to a halt on the highway.

Thankfully, they had lost their quarry but they still had to be concerned about the police. That concern became secondary, however, when Encizo realized there was a bigger problem now before them. A small Italian-made panel truck pulled alongside them on the cross street shortly after Encizo blew the red light and rounded the corner. The truck slammed them into the curb. Both tires on the passenger side burst and the rear door caved in, nearly carving Mazouzi's thigh to shreds, the impact moving him just far enough out of reach to avoid injury. Ubuntu tried to take advantage of the situation and grabbed for the pistol Mazouzi still held in his left hand.

Encizo and James were no longer concerned with the trouble in the backseat as the bent rims entangled with melting shreds of rubber jumped the sidewalk. Encizo swerved to avoid hitting a pedestrian just exiting a shop. The Cuban slammed the gearshift into Reverse and powered the tail of the vehicle around until they could come to a nice, controlled stop by smashing the rear end into a light pole.

The impact threw both Mazouzi and Ubuntu into the back of James's seat and the gun flew from Mazouzi's fingers. The men scrambled to retrieve it from the floorboards even as Encizo and James went EVA with weapons ready. The panel truck screeched to a stop, the rear door rolled upward and six figures with semiauto pistols emerged from the truck.

James took up position behind the door of the Peugeot, braced his arms between the door and partially mangled frame and sighted on his first target. He squeezed the Baretta's trigger, the twin reports barking in the crisp evening air as the 9 mm slugs found their mark. The gunner took both slugs in the left chest, the impact exploding his heart and slamming him into the tailgate of the truck.

Encizo leveled his Glock 21 at two men advancing side by side. He grimaced at their sloppiness even as he unleashed the first .45-caliber slug, intent on making every shot count given his limited ammunition. The bullet left the chamber at a velocity of 350 meters per second and blew the target's skull apart on impact, splattering his partner with gore. The second hard case managed to get off about a half-dozen slugs that came dangerously close to Encizo, but close wasn't going to cut it in this round. Encizo dropped him with a double-tap to the chest.

The remaining trio grabbed cover behind a couple of vehicles parked at the curb just ahead of the wrecked Peugeot. In the lull, Encizo managed to catch Mazouzi as he hammered the side of Ubuntu's face with repeated elbow strikes, splitting the man's cheek and lip. The fourth blow knocked him half-senseless and Mazouzi used that advantage to retrieve his pistol. He slammed the butt of the weapon against the bridge of Ubuntu's nose and then cleared out of the backseat.

Mazouzi rushed down the sidewalk and directly into the view of the three remaining gunners, who'd sought shelter behind the cars. They turned their pistols toward Mazouzi, who made the corner just in time to avoid being hit by a half-dozen rounds, but failed to notice that James and Encizo—at first having thought Mazouzi crazy but then realizing the genius of his providing a distraction—had advanced on their flanks with pistols blazing. James got one with a shot to the back of the head, and a fifth fell when Encizo blasted him through the spine so close that it exited through the man's spleen. The surviving gunner tried turning his pistol back toward the Phoenix Force pair but he was far too late. They hammered him with several rounds in the gut and chest, along with one by James that entered his left eye and scrambled his brains.

The engine on the panel truck *varoomed* to life and the vehicle pulled away, albeit somewhat slowly.

James leaped into action, rushing the truck and leaping into the back before it could make too much distance. Encizo shouted a warning at his friend but it went unheeded and with the increasing speed he knew he wouldn't be able to catch up; there was also Ubuntu to think of, not to mention one of the two squad cars that now rounded the corner with a squeal of tires and made a fast approach directly toward him.

The squad slid to a halt at a respectful distance and a pair of uniformed officers jumped from the vehicle and drew on Encizo. Before he could react, they were all distracted by Mazouzi shouting something in Arabic and waving at Encizo while holding up his badge. He then jabbed his finger at the retreating panel truck before switching back to English and ordering Encizo into the squad car.

Further heated debate continued inside the squad car, but Encizo, seated in the right rear of the vehicle, kept his mouth shut. Better to let Mazouzi handle whatever inquiries came his way, and from what the Cuban gathered listening to the conversation the two policemen were making several. Mazouzi shouted to make his voice heard, jerked his thumb behind them and then the cop riding shotgun picked up the radio and began to shout at the dispatcher.

"I told them to pick up Ubuntu."

"What about my friend?"

"I told them to follow him."

"I thought you didn't want to have to explain any of this," Encizo said.

Mazouzi frowned, his expression unreadable as he replied, "Since when do we ever get what we want in this business, American?"

CALVIN JAMES REALIZED that what he'd probably done here had been a bit rash.

Hell, it had been downright stupid.

The panel truck was now swerving through traffic erratically, and James had nearly been knocked off the back when the rear door started to come down on him. He'd rolled inside at the last moment to avoid being pinned to the floor or—worse—knocked from the truck and dragged an unknown distance. From the speed they were traveling, James guessed the driver hadn't gotten back on the highway, so at least there was a small chance the cops might flood the area looking for the truck.

Not that he had any idea what the resources were of the Casablanca police, or even if they knew about him. James didn't doubt Mazouzi would issue an APB on the panel truck, even if not under his own initiative then definitely under the insistence of Encizo. James realized he'd broken the cardinal rule in leaving his partner behind but the situation had called for him to make a split-second decision and that meant he didn't have the luxury of second-guessing it now. James had done what he had in search of answers. Someone had been waiting for them, either because they'd known all along that Phoenix Force was in country, or they'd had Mazouzi under observation.

The latter seemed the most likely scenario given that Stony Man certainly didn't have any leaks. They had spent several hours at the safe house against McCarter's better advice, which meant someone could've easily had time to rat them out. But to know the specifics of the thing, like where'd they be and who they were looking for? The only two who'd possessed that information in advance had been Mazouzi and Trebba, and these goons hadn't shown the slightest trepidation trying to shoot Mazouzi.

That left Trebba, and James began to wonder if they hadn't found the leak.

Of course he had to consider the other possibility, that Abbas el Khalidi had extensive resources—just as Mazouzi had warned—that he'd somehow learned of their mission or somebody had observed them and reported back. For all the Phoenix Force team knew, this was standard practice and it wouldn't be unusual for a guy like Khalidi to have spies and informants in every nook and cranny of the city. It didn't seem probable, though, and like his teammates, James didn't much believe in coincidence.

The jolt of the truck brought him back to his senses and James wondered for a moment if he'd drifted off. He looked down at his arm and did a double take—it was blood. He felt around to see if it might have come from one of the men they'd shot, but a quick assessment of his body revealed it was his own. He located the source of the bleeding and breathed a sigh of relief when he realized it was a flesh wound on his left forearm. He couldn't tell if it had come from a bullet or some sharp piece of metal on the car, but he was figuring the latter since he'd been shot several times before and it had never really manifested this way.

James shook it off. He couldn't do much about it now so he reached into the thigh pocket of his cargo pants and withdrew a combat compress. He ripped the paper with his teeth, pressed the compress to his forearm and wrapped it with the attached bandage. That would at least staunch the bleeding until he could have it attended by a physician or numb it with a local and suture it himself.

James cursed as his head suddenly impacted the back wall, just hard enough to jar his teeth, and then he changed positions to his hands and knees. The truck lurched again and James started to wonder if the driver weren't inebriated or something. Then he heard the siren. The cops! The cops had given chase. Bless that Zafar Mazouzi anyway. James's elation was short-lived as he was slammed into the floor of the truck by a sudden turn and then the feeling of impact—he'd be tossed around inside this thing like a lone pickled herring in a jar unless the cops could end this pursuit shortly.

Then he felt his stomach roll into his throat as he realized the panel truck was rolling, probably down an embankment of some type.

"¡MADRE DE DIOS!" Encizo exclaimed. "Take it easy! One of our friends is in there, you clowns!"

Mazouzi put a restraining hand on Encizo's arm but the Cuban shook it off.

The cops came to a screeching halt as the truck they'd been pursuing took the entrance ramp to the freeway too wide, skidded out of control and then toppled over the side of the ramp and slid down the concrete slope. Sparks flew from the panel truck as it slid another thirty yards or so under its own impetus, finally jolting to a halt.

Hell, if James were inside that truck and Encizo had no reason to think otherwise, the poor bastard was probably getting bounced around like a doll.

"You stay here," Mazouzi said as the squad came to a halt.

"Like hell," Encizo said and he was EVA.

The Cuban moved with the trained reflexes of a combat veteran, even outpacing the two younger cops in the front seat. He was halfway to the truck before any of the police had even made it out of the car, pistol in hand and ready for action. He side-vaulted the guardrail, ignoring the pain in his wrist as he went over and half skidded down the slippery concrete. The rear wheels of the panel truck were still rolling and steam poured from the engine even as Encizo reached the rear of the truck.

He grabbed the strap and hauled the door upward, letting his eyes adjust before he spotted the motionless form of his friend lying toward the back.

"Cal, you okay?"

Encizo could feel his heart skip a beat at first, fearful his friend was dead or severely injured, but then the groan from James brought a warm feeling to his center and he smiled.

"I feel terrible," he quipped.

"Hang tough, buddy," Encizo said, holstering his pistol and then stepping gingerly into the back and picking his way over the broken wooden struts and bent aluminum shell. He eventually reached James, helped the man to his feet and then, careful to avoid the injured forearm, draped the opposite arm around his neck and assisted him out.

They emerged to find the two uniforms helping the driver from the cab while Mazouzi looked on. The Maroc cop turned on the pair and for just a moment Encizo thought he saw something bordering on relief in the man's eyes. Despite the fact he couldn't claim to condone their actions or lend assistance, even admit to his superiors that he knew them, it seemed Zafar Mazouzi felt some sort of responsibility toward them all the same—almost as if they were a litter of puppies he'd adopted or something strange like that.

"You okay, Mr. White?" he asked.

James nodded wearily and then Mazouzi turned on the driver and began to shout at the man in Arabic. The driver had a cut over his left eye but appeared otherwise unharmed and Mazouzi didn't mind being a little rough on him. Not as rough as he'd been on Ubuntu, obviously, especially in light of the fact he was operating in front of the two uniformed officers, neither of whom looked as if he'd been out of high school more than a few years.

As Mazouzi questioned the driver in short, vociferous phrases, more units were now arriving. James and Encizo figured the jig was up now. They'd probably be arrested and have their weapons confiscated. If they weren't summarily judged and executed by firing squad, not an entirely implausible possibility in Morocco, they would at best be ejected from the country on the next hop out.

"So much for not drawing attention," James said.

THE FIVE MEMBERS OF Phoenix Force sat clustered in an isolated cell room at the main police headquarters.

Even from there they could hear the incessant shouts of at least three men, possibly more, and one of those men was Mazouzi. There was little question in the minds of any of the men that the discussion centered on the presence of five American commandos operating secretly within the country with the aid, if not blatant support, of a Moroccan police inspector. There was a pretty good chance, as well, that word had already reached Stony Man.

"If this goes south," McCarter had said earlier, "we'll never hear the end of it from Able Team."

At first, McCarter had danced around the idea of finding a way to break free but he'd changed his mind on the advice of Mazouzi. The Moroccan had pointed out that first, they didn't have anywhere to go and unless they had other contacts it wouldn't take long for police to locate them. It wasn't as if they didn't stand out like sore thumbs, even among the tourist population.

"Second, and more importantly," Mazouzi had said, "I still have points in my favor."

"What's that?" McCarter had asked.

"My status with Interpol, while it has been a secret, is still an *official* status and I am under their protection. It's possible this will have some impact when I talk to the chief of police, especially since my country does have treaty stipulations for the operation of Interpol agents within the country."

McCarter realized the guy had a very good point and decided not to argue with him. Instead, he'd instructed the team to go quietly and do whatever they were told. At first the suggestion had been made each of the Phoenix Force members be separated and interrogated individually, but McCarter had advised in no uncertain terms that wouldn't happen. Whatever else occurred, they couldn't afford to allow themselves to be separated for any length of time. Phoenix Force operated best when they were whole and complete—they had tried a different way once and it hadn't worked.

It wouldn't happen again as long as they were in Morocco…or for the duration of this mission, for that matter.

The shouting finally ceased and a minute later Mazouzi appeared with one of the uniformed officers, who served as jailer. He nodded at the officer, who immediately gestured to another guy. There was a buzz and a moment later Mazouzi swung the door outward.

"Let's go," he told them roughly. "Quickly and mind your step."

"We're leaving?" McCarter asked.

"I'm to take you directly to Mohammad V International. There you will wait until you can catch the next flight to New York City."

"Now wait a bloody minute—" McCarter began.

"Move!" Mazouzi shouted.

The echo of his booming voice reverberated down the

length of the concrete-and-steel corridor of the cell block.
McCarter started to open his mouth again but then thought
better of it. Mazouzi was up to something; there was no
way he could have arranged for their release so quickly.
No, he had something else up his sleeve, and McCarter
remembered his instructions that whatever happened they
were to cooperate with any orders given by the Casablanca
police officials. Apparently that included Zafar Mazouzi.

Once they were out of the station they were ushered to
a waiting compact bus. When the five men were aboard,
accompanied by Mazouzi and four armed officers, the bus
pulled from the curb and headed for the airport.

"How far is it?" Manning asked.

"We will be there soon," Mazouzi said.

"I can't believe this," McCarter said. "I can't bloody
well believe it. You dirty bugger, you promised us—"

"Nothing," Mazouzi interrupted. "I told you what I
needed to tell you to get your cooperation. Nothing more.
Now shut your mouth."

McCarter decided there was no reasoning with the guy
and fell silent. The men looked out the windows, each lost
in his own thoughts but all convinced they were getting
off lucky. They had been in similar situations before but
Stony Man had always managed to invoke some diplomatic miracle that got them out of hot water. It looked as
if somebody else was writing the rules this time.

When they reached the airport ten minutes later, Mazouzi
ordered them off the bus and he led them inside. Only one
of the officers accompanied them. Mazouzi leaned close
to the officer and whispered something. The man nodded,
turned and headed toward the block of terminals indicating international departures for North America. The airport
was crowded and as soon as the officer was indistinguish-

able among the throng of travelers, Mazouzi turned to the five warriors.

"Follow me, quick."

Hawkins slapped his fist into his palm. "I knew it! I knew this guy was a cowboy at heart."

"What the hell is going on?" McCarter said as he rushed to keep pace with Mazouzi's long, measured strides. "You expect us to trust you after what you did to us?"

Mazouzi smiled. "I told you that I promised you nothing."

"What are you saying?" Manning asked. "You mean you're *not* sending us home?"

"Of course not," Mazouzi said. He let out a small chuckle and said, "I've never worked with men as dedicated as you. You fight like devils and you look out for each other. Only men like you can help me find el Khalidi."

"What about you?" McCarter said. "You're a bloody cop here."

"No longer," Mazouzi said, eyes straight ahead.

CHAPTER TWELVE

David McCarter had to admit that of all the things he'd expected out of Mazouzi, this hadn't been one of them. Not only had this tough, grisly cop gone to bat for them against his superiors, but he was now also risking his own hide to ensure Phoenix Force succeeded in its mission to end Abbas el Khalidi's regime. McCarter understood some of the things that might have motivated a guy like Mazouzi, but it wasn't until they were away from the airport and traveling south away from the city that Mazouzi explained it in detail.

"There is a good reason Interpol recruited me to track Khalidi's whereabouts." Mazouzi said something in Arabic and continued, "You would most likely translate this word as *outsider* in your language."

"Outsider," McCarter replied and scratched at his chin. "Yeah, I guess I can relate a wee bit to that."

Mazouzi nodded. "Interpol has never been good at catching criminals outside of Europe, since that is their central concern. Their operations in places like South America and Africa are ineffective, and in Southeast Asia they are practically nonexistent. Many of my colleagues take bribes or trade favors, looking the other way or being too lenient on the criminals, but I do not believe this is my duty as a policeman. I answer to a higher authority, responsible to not just Allah, but also my fellow Muslims. We are not all terrorists, you know."

"I know," McCarter replied. "Do you think one of your colleagues betrayed us?"

"I think it is possible," Mazouzi said.

"Our money was kind of on your friend Trebba," Calvin James suggested.

"Do not believe this. I have worked with him for more than fifteen years. He has never betrayed me and no operation we were on where only he and I were privy to details was compromised. You must remember that el Khalidi has many, many spies in this country, as well as around the world. Among the civilian populace he boasts the reputation of a generous and righteous man, but among us within the law, well…let us just say that we know him very differently."

"Then how did both our teams get blown?" McCarter asked.

"It's possible we could've gotten some answers from Sahib," Hawkins interjected. He directed his next comment to Mazouzi. "Unfortunately, your people snatched him from us before we could interrogate him."

"It is also possible that we shall never know," Mazouzi said. His easy reply made it clear that Hawkins's observation hadn't offended him. "It is important that you remember Trebba knew Sahib was an important asset and therefore Khalidi would know it, as well. He was probably having Sahib watched. The important thing now is for us to find Khalidi and shut down his transshipment pipeline to Europe. This is the priority."

"You think so?" McCarter asked. "Because not that we're all not real grateful for saving our arses back there, but our priority is stopping his human-trafficking shipment out of the United States."

"All the more reason to shut down his pipeline. It is the money in drugs that interests el Khalidi most. Remember that in your country, and some others, he is vulnerable and so must hire outsiders to do his dirty work. Here in Morocco, though, he is protected and operates with a free hand. If Trebba knew Sahib might be a good source of information you can be sure el Khalidi knew so, too."

"Which probably explains how we got made," Manning concluded.

"But what about us?" Encizo asked. "How could el Khalidi possibly have guessed correctly twice?"

"I think we were being watched," Mazouzi said.

"In which case we might still—"

"Yes." Mazouzi's eyes flicked to the rearview mirror at Encizo's remark. If they were being followed he made no sign of it.

Mazouzi drove for fifteen minutes until the city became scattered villages and eventually open land. He then took a nondescript exit and drove along a dusty, barren road for approximately five miles that twisted and turned through a rise in elevation, until they reached another road that Phoenix Force almost missed as being a road. Another mile over bumpy terrain surrounded by dense woods terminated at a clearing.

A squat, house—brown in color and made out of what could have been adobe but was more likely composite materials of some kind—sat in the center of the clearing. It looked well kept and when Mazouzi escorted them inside they were all surprised to find the place in meticulous order. On the walls of a central room were maps of different parts of the country and one wall boasted a massive world map with red pushpins in specific countries across the globe. The remainder of the maps were of Casablanca and surrounding areas.

The table sported everything from documents to computers to grease pencils and more. The fact that all the doors were heavy, wooden exteriors with obvious metal cores hadn't been lost on any of the men in Phoenix Force; neither had they failed to notice the three large exterior rooms, each with three cots that bore sheets, pillows and blankets, two full baths and a huge kitchen facility.

After taking a good look around the place, McCarter eyed Mazouzi. "I take it this isn't just your run-of-the-mill getaway place."

Mazouzi smiled. "I've been stocking it in my spare time since my recruitment. I used the pay I collected from Interpol to buy it. It belonged to a family in Casablanca that had it built and intended to move in. The man of their house was killed in a robbery that went wrong, and when I learned of it I offered to buy it in a private sale. Every month I pay them cash and they credit my account. It is a very good arrangement."

"No doubt," Hawkins said.

"Looks like it's already seen quite a bit of use," Manning remarked.

"I have found it necessary to collect these things since I began to watch Abbas el Khalidi much more closely. Some of the intelligence I gathered was before Interpol came to me, but most of it was collected after my recruitment."

"Couldn't have done a better job if you ask me," Encizo said, visibly impressed by the layout.

"So I'm curious to know why you didn't just bring us here to start with," McCarter said.

"This was my final option." Mazouzi looked around and sighed. "It was intended to be a last place of refuge if something like this ever happened. If I'd brought you here immediately and we were under observation, then our enemies would have learned of it and would in turn have told el Khalidi."

"But this way nobody knows about it," Manning concluded.

"Right."

"Smart," McCarter said. He gestured around the room and said, "So I'd guess that among all of this stuff you've got something solid on Khalidi's movements."

Mazouzi nodded. "I know much, in fact. But as I said before I did not know if I could trust anyone with the information. Now that I have seen you and your men in action, I believe you are capable of doing exactly as you say you can do. Finally we can end el Khalidi's reign and put him in prison for life."

"Our intent isn't to put him in prison, mate," McCarter said.

"Your orders are to kill him."

"If the opportunity presents itself, yeah."

Mazouzi nodded. "I believe I can understand why you have these orders. But I'm still bound by my oath to not take a kill without provocation."

"Look, partner," Hawkins said, "we appreciate all you've done to help us but you got to understand that this guy poses a significant threat to our country. From everything we know so far, he's employed terrorists or members of al Qaeda to run his business concerns in the U.S., as well as caused the death of at least two of our congressmen."

"And let's not forget that of all the slave trading he's chosen to finance his efforts with, he's targeted children," James added. "That's the most reprehensible kind of slavery, in my opinion."

Mazouzi looked at each of the Phoenix Force warriors in turn and something definitely changed in his expression. Up until this point, Mazouzi had come off as somewhat of a type A personality, but now the men saw something different in him. This Mazouzi was not the same one who had met them at the airport; something had almost seemed to liberate him from whatever emotional or mental bonds had held him back. Whatever happened now, Phoenix Force was confident that they could get the cop's full cooperation. In the next minute, he demonstrated as much.

"I have collected much information," he said as he sat at one of the computers and powered it up. "The main problem is I do not know exactly how to organize it. There is much scattered intelligence from many sources. My own notes have even been entered on this computer but I do not have any way of running it through the Interpol systems for comparison."

"Does this computer have internet access?" Manning asked.

Mazouzi nodded. "Interpol provided me with an interface card that communicates with a secure satellite. I am not the most technical man, please understand. I had to take courses at local school in order to learn the most basic tasks, although I will say I am more proficient than I used to be."

Manning turned to McCarter. "If he has access to a satellite…are you thinking what I'm thinking?"

McCarter nodded and said to Mazouzi, "I think we can help you with this."

AARON "BEAR" KURTZMAN had never been much for pomp and circumstance.

His mind was a steel trap and most of the time the head of Stony Man's information systems and cybernetics team tried to keep his approach simple and direct. At its core the team members who reported directly to Kurtzman included Carmen Delahunt, Akira Tokaido and Huntington Wethers, although there were many more experts who contributed to Stony Man's excellent information network. Every scrap of processed information in the Western Hemisphere came through Stony Man's massive computer systems. This information was evaluated, sorted, organized and stored, if applicable, within a variety of relational database management systems.

Whenever they could virtualize their systems to conserve space, such as the untraceable hacks they maintained in other federal agencies like the FBI, DIA, NSA, DARPA, CIA and Justice Department, they would do so. However, some information had to be stored locally and that required a significant amount of power and processing. Within the Annex network alone there were massive circuit boards that contained hundreds of central processing units capable of performing billions of computations per hour. These systems worked symbiotically with each other to provide the information-network platform needed to deliver real-time systems data solutions to Kurtzman and his team.

In turn, Kurtzman could collect and assess any data sets or subsets and perform an intelligence analysis that he could then provide in streamlined, focused reports. These reports were the critical pivot points on which Price and Brognola made their decisions, deciding which threats to assess and keep close in the event they had to activate one or both of the field teams to tackle specific problems.

Given all of that, then, it was child's play for Kurtzman to collate and organize the information sent from Zafar Mazouzi's personal computer system into an intelligence brief that Price could evaluate. She entered Kurtzman's office just as he was putting the finishing touches on a new digitized version of the map on the massive touch screen that spanned one wall of his office that had been positioned at a height to accommodate his wheelchair.

Kurtzman reached up and touched a point on the screen near Berlin, and a red dot appeared there. He then slid a virtual document from one corner of the screen into position in an open area where the Pacific Ocean would have been and moved one corner of the document to expand it so that the text was readable.

"I got your email," Price said. "What's up?"

"I just finished disseminating the information sent by Phoenix Force that Mazouzi's been collecting for the past five years or so. This here," he said as he pointed to the map on the wall, "displays all of the cities where el Khalidi's people are delivering drugs. So far Interpol's managed to succeed in tearing down two of the major distribution points, although they believe whenever one gets shut down that Khalidi's contacts simply set up new points somewhere else and communicate those back to Morocco."

"So these are only distribution points?" Price asked. "There's no processing or manufacturing going on?"

"Not as far as we know."

"That means the processing has to be taking place in Morocco."

"Not so fast, my dear," Kurtzman replied as he wheeled over to his desk. As he began to type on his keyboard, he said, "We still don't know that the drugs are originating from Morocco. That would only be an assumption based on partial intelligence, and we shouldn't jump to such an assumption so quickly."

"Good point," Price said as she looked at the map again. "You're thinking there could be other points of origin?"

"I didn't necessarily say that, either," Kurtzman replied with a grin.

"Are you just messing with my head because it's early in the morning and I haven't had my run or coffee yet?" Price asked good-naturedly.

"Oh, were it that simple," Kurtzman teased.

This kind of banter couldn't be described as anything

new. Kurtzman and Price spent many hours together, and as a result they had developed a very close, albeit platonic, relationship. They treated each other like siblings and consequently bickered like them at times. Nobody else within Stony Man got between the pair, including Brognola. It was a friendship that had been forged from a long-standing need for human contact under the most stressful and at times downright hectic environments, and the confidences they put in each other were vital necessities.

"I'm just saying the drugs might be harvested and processed in their source countries and Khalidi simply arranges shipment," Kurtzman continued.

He finished typing and a picture came up on the wall of a square-faced man with dark skin, a neatly trimmed beard, wild curly dark hair and bifocals. "I'd like to introduce a possible new player to the game. This is Ebi Sahaf, a native of India who studied at the University of New Delhi. Up until a few years ago, Sahaf worked for a variety of agencies as a technical expert. He's well-known enough that I've even read some of his white papers on various topics regarding technology applications for structural engineering. In short, the guy's a genius."

"What's his connection?"

"Eight years ago he left India and moved to Casablanca. Guess who he took a job with?"

"Khalidi."

"Give that woman a prize." Kurtzman tapped another key and a slide show began with a series of photos of Sahaf. "These were pictures taken by various news agencies not long after Sahaf went to work for *Abd-el-Aziz*. Officially, Sahaf was hired as a low-level technical adviser to Khalidi's news organization."

"An odd job for a man of his caliber to pack up and move thousands of miles for," Price remarked.

"My feeling exactly," Kurtzman said. "What's interesting is these photos were taken in many different countries. Coincidentally, the computer algorithms I had Carmen run on the meticulous log Mazouzi kept on Khalidi's movements revealed dates that corresponded directly to dates where Khalidi was out of Morocco.

"I then cross-referenced those dates against the dates Interpol logged Khalidi traveling abroad and it turned out the dates Khalidi was in these other countries are within the same range of the dates photos were taken of Ebi Sahaf."

Price nodded. "Hmm…so it's obvious Sahaf and Khalidi were traveling separately while the whole time Sahaf has secretly been advising him. Were there any pictures taken of them together?"

"No," Kurtzman said. "I thought that was pretty strange but all I can assume is they never communicated personally with each other. My guess would be they used email aliases or perhaps encrypted voice communications to speak."

"And being seen together in Casablanca wouldn't have been unusual so they didn't need to be careful there," Price said. "It would've been plenty easy for them to meet discreetly."

"Right. Now here's the whipped cream and cherry on top," Kurtzman said. "About five years ago, Ebi Sahaf simply dropped off the radar. He didn't publish any more articles, he didn't make any more public appearances or speak at any conferences and he hasn't been active on any of the engineering-community sites as he once had been.

"No interviews, no articles, no public-speaking engagements. Nothing."

"Hiding?"

"Maybe, although I'm betting it's in Morocco somewhere," Kurtzman said. "The only activity I can find on him, financial or otherwise, is he's renewed his passport annually and on occasion there are small charges to a number of his credit cards."

Price nodded. "Uh-huh. Sounds like just enough activity so that people think he's alive and well but in actuality he's not really active at all. So what do you think? Maybe that Khalidi killed him?"

"No way. A guy like Sahaf is way too valuable to kill. One thing we know for certain is that Sahaf is a devout Muslim."

"Really? That *is* a surprise," Price replied. "I'd think he'd be a Hindu."

"As would most, although that's apparently not the case here. I believe Sahaf's disappearance is by design. I think he went underground and that he's working secretly for Abbas el Khalidi."

"To what end?"

"Well, figuring that out is the real trick, isn't it?" Kurtzman shook his head and stared absently at the map. "But if I had to venture a guess, and it's only a guess, mind you, I'd have to believe it has something to do with Khalidi's transshipment pipeline. Maybe he's helped Khalidi build a secret processing plant or devised some unique way of smuggling the drugs out of Morocco. Hell, for all we know they might be building a nuclear bomb to sell to al Qaeda for funds. It's hard to tell. Whatever they're doing, though, you can bet that Sahaf's working for Khalidi."

"Okay, I'll let Phoenix Force know what you've come up with," Price said. "If Khalidi's been too careful to pin down, maybe they can pick up Sahaf's trail and that will lead them to the heart of whatever Khalidi has up his sleeve. Good work, Bear!"

Kurtzman yawned as he folded his massive arms over his muscular chest. "Thanks. Now I'm going to bed."

CHAPTER THIRTEEN

Casablanca, Morocco

Abbas el Khalidi didn't know at first how to process the news delivered by one of his spies.

They had originally told him that the local operations were not in jeopardy and then come back to say that the police, accompanied by unidentified individuals, had been going after the street-level dealers. In fact, two of these men—Mahmed Paran, aka Sahib, and Osama Ubuntu—had been grabbed by members of the Casablanca police force and were now being held in a secure facility pending charges. Ubuntu would probably beat any conviction since there were at least a dozen witnesses who said he was grabbed by the police without provocation, and one of the attorneys who was secretly on Khalidi's payroll indicated Ubuntu had suffered police brutality. Paran, on the other hand, had been in possession of an unlicensed firearm and that was a very serious charge in Morocco. Only time would tell if he would be freed since no bond was permitted for a firearms case.

And at the center of it all was the Maroc cop, Zafar Mazouzi. Khalidi hated that bastard, hated him for his interference into Khalidi's operations, as well as the sneaking around he'd been doing. Khalidi's people had advised him of Mazouzi's self-appointed mission and he'd heard stories of how Mazouzi mysteriously showed up at one of

Khalidi's street operations after another to shut them down. Mazouzi had become a thorn in Khalidi's side but the drug lord had opted not to do anything about it. The death of a cop, even one who wasn't appreciated by his colleagues because he chose not to partake in the widespread graft, would draw enough unwanted attention that Khalidi had actually issued an order to his connections *not* to touch Mazouzi. In fact, Mazouzi probably didn't know that Khalidi had put certain personnel inside the police in place to make sure nothing bad happened to him.

Well, he'd now lifted his beneficence and ordered every man on the street to keep an eye out for Mazouzi. If he was seen, the order was to terminate the man's life if it could be done without risking the operation to exposure. They were at a critical juncture with their new secret facility in Rabat and he couldn't afford to draw any attention to himself or Ebi Sahaf. For the moment, however, he would not allow this to concern him. Of more danger to their operations were the mysterious strangers, and that was something he needed to address. Normally he would've put Sahaf on such a problem but he had enough going on with the facility and trying to determine what Biinadaz had been planning in America.

That was fine—Abbas el Khalidi had the perfect man for the job. He stood and welcomed the man with a traditional greeting as he entered the office. Hasidim Trebba returned the traditional hug and kiss, and then took the seat Khalidi waved at him. Khalidi returned to the chair behind his desk and offered a drink to Trebba, who politely declined. Trebba was one of the few who did not sneak a little alcohol now and again. Khalidi knew of the inconsistent Islamic view toward consuming alcohol, although he did not personally believe it to be the sin as did some of his employees. Not that Trebba would ever have dared point it out to him. That was one of the reasons he liked the cop, because he had respect and class. He wasn't like most of his comrades, and Khalidi had spent much time around the police, inserting himself into their ranks right under their proverbial noses.

"Thank you for coming on short notice, Hasidim."

"Thank you for inviting me," Trebba replied.

"I must apologize for dispensing with the pleasantries but unfortunately this is much more a business call than a social one."

Trebba inclined his head to indicate he understood.

Khalidi continued, "I would not ordinarily ask you to risk exposing yourself like this but it's somewhat of an emergency."

"Perhaps I can hasten your attempts to explain."

"Oh?"

"You are worried about the disappearance of Zafar Mazouzi, no?"

Khalidi couldn't help but smile. "I see you're still as observant as always."

"Policemen must be observant," Trebba said, making a show of inspecting his fingernails. He stared Khalidi in the eyes and opined, "I don't think we should be concerned with his disappearance as much as that of the Americans."

"So the foreigners my spies tell me about are from America?"

"Some sort of strike team," Trebba said with a casual wave, "although I don't think we have to worry about them."

Khalidi felt the blood rush to his face. "My dear Hasidim, if the Americans know enough that they would send secret operatives to Casablanca, then I would have to disagree with your assessment. How could you even suggest they are not a threat?"

"I wasn't suggesting they weren't a threat," Trebba said. "I was merely expressing an opinion as to their presence and its impact on your operations. You have nothing to fear from these men. They have run to ground, just like Mazouzi, and I would not at all doubt they are all hiding together somewhere and waiting for you to make a move."

"So you don't believe they know anything about me?"

"Why should they? And even if they did, Abbas, who cares?" Trebba held up a finger with each point. "First, they have very few resources in Morocco at this point. Zafar made sure of this after he resigned his post and then stole away with foreigners who are in the country illegally. Second, there is very little chance they can move about this country very long without drawing attention, and because of the crimes they've perpetrated against Moroccans there is a shoot-on-sight order in effect. Finally, they have found nothing that can be traced directly back to you and therefore you have no reason to worry about your activities being exposed."

"You make valid points," Khalidi said after considering Trebba's argument. "However, the fact they are still alive is of great concern to me. Live men can pose a threat to my plans even by making trouble for us in other areas."

"You should let me take care of that."

"How, if you cannot even find them?"

"Sooner or later, Zafar will come to me. He trusts me. In fact, I'm probably one of the few he trusts. Your order to look out for him, make sure no harm befell him, was more prophetic than you might even understand because it could prove to be your greatest weapon against him."

"I only wonder, and you will forgive me in advance since I mean no offense by this, how trustworthy *you* are."

"Me? What have I ever done that you would mistrust my loyalties?"

"You're proposing this very moment to betray and kill a man you've known for nearly twenty years," Khalidi replied. "Is it so hard to believe that this would give me pause to think?"

Khalidi hadn't made the statement as much because it did concern him as he wanted to gauge Trebba's reaction. How Hasidim Trebba had come onto Khalidi's payroll had always been somewhat of a mystery to him. Someone had given Trebba critical information, enough that when Trebba began to poke around he discovered it was Khalidi behind the main drug pipeline out of the country. Khalidi had originally marked Trebba for elimination, putting out a contract on the cop's head worth one hundred thousand dollars. To his surprise, Trebba had proved resourceful enough to show up in Khalidi's private hotel suite one night in Spain, of all places, and make Khalidi an offer that no businessman in his right mind would have refused. Trebba had offered to act as Khalidi's eyes and ears inside the Casablanca police in exchange for the hundred grand Khalidi had put on his head.

Of course, the money had turned into nothing less than a salary and over the past five years—basically since he'd sequestered Ebi Sahaf to oversee construction of the underwater complex in Rabat—Trebba had made about a half-million dollars to act as Khalidi's eyes and ears inside the Maroc law-enforcement community. It then didn't come as any surprise what Trebba proposed next.

"I could be persuaded to take care of this problem once and for all," Trebba said. "If, of course, you were willing to make it worth the risk."

"What do you propose?"

"You've made all the deposits to the numbered account in Zurich? I know, I've been keeping tabs."

"Yes."

"There's now a half-million dollars in the account."

"Yes. Get to your point, Hasidim. I'm a patient man but a busy one."

"Triple the current amount and I will dispatch Zafar Mazouzi," Trebba said quietly. "Once and for all."

Khalidi produced a scoffing laugh. "You want me to pay you a million and a half dollars for the head of one man? An ex-cop who has all but alienated himself from the Casablanca police?"

"Don't forget that if I kill Zafar I have to eliminate his American friends, too. I should think six men are worth at least that much. Not to mention that once I do this I will have to leave the country. Five hundred thousand is hardly enough to live on comfortably for the rest of my life, even in South America or Pakistan."

Now Abbas el Khalidi could see that this was exactly the kind of opportunity Trebba had been waiting for. He'd probably known about the arrival of the Americans before they even entered the country and yet he'd chosen not to say anything until now. He was as cold and calculating as his reputation for brutality on the streets; this both pleased and frightened Khalidi because he wondered what other treachery Trebba might justify if the sides were ever reversed. Still, he made a good point and Khalidi had been in business long enough to know that opportunities like this only came along so often. Besides, if Trebba got himself killed trying to execute Mazouzi or the Americans it wouldn't be sweat off his brow. There wasn't anything to connect Hasidim back here.

"You know, now that I consider it this *would* be a small price to pay," Khalidi said with a smile. "Very well, Hasidim, you have your wish. Kill Mazouzi and the Americans and I will pay you your price."

Trebba nodded. "Consider it done."

"I DON'T LIKE THIS PLAN," McCarter told Mazouzi. "Too much risk with too little return on the investment."

"I understand your concerns," Mazouzi said with a nod of acknowledgment. "However, I must remind you that I'm very much an outcast here in Morocco, and in Casablanca even more so. The only option left to us to make el Khalidi expose himself is by hitting those things most important to him. We must shut down his factory operations in Safi first. That will force him to change his current method of operation, and I think he will make a wrong move."

"And you're certain this factory is one of his?" Encizo inquired.

Mazouzi nodded and tapped the map on the table with emphasis. "Safi is the capital of the Doukkala-Abda region. There is much activity there, many businesses that export many things. The main commercial export is fish, sardines in particular."

"Sorry, but you've lost me," Hawkins said around a bite of sandwich. "What does any of this have to do with Khalidi?"

It was Encizo who answered. "Boats."

"Come again?" James said.

"Boats. The main export is fish, right? That means boats are in and out of that port all the time. It also means that foreign boats draw lots of attention but local fishing trawlers don't get a second look. If Khalidi has a manufacturing point operating out of Safi, he could well be moving processed drugs to some other point by water, then in turn move them out of the country to the transshipment points along the European pipeline."

"Right," Manning said with a nod. "The boats then get off-loaded before European customs can actually inspect them."

"So let me see if I got this straight," McCarter told

Mazouzi. "You're proposing that Khalidi's operating a bunch of fishing trawlers that he sends out and they load up drugs from oceangoing vessels and bring them back to Safi. The drugs get refined and processed, then get sent back out by these same fishing boats and once more loaded onto outgoing vessels bound for Europe."

Mazouzi nodded.

McCarter looked among the rest of the group and said, "Pretty bloody clever if you ask me."

"I don't know," James said. "Seems a little too risky to use the same boats to move the drugs both inland and out."

"You got an alternate theory?" Manning asked.

"I just think," James continued, "that would be enough traffic to draw attention. Now if he was just using Safi as a port to bring the drugs in or send them out alone, or even just to process them, that would be something else entirely."

"Well, we aren't going to find out sitting around on our arses," McCarter said. He looked back to Mazouzi. "So what did you have in mind?"

"The factory is probably well guarded," Mazouzi said. "I think it would be better if we go in at night. I have all of the equipment you will need but weapons are a bit more of a problem."

"Not to worry," McCarter said. "We know how to take care of that."

"Assuming you can get us back to the airport," Manning said.

"This will not be a problem," Mazouzi said with a nod.

"I don't think we should all do that," Encizo replied.

"You have somewhere else to be, Mr. Gold?" McCarter said.

"In fact I do. I'd suggest while some of us go back for our weapons, we send a detachment to recon this factory. I mean, why take chances? We don't have much intelligence on it and we know Khalidi has significant resources. I'd think it would be smart to take a look at this place before we decide to put our necks on the chopping block."

"He does have a point," Hawkins said to McCarter.

The Briton considered his options. It was true that so far Khalidi had managed to stay one step ahead of them. Supposedly he no longer had a line on them, but McCarter couldn't be sure how long they could stay under the radar. They were operating solely off Mazouzi's intelligence, which wasn't very much, and they had already seen their presence in the country was compromised. Operating in smaller teams, while it bothered McCarter a whole hell of a lot, would have to continue by necessity for the moment. Time was a luxury they no longer had, and the more time they spent together doing jobs they could do just as quickly and efficiently in teams, the more chance they wouldn't find Khalidi's operation in time to shut it down.

"Okay," McCarter said. "Mr. Gold, you'll accompany Mazouzi back to the airport and show him our reserved hangar. Bring everything, and I mean *everything*."

Encizo nodded.

McCarter turned to Manning. "You and I will get some wheels and take a trip down to Safi. The drive's not more than an hour—" he looked at Mazouzi "—and I'm sure we can find some small agency to rent us a car without asking a lot of questions."

Mazouzi nodded. "It would be better if I loaned you my vehicle and rented one myself. This will not draw attention."

"Fine," McCarter said.

"What about us?" Hawkins asked in reference to himself and James.

"I want you two to go easy for now," McCarter said.

"You guys took it rough in this last round and some rest will do you good."

"But—" James began.

"No arguments, Mr. White," McCarter interrupted, the edge apparent in his voice. "We'll be hitting this factory in a few hours and I need each of you at your peak…or at least as close to it as possible. Besides, we need someone here to man headquarters and wait for communications from the Farm on the intelligence we sent. All teams will check in with headquarters at half-hour intervals. This way if there's any trouble we'll know about it soon enough. Understood?"

They nodded in unison and then McCarter stood. "All right, those of us on field duty get ready to mount up. We've got a bloody hell of a lot of work to do and a short time in which to do it."

THE LATE HOUR passed into early morning without incident and it was almost 0200 hours local time when the members of Phoenix Force were reunited.

"The place is pretty much laid out according to Mazouzi's intelligence," McCarter told his teammates. "There's a light crew on at night, so we're guessing that if there are drugs running through there that's probably the time they'd be processing them."

"So most likely there aren't any innocents to get in the way," Hawkins said.

McCarter nodded.

"What about other civilians?" James asked. "Those who don't work there but might just happen to wander near the place, for example."

"Won't be any concern," Manning said. "A number of other factories surround this one but they're far enough away that even stray shots shouldn't pose a danger to by-standers."

"What about sentries?"

"Half dozen walking the perimeter," McCarter said. "They try to look like uniformed security but I don't doubt they're just hired guns."

"You saw no weapons?" Mazouzi said.

McCarter shook his head.

"Do not let this deceive you," the cop replied. "While the restriction on firearms in Morocco is strictly enforced and most firms do not offer armed security because of the liability, anyone Khalidi has watching his assets will be armed."

McCarter nodded in understanding. "Not to worry, we'll be going in hard and fast."

"Well, we rounded up plenty of firepower and all of the ammunition available," Encizo said. "Shouldn't have any trouble on this run."

"Good deal. Let's start gearing up and do a weapons check. Bring plenty of spare magazines and change to full combat attire." McCarter made a gesture and added, "I don't want to risk being outgunned this time."

"Do you have a spare set of fatigues for me?" Mazouzi asked.

"No," McCarter said with a lopsided frown. "I'm sorry, Zafar, but this is where you get off the train. I can't allow you to tag along."

Mazouzi's face changed color. "What? But you are operating from my information!"

"And we appreciate it, but we can't risk you getting caught," McCarter said. "If we get hammered at least you can disavow any knowledge of our actions and make the story somewhat credible."

"Don't insult my intelligence, Brown," Mazouzi said.

"Everybody knows by now that we're in league with each other."

"Look, Mazouzi, I'm not going to argue the bleeding point with you," McCarter replied in a flat tone. "You're not going along on this one and that's the end of it."

"Then I will go alone."

McCarter said, "I can't stop you."

"No," Mazouzi said, anger flashing in his eyes. "You cannot."

"I won't try."

Mazouzi expressed suspicion now. "I don't trust you."

"Sorry."

"What are you planning? You are not a man that would give up so easily?"

"You're a free agent just like me. Although I'd think you might try to gather some additional intelligence."

"How?"

"Maybe reach out to your friend Trebba, since you seem to trust him."

"Yes," Mazouzi said. "I had not considered this before."

"Just do me a favor?"

"I think you're about out of favors, American," Mazouzi said.

"Maybe so," McCarter said. "But all the same, watch your arse, mate. I'd hate to lose an ally like you on our account."

"Sometimes, Mr. Brown, you and your friends surprise me."

"Really," McCarter replied with a smile. "I've never heard that before."

CHAPTER FOURTEEN

Dressed in flat black combat fatigues and stocking caps, with camouflage paint smeared on their faces, the five warriors of Phoenix Force prepared to launch their assault.

David McCarter peered through the night-vision binoculars, part of the gear that Encizo and Mazouzi had retrieved. In addition to the surveillance equipment, each team member had equipped himself with a select arsenal and plenty of ammunition. The entire armament, really, had been supplied by Stony Man's contacts within Morocco—no small feat considering they had very few allies in the otherwise primarily Muslim country. While Morocco and the United States were on relatively friendly terms, the religious differences still contained within them a level of tension that could not be overcome by mere political affiliations.

Not that Morocco hadn't shared in a considerably decent share of the profits from tourism, a large amount of the tourist population being Westerners. In fact, a number of flights came into and left Morocco daily from cities like Los Angeles, Miami, New York and Philadelphia, with plenty of money being left behind as evidence of just how well the business thrived in Morocco.

And then there were the many exports shipped daily to the United States, a lot of the products bought at elevated prices. American companies even operated a number of properties and interests within Morocco, providing hundreds of jobs to Moroccan citizens and bearing nowhere

near the liabilities and regulatory compliance issues in
that nation as they had to bear within their own country.
So much for a democratic republic that believed in economic freedom and capitalism—shipping jobs overseas
had become the norm for companies in America rather
than the exception.

McCarter didn't really care about such matters, however, at least not when it came to missions. The objective always remained the same for the team leader. He
headed a unit of crack antiterrorists, one of the finest in
the world, and that kind of responsibility meant he had to
keep them alive. That was goal number one. McCarter let
that always stay as an item of alert and necessity in the
back of his mind, bringing it to the forefront in the moments he needed it.

This had proved to be one of those moments as he
took, for the second time in these early-morning hours,
a good look at the sentry patrols. His earlier assessment
had not revealed any weapons on the uniformed security
that patrolled the ten-foot-high chain-link fence surrounding the factory, but on this pass, after considering the advice Mazouzi had given him, McCarter realized he hadn't
looked as carefully as he might have had he known then
what he knew now.

"Looks like our Moroccan friend was right again," Mc-
Carter said. He passed the NVDs to James, who lay on the
roof of Mazouzi's SUV alongside the fox-faced Briton.

James peered through the binoculars in the direction
McCarter pointed and after a minute of study he lowered
the night-vision device and nodded in agreement. "Yeah,
those sentries are definitely armed. You can tell just by
the way they're carrying themselves. Probably semiautomatics beneath those uniform jackets."

"That was my thinking," McCarter said. "Might even have machine pistols or bloody SMGs for all we know."

"I'd say there's no point in taking chances," James said.

McCarter frowned. "I know what you're going to say, Cal, and I'm still concerned. Sniping our enemies without knowing if they are our enemies makes my arse itch."

"There's no doubt these men are working for Khalidi," James said. "I believe Mazouzi's intelligence. He hasn't been wrong so far and moreover I think that there are drugs inside that warehouse. Look at the other factories and plants. Do you see any security?"

"No," McCarter said and knew he had to admit his friend was right.

"And do you know why?" James persisted. "Because there are no illegal operations going on inside of them. They have security for a fish-packing-and-processing warehouse. Really? I mean…come on!"

"Still doesn't make me want to be responsible for killing innocent people."

Now James could no longer contain his smile. "Me, either. That's why I told Rafe to be sure to grab some k-darts. I figured they'd come in handy."

McCarter noticed James's grin now and coupled with the k-darts comment he knew the guy had been putting him on all along. While it wasn't really something to joke about, McCarter was definitely feeling better. The "k-dart" referred to ketamine, a drug commonly used to tranquilize animals. In this case it wasn't really the truth since k-darts didn't contain any ketamine due to its side effects. Still, the name had stuck for the more human-friendly cocktail that included valium, Sodium Pentothal and chlorpromazine in a mixture guaranteed to put out a three-hundred-pound male in about twenty seconds.

"Think you're bloody clever, don't you?" McCarter said

as he keyed the short-frequency radio attached to a throat mike. "Sigma One to Sigma Three. Do it."

The design of Akira Tokaido, the radio had a special chip inside it that turned the transmission to static by digitizing the transmission and encoding it with short bursts. This made it next to impossible to pick up with other short-range radios, even on the same frequency, since ninety percent of such radios were analog. Of course there was a small chance their conversations could be overheard, still, since there was no "real" way to encrypt an open-air transmission, but the possession of such equipment wasn't typical among criminals and terrorists.

In any case, McCarter knew his transmission had gotten through when Sigma Three came back with the reply: "Roger."

GARY MANNING, aka Sigma Three, had taken up a position atop a parked semitrailer nearly one hundred yards from the factory.

He sighted through the scope of the MSG90 sniper rifle, tracking his first target—a uniformed sentry on the southwest side of the perimeter fence. Hitting the sentry wouldn't be the tricky part, hitting the sentry without the dart connecting with a piece of the chain-link fence would be the real trick. If he'd been firing a high-velocity projectile it wouldn't have concerned him, but this would take a much more deft hand.

The MSG90 would help Manning do that job. A militarized version of the Heckler & Koch PSG1, the MSG90 had become a favorite among the members of the Stony Man teams. Not only was it rated as one of the most highly accurate sniping rifles in the world, but it was also one of the most reliable. It sported a high-capacity magazine of twenty rounds, currently seated within the cargo pocket

of Manning's fatigue pants, but also a 5-round magazine
that presently contained the k-darts.

Manning estimated the windage once more as he took
a deep breath and let half out, locking the stock tighter
against his shoulder and pressing his cheek to the same.
The illuminated reticule of the Hensoldt ZF6 15 × 56 mm
scope glowed. There hadn't been an actual nighttime scope
available so this would have to do. Manning gave it one last
check and then squeezed the trigger. The weapon made almost no sound since the k-dart was propelled by a subsonic
cartridge—anything more would have been nothing short
of disastrous and would have destroyed the efficacy of the
chemicals within it, if not the projectile itself.

The k-dart hit the target, the impact obvious from the
way the sentry stopped suddenly and reached to his neck.
Manning began to count off the seconds, not moving or
making a sound, watching the sentry's motions through
the scope. It would take approximately fifteen seconds
for the drugs to take full effect, and it was about that long
when Manning spotted the sentry drop to the ground in
an unconscious heap.

"Go," he whispered.

As soon as Encizo and Hawkins heard the signal they were
up and moving toward the gate. The four roving sentries
were spread far enough apart, and the external lot poorly
lit enough, to permit the pair to breach the chain-link fence
before they were spotted. They crossed the open space—
the riskiest part of their venture—within a few seconds
and Encizo set up covering position while Hawkins went
to work on the fence with a pair of tin snips after testing
to ensure it wasn't electrified.

"Ten seconds," McCarter's voice announced in their
headsets.

Once they were inside the fence line, Manning was supposed to take out the sentry in the northwest corner. That would buy McCarter and James the time they needed to advance on that position, and Manning would follow up to complete their entry action.

McCARTER AND James broke cover as soon as they saw the sentry on the northwest corner fall.

The pair had advanced about half the distance to the hole in the fence when autofire began to rake the rough concrete around them. Muzzle-flashes winked from small ports within the building and bullets chipped concrete and dust around them. One burned so close that James heard it buzz past his ear.

"Sigma One to Sigma Three," he said into his microphone. "We're taking fire. You got eyes on it?"

"I copy, Sigma One. Working on it."

GARY MANNING FLIPPED out the 5-round magazine, withdrew the high-capacity magazine and slammed it home. He jacked the charging handle to eject the next k-dart from the chamber. When the bolt came forward it slammed home on a 7.62 × 51 mm NATO round. Manning put his eye to the sight and swept the muzzle along the perimeter of the factory until he spotted the first muzzle-flash. Through the scope, in the light of the flash, Manning saw the silhouette of the first target's head.

Manning jammed the stock tighter against his shoulder in the knowledge that this time the rifle would definitely have a kick to it. He let out half a deep breath, reassessed the silhouette one last time and then squeezed the trigger. With less than a 1.5-pound pull it didn't take much, and it was this particular feature that made the MSG90 so accurate. The bullet left the barrel at approximately 870 meters per second and hit with stunning effect. Manning watched in the scope as the target's head seemed to explode under the impact of his marksmanship, the geyser of blood, bone and flesh evident even from this distance.

Manning swung onto the second target, acquired the desired site picture and squeezed the trigger. The effect produced roughly the same results, although Manning couldn't see quite so many details as the first. He called an all-clear signal into his radio and then continued scanning the parking area and perimeter of the building for any further trouble. He was supposed to rally with his teammates in the next minute or so, but Manning wasn't entirely sure he could do that; if he left this position they wouldn't have any cover.

Well, to hell with it. Orders were orders and he had no intention of taking it upon himself to disobey McCarter. He'd make the rendezvous come what may.

JAMES AND McCARTER scrambled to their feet and continued toward the point of ingress as soon as Manning advised them it was safe.

McCarter was damn glad to have the Canadian on their side. In light of the fact they'd nearly gotten their butts shot off by hard cases inside the processing factory, he wondered if his decision to have them rendezvous before commencing their assault on the main building had been wise. It would've been better to let Manning hold the high ground and take out any opposition they hadn't accounted for.

Well, too late to change tactics now—Manning was probably already on his way to them.

As if reading his thoughts, McCarter had barely had time to consult with Hawkins or Encizo before they saw a shadowy figure sprinting toward their position. They held their weapons at the ready until it became obvious it was Gary Manning. Once they were gathered, McCarter gave the signal and they were on the move again, putting at least fifteen yards between each other as they converged on the factory.

In fact, the place turned out to be more of a fish-packing-and-processing plant than a factory. The smell of dead and rotting fish nearly overpowered the five men, even stronger this close to the outskirts. It was so strong at this point it seemed practically toxic to him, and McCarter figured if the enemy didn't get them then the odor damn sure might.

"Whew!" Hawkins said as he pressed his back to one of the steel beams that framed the external walls. "Maybe we should've brought our protective masks."

"Really," James added. "I didn't think we'd be subjected to an NBC hazard."

"Quit your bloody yakking and get to it," McCarter ordered.

Manning stepped around the other four and knelt just to the left of a heavy door. He unslung his shoulder bag, withdrew two pieces of M-118 block demolition explosive. Designed to cut steel, the sheet explosives were more expedient than C-4 plastic blocks. Manning affixed M-8 blasting cap holders into the ends and then primed them with the electric caps themselves, to which he had precrimped the electric wiring. Manning waved his teammates back as he fed out some of the firing wire and then quickly and efficiently twisted it around the terminals of the M-34 blasting machine.

Manning nodded to the rest of the Phoenix Force warriors he was about to blow the door, moved farther to get outside the effective back-blast range and then depressed the handle several times. The blasting machine did its job, sending enough juice through the firing wire to blow as many as fifty blasting caps spanning a five-hundred-foot length. The sheet explosives did the trick nicely, cutting through the heavy metal of the door without effort.

Smoke belched from the red-hot openings and the door fell outward, smacking the pavement with a clang.

"Do it!" McCarter said.

Encizo took point, followed by Manning, McCarter, Hawkins and James on rear guard. They went through the door one behind the other and fanned out. Most of the interior was dark although some sections were illuminated by overhanging lamps. It wasn't exactly bright inside, but just enough for them to see without requiring night-vision goggles.

Manning spotted the first resistance in the form of four security officers descending a rickety set of metal stairs, submachine guns held at the ready. They leveled the SMGs and opened fire on the invaders but Phoenix Force already had the space and element of surprise on their side. Manning got the first one with a 3-round burst through the chest from his FN-FAL battle rifle. The impact flipped the gunner over the back side railing of the steps and he rocketed to the pavement.

McCarter felt rounds buzz the air around him and hit the bone-crushing pavement in time to avoid being cut in two by swathing autofire. He rolled to cover behind a big, heavy machine he didn't recognize and came to one knee with his MP-5 ready. McCarter swung the sights into acquisition and squeezed the trigger, delivering a continuous barrage of 9 mm Parabellums in the direction of the "security" guards—as if he'd ever seen legitimate security carrying full-auto weaponry.

Yeah, this was definitely one of Abbas el Khalidi's places.

McCarter's shots hit home and blew the top of another

gunner's skull off. The man dropped his SMG, teeter-tottered a moment and then gravity took over. He bounced down the metal-grate steps and landed at the bottom in a heap.

Encizo and Hawkins got the other two in a cross fire from two different angles. Encizo had triggered his MP-5 in short bursts, aiming for effect, while Hawkins opted to cut the enemy to ribbons with a sustained sweep from an M-16A3. The two remaining guards danced under the impact of 9 mm and 5.56 × 45 mm rounds, the bullets ripping flesh and bone from their bodies without mercy. At one point the pair ran into each other, a sight that would have been funny if it weren't so grisly, and finally they bounced down the steps. One of them reached the bottom and sprawled across his comrade while the other somehow got wedged halfway down and stopped there.

Calvin James felt a little left out at first but that quickly changed.

He heard the scrape of footfalls behind him and whirled in time to see two more uniformed security attempting to sneak up on him. James produced a fierce, sustained scream—a diversionary tactic that froze the two in their tracks for a moment and caused them to produce looks of perplexity—even as he leveled his M-16A3/M-203 and opened fire. The guards realized their mistake a moment too late and instead of attempting to repel James's fire with some of their own, survival instincts took over and they scrambled for cover.

Too little, too late.

James caught the first man with four rounds to the right side of his opponent's body, the impact driving the man backward and slamming him to the painted concrete floor. His partner managed to get partway to a metal support beam before a round shattered his lower leg bone. The guy let out a scream and dropped his weapon. The scream died in his throat as James pumped his stomach full of lead, the exit wounds leaving splotchy patterns in his lower back. He collapsed to the ground, now slick with blood around him.

The reports of the weapons finally died and in their place were sounds of vehicles pulling up out front. Through the open doorway Manning had blasted, McCarter saw the flashing blue lights of police vehicles.

"Cops? How the hell did they—" Encizo began.

"We've been set up!" McCarter yelled. "Anybody know another way out?"

"Probably won't matter," Manning replied. "If they knew we were coming, they'll surely have the place surrounded."

Bloody hell! McCarter thought.

They were trapped inside the factory with an army of cops outside and who knew what kind of numbers the enemy still had inside.

"One way or the other, it's going to be a very long night," Calvin James said.

CHAPTER FIFTEEN

While he didn't want to believe it, Zafar Mazouzi knew the chances he'd been blown by Hasidim Trebba were pretty good.

What troubled him more than that, however, was that Trebba would actually think his comrade stupid enough not to know it. Trebba had always been a loyal friend, but Mazouzi knew he was crooked like so many other men. That he would betray his old friend wasn't something Mazouzi had ever thought he'd have to worry about.

Until now.

Their friendship hadn't been any accident. Mazouzi had already been on the force about four years when they met. He could recall Trebba's first day on the job, a fresh-faced rookie straight from the academy—what had passed for a police academy, back in those days, was laughable even by today's standards—filled with questions and idealism. It hadn't taken a young, impressionable type like Hasidim long to fall into the ways of so many other Maroc cops, and Mazouzi couldn't really say he blamed Trebba for going along with his brothers.

Graft wasn't as uncommon in police departments around the world as most wanted to pretend. Favors of every kind went on all the time, most of them within that blue line, sure, but it happened with much more frequency than most wanted to admit. No police department in any country on Earth could declare itself completely immune from corruption; if it could there wouldn't be any need for internal affairs or any of the other half-dozen units known by other names that policed the police. The sad part was that corruption and graft were oftentimes as much a part of an internal-affairs unit as they were a problem for standard cops.

Then again, such activities were still a very small part of a much larger organization that tried to portray a pure image, unspotted and unblemished by the stain of improprieties. The very idea stank in the nostrils of the politicians who knew better, at least the ones who weren't neck-deep in corruption themselves, and they were typically the ones who liked to go after the unjust among the ranks of the police.

In all of this, it wasn't as if the law-enforcement community in Casablanca was any worse or better than other departments of similar size and construct. At the end of the day, the department had many excellent officers among its ranks. For the most part they went out on the streets and did the best job they could with limited resources. Budget constraints were the worst enemy of police officers everywhere, and it was these kinds of things that had led to widespread graft among the cops. Hell, what cop didn't take everything from the free meal to the free blow job; it really wasn't harming anybody and it kept the playing field somewhat even.

It wasn't until one cop betrayed another that things turned ugly, and Mazouzi knew just by the look on Trebba's face that his longtime friend and partner had betrayed him.

They agreed to meet in a small, remote restaurant on the southeast fringe of the city. This area wasn't heavily populated so there weren't many cops here, and Mazouzi had chosen it by design. Trebba insisted they meet away from the city entirely but Mazouzi refused, content in the knowledge that if Trebba had betrayed him—he knew he'd be certain once he saw the guy and could watch his mannerisms, listen to him speak and look him in the eyes—he at least wouldn't attempt to murder him while they were in public.

Mazouzi arrived a few minutes early and watched the street from the overhang of a small clothing shop directly across from the restaurant, which was open twenty-four hours a day. They were coming into the early-morning hours and, it being a Saturday, the denizens of the area would soon close up their shops and attend prayers at local mosques. When they were through, they would reopen their shops and the day would commence in a business-as-usual fashion.

Mazouzi saw Trebba's car first. He watched his friend get out, look around and then light a cigarette before he went inside. Mazouzi had been to the restaurant many times before, knew the owner's entire family personally, so he felt comfortable with the area. If Trebba planned to kill him here he would have to use outsiders and Mazouzi would be able to pull them out of the crowd with one look.

He did so immediately, noticing the onyx Mercedes pull to the curb four cars behind Trebba's city-issued Citröen Visa. From that vantage point, Mazouzi observed two men inside. One of them lit a cigarette and his face came into visual for a moment in the brightness of the flame. Mazouzi searched his mental files and ten seconds later came back with a name: Aziz Saqaf. Saqaf was an Egyptian-born Arab whose parents immigrated to Casablanca when he was a baby. He'd been in trouble with the law since he was old enough to pick pockets, and now he worked as an assassin for Sahib, aka Mahmed Paran, believed to have been responsible for at least two dozen murders, but none of the evidence was strong enough to prove his guilt in court. So he'd remained on the streets to terrorize everyone from competitors to innocent bystanders who just happened to be in the wrong place at the wrong time.

This could be no mere coincidence.

Trebba had turned the Americans on to Paran first, and now here he was with two of the drug dealer's goons on his tail. There was no way they could have followed Trebba here without his knowledge; the Hasidim Trebba that Mazouzi knew was entirely too experienced for that. It also wouldn't make any sense. Even with Paran in custody, there was no way that Saqaf or anyone else within Paran's organization would've automatically connected Trebba to the events that took place at the Nephdat Club.

No, the only reason a guy like Saqaf would be here was if he'd been invited to tag along and if there had been plenty of money passed along with that invitation.

Well, Mazouzi knew exactly how to deal with this kind of scum. He turned and angled up the sidewalk, watching the vehicle for any movement and managing to get past Saqaf and his passenger unobserved. Mazouzi proceeded another half block and then turned to his left, crossed the street and headed back in the direction he'd come on the opposite side.

When Mazouzi was within a few dozen yards of the vehicle, he withdrew his Walther PPK and surreptitiously palmed a sound suppressor in his other hand. He screwed the device onto the barrel, waited until he was parallel with the back door of the Mercedes and then pivoted ninety degrees and walked straight on to the door. He opened the handle, jumped into the backseat and pressed the barrel of the suppressor directly behind Saqaf's right ear.

"Good morning, Aziz," Mazouzi said with mock cheer.

The passenger started to reach for hardware but Mazouzi

warned him off with an "ah-ah" sound, as if scolding a puppy or infant looking to get into mischief.

"You're not that fast, asshole," Mazouzi said. He looked at Saqaf, whose eyes pinned him in his rearview mirror. "You know, I had hoped that it wouldn't come to this but then it occurred to me—Abbas el Khalidi has never really been known for playing fair. Has he?"

Saqaf tried not to let the mention of Khalidi's name appear to affect him, but for just a moment, Mazouzi's cop intuition took over and he saw the flicker of recognition in the drug assassin's eyes.

"I can see what you're thinking, Aziz. You wonder how I know el Khalidi's behind all of this. Who else? It's no secret that your boss was once an employee for el Khalidi, one who was publicly disgraced when it was discovered he used drugs. Or did he? Maybe that was just what el Khalidi *wanted* everyone to think, since we all know that Sahib's been able to operate on the streets for the past ten years and nobody's been able to touch him.

"And then there's you, of course. How much did my old buddy Hasidim pay you to follow him here? Were you supposed to kill me as soon as I showed up or after I met with him, when I was feeling comfortable enough to make a mistake?"

"You are not as clever as you think, cop," Saqaf finally said. "You will die. Whether now or later, you will not escape death."

"Spare me," Mazouzi interjected. "Guys like you are pathetic, Aziz. You lick the boots of whoever can provide your next meal and you think nothing of killing on a whim. You like to kill, I think. It gives you some sort of high, doesn't it?"

"Who do you think you're fooling, old man?" Saqaf said. "You're still a cop, so straight it's like you've had a cock stuck up your ass the entire time you've been on the streets. You're a maverick, an American wannabe cowboy who betrayed your own people for the Westerners. Yeah, Hasidim told us all about you."

"How much did he tell you?"

"Enough that I know you don't have the balls to pull that trigger. You won't kill me in cold blood."

"Maybe not," Mazouzi said. "Then again, maybe so."

The snap of the report from the PPK was like a firecracker within the confines of the Mercedes and it caused Mazouzi's ears to ring. The left side of the windshield was suddenly covered in blood and brain matter, some of it sticking to the glass like the remnants of gelatin in a bowl while some ran in gory streaks into the recesses of the dash.

Mazouzi turned the smoking muzzle in the direction of the passenger, a man he didn't recognize. Probably one of the men on Saqaf's little hit team. Mazouzi didn't let the man see his fear, neither did he give any indication of the burn in his throat where stomach acid threatened to burn a hole in his esophagus. Mazouzi knew he'd just crossed a line with that one simple act. Any hope of his coming back from that dark point had just passed. How easy had it been to take a life? How easy had it been to become the one thing he most despised, a heartless and ruthless murderer who did not hold human life in esteem above his own aims?

How was he any different from Abbas el Khalidi—or did it even matter?

Perhaps he could find some small piece of redemption by sparing the life of the much younger passenger. He could see the shock and fear and awe in the man's expression. Hell, he couldn't have been more than twenty-five, a fresh-faced punk who dreamed of being a big-time thug like his boss. At least now he could see how it might end for him, studying the dead carcass of Saqaf firsthand might make him rethink his career choice.

"Give me your pistol," Mazouzi instructed the thug. "And do it slowly…I'm in no mood for games."

The guy did exactly as he was told, reaching gingerly into his coat whereas earlier he'd clawed for the piece, and eased the weapon into view. A punk pistol it turned out to be, Makarov knockoff of perhaps Hungarian or Polish make, that actually chambered 9 mm shorts. Mazouzi relieved him of the gun and stripped it into several pieces with one hand before tossing it out the window. He kept one eye on the man, though, not willing to give up anything to assumption. Sloppiness could get him killed very fast in the rough-and-tumble society of the Casablanca underworld.

The weapon now disposed, Mazouzi looked into the frightened eyes of the young man he had at gunpoint. "I have a choice to make now, a choice that depends on the choice you make."

"What do you mean?" the young man asked in a shaky voice.

"You still have a lot of years ahead of you," Mazouzi said. He gestured to Saqaf's corpse and said, "Is this where you want it to end? Like this, eh? Your choice is to join your boss here in hell. Or you can walk away."

"Die or be hunted by el Khalidi for the rest of my life," the man said. "Some choice you are giving me, cop."

"So it is el Khalidi behind this," Mazouzi replied with a smile. He took great satisfaction in seeing the look of horror spread across his prisoner's features. "Thanks for confirming it. Now you really have only one choice to make. Get out of Casablanca and don't ever return."

"Are you kidding?" the man asked with a snort of derision. "Getting out of the city isn't enough, cop. I will have to leave the country if I wish to escape el Khalidi."

"I wouldn't worry too much about that. Abbas el Khalidi isn't long for this world—of this much I can assure you. He has made enemies with many powerful people, including some Americans I know, and if I don't get him and they don't get him, somebody else will get him. It's only a matter of time." Mazouzi inclined his head in the direction of the restaurant where Hasidim awaited him. "What was the plan supposed to be? Kill me on sight or wait until after the meeting?"

At first the young man hesitated but a tap on his cheek from the pistol got him talking soon enough. "We were to wait until you finished meeting and split up. Then follow you back to wherever you were hiding."

"And do what?"

"That's it," he said. "We had no orders to kill you, only to call someone once we knew where you were staying."

So that was it. Either Hasidim had planned to do the job himself or he would send an unknown to finish his dirty work. If he had hired these two only to follow and report back, that meant he was probably taking his orders from the same people they were. And those people were either working for Abbas el Khalidi or it was Prince Story personally at the head of the line. Well, that was just fine with Mazouzi. He preferred to deal with this problem himself, and he could have it wrapped up before the Americans even needed to know about it.

So much the better.

Mazouzi reached into his pocket and withdrew a pad and pen. He handed them to the man and ordered him to write down an address. "How were you supposed to deliver the information?"

"We were given a number and told to leave a message."

"Where at?"

"Some hotel," the guy replied.

Mazouzi looked sideways at him. "You weren't supposed to call him directly?"

The guy shook his head. "No, he said it would be too risky and someone might be watching for that. We were supposed to leave a message with wherever it was you led us. To say that's where the business meeting would take place."

"How droll," Mazouzi said. "So you weren't going to talk to him directly."

"No."

"Good, then it doesn't matter who calls the number and delivers the message." Mazouzi slid the pistol into his jacket and said, "You get to live today after all. In two hours you're going to call that number and give that address to whomever answers. And then you are going to leave this city and never return. You understand? Because if you do your life won't be worth anything. If you don't follow instructions, I will find you and kill you, so I would suggest you don't betray me. This is a golden opportunity to change your fortune. Don't be stupid and let it pass you by."

The man nodded with an expression that implied his emphatic understanding. Mazouzi, convinced the guy would do exactly as he was told, slipped from the vehicle without another word. He walked up the sidewalk and put on his poker face. It would take every skill in his personal bag of tricks when he met with Trebba. If he'd learned anything about his friend—check that, his *former* friend—it was that Hasidim Trebba wasn't an idiot. The guy had a sixth sense and he would pick it up immediately if he thought Mazouzi was conning him. After all, he'd been playing that game much longer while Mazouzi was a newcomer to some of it. But Mazouzi also had a trick or two up his sleeve, and he'd played a few games of his own.

Every Maroc cop learned to do so if he wanted to live long, and the ones who knew best how to bullshit were usually the ones who survived to collect a meager pension, at best.

Mazouzi decided the best way to fool Trebba would be to make the guy think he was a last resort, that Mazouzi had reached out to every other resource and been turned down. Trebba liked to be the hero and this would appeal to his baser instincts. Maybe it would be enough to make Trebba think he'd devised a foolproof plan, but maybe Trebba would see through the disguise immediately and Mazouzi's plans would fall apart.

Either way, this was going to end with el Khalidi dead and possibly, just possibly, Trebba dead, or it was going to end with Mazouzi's dead body rotting away somewhere in the Moroccan wilderness. He was ready for it either way.

Hasidim Trebba smiled immediately upon seeing Mazouzi. With that one look, Mazouzi knew it was all true. Trebba had betrayed him and intended to kill him, or would report back to Abbas el Khalidi, who would order somebody to kill him, and that was all there was to it.

Mazouzi let out a little shudder as they hugged each other in traditional greeting. Then they sat at the table Trebba had reserved and ordered strong coffee and made small talk awhile before the conversation turned quiet as more sensitive matters ensued. "What is my situation at headquarters?"

"Your situation?" Trebba looked around and then tendered an expression of incredulity. "Your situation is all fucked up, is what your situation is, Zafar. You resign in disgrace from the force and then you bungle the job with the Americans. There's a city-wide manhunt for you, and before long it will probably spread to the rest of the country. Why would you ask such a stupid question?"

"I know the situation isn't good," Mazouzi said. "But you are the last person I can turn to. You are the only one I can trust, Hasidim."

"You have put me in a very bad situation, Zafar. Do you know this?"

"I know, I know." Mazouzi nodded and lowered his eyes. He made a show of looking around and then in a conspiratorial fashion he said, "I hope you can one day forgive me. I did not mean to drag you into this. But of everyone I have turned to you are the only one who did not deny me. To the rest of my supposed friends, I don't even exist."

"We've been through much together," Trebba said and he tapped the top of Mazouzi's clutched hands with the side of his fist. "We will always be brothers. Where are you staying?"

Mazouzi hesitated a moment and when he saw Trebba noticed he was balking, he covered it quickly. "I don't think I want to tell you."

"Why not?"

"Because it could make things worse for you," he said. "If I tell you and you are asked, then you may be forced to say for your own protection."

"So you *don't* trust me."

"No...no, that is not true." Mazouzi feigned protest. "It is because I trust you that I don't tell you this. Because I know you are honest and a good cop. Look, Hasidim, I know we've had our disagreements over the years because you chose to do the job one way and I another, but that is no reason for me to now put you at risk unnecessarily. You see what I mean?"

Something in Trebba's expression changed and Mazouzi could tell that he'd bought the story. Now it was time to add the last ingredient, one that stirred the pot and would make the call placed by Saqaf's associate in a couple of hours all the more convincing. "I am putting some money together, funds that will get me out of the country. Do you think you can help me?"

Trebba didn't hesitate to jump at the bait. "Of course, Zafar, of course."

"Thank you," he said, looking as relieved and conciliatory as he could manage even while it sickened his stomach. "I will call you and tell you where to meet me with the money when the time is right."

Mazouzi stood and Trebba looked at him with surprise. "You are not going to stay and eat?"

"I must keep moving. I will call you very soon."

"I understand," Trebba replied. "I know you are not a terribly religious man, Zafar, but I bid Allah go with you."

And I bid you go straight to hell, Mazouzi thought.

CHAPTER SIXTEEN

Phoenix Force could stand rock-steady in the face of adversity most of the time, but the situation was different—completely different—when it came to the cops. Maybe the police had been sent here by some deception on the part of Abbas el Khalidi, maybe Mazouzi had sent them out of malice for McCarter not letting him tag along. Whatever the case, though, the cops were just doing their job and it was a hard-and-fast rule among the Stony Man field teams that conflict with law enforcement must be avoided at all costs.

Even in a foreign country, none of the Phoenix Force warriors wanted to be responsible for drawing the attention of cops, and they found the idea of killing cops, even dirty ones, even more distasteful. Better to deploy a nonmilitary option in such circumstances. It was a good policy, really. It was tough enough to stay one step ahead of the terrorists and criminals in the international community, but it was quite another to have both sides of the law with which to contend.

"Options?" McCarter asked his teammates.

"We could surrender," Hawkins said.

Manning cast a sour eye. "I don't think that's what he had in mind."

"Maybe Hawk's right," Encizo said. "Maybe if we surrender we can somehow talk our way out of it. Get Mazouzi to help."

"You're kidding, right?" James asked in disbelief. "Mazouzi's completely on the outs with his people. We're on our own, gents."

"Well, then, it's time for me to make a command decision," McCarter said. "And I bloody well decide we look for a way out that doesn't bring us in line with the cops. Failing that, we may just have to shoot our way out—"

Before he could finish the statement, it seemed the police had their hands full and without any help from Phoenix Force. They really couldn't see what was happening from their vantage point, but it was obvious the cops were taking fire from guns inside the processing plant. Through the open door, the lights revealed the situation in all its horror. Officers were falling under a merciless onslaught of automatic-weapon fire coming from somewhere above them. Men had obviously stepped in to replace those Manning had dispatched with the MSG90, and a brief exchange of glances confirmed the same idea had dawned on the Phoenix Force warriors at once.

"Whoever's beating on the cops out there thinks that we…" Encizo didn't have to finish the statement.

Indeed, it was obvious that from the moment Phoenix Force began their assault that the security forces defending this massive facility thought they had simply been the advanced team. The police were now being punished for what Phoenix Force had started, and based on the commotion and sounds of battle coming from outside, it didn't sound as if it would take long for the cops to wind up on the losing side.

"We need to stop this and right bloody now," McCarter said. "Let's move out."

The five warriors turned and fanned out across the facility, keeping in their assigned teams with Manning on munitions duty. While the Canadian explosives expert planted charges from his bag of tricks throughout various structural stress points, the remainder of the team members would spread out through the plant and dispatch the gunners who were now shooting up the Moroccan cops.

Under the cover of the autofire coming from above and the shouts of confusion, agony and death reverberating through their ears, McCarter and James advanced up the metal stairwell toward the second floor with weapons held ready at eye level. McCarter had selected an FNC from Encizo's picks for this mission. A favorite of Stony Man's cofounder and avenging angel of American justice, Mack Bolan, the Belgian-made carbine was the dream child of Fabrique Nationale de Herstal. It chambered 5.56 mm and functioned on a gas-operated, rotating bolt system. With a cyclic rate of fire exceeding 650 rounds per minute and a muzzle velocity just shy of 1,000 meters per second, the FNC had rightly earned its reputation as one of the most rugged and versatile assault rifles in the world.

McCarter and James cleared the stairs and emerged on the second floor to find row after row of fish-packing machines, spare parts and some general office spaces. From the massive row of glass cubicles against the west wall they could see a number of shadowy figures firing from specially designed ports.

"Those aren't part of the normal construction," James whispered.

"Probably Khalidi's idea," McCarter replied. "Cheeky bastard. Let's see if we can't help out those poor buggers below."

James nodded and the pair split in opposing directions, determined to flank their enemy and take them down before they could do any real damage.

McCarter sensed movement and turned to see Encizo and Hawkins emerge on the second floor from what had obviously been another stairwell access. Hawkins spotted McCarter first, so the Briton made a twirling motion with his finger, pointed at his eyes and then gestured in the direction of the enemy gunners. Hawkins nodded and turned to Encizo with the plan, and within a moment Phoenix Force advanced on their opponents.

In the lull of the firing, caused by two of the eight who had stopped to reload, one of the "security guards" noticed the approach of four silhouettes. He tried to shout a warning at his comrades, but most of them were still in the process of pouring a lead hailstorm on the cops below and oblivious to all else. Too bad, because the comrade who had tried to save their lives was the first one to buy the farm when James braced his M-16A3 in a V-shaped protrusion on one of the machines, sighted down the receiver rail and squeezed the trigger.

The 5.56 mm slug punched through the target's cheek at the same moment he leveled the muzzle of his reloaded weapon in James's direction. The bullet clipped off the bottom of the man's face, smashing his cheekbone and blowing out the opposite side just below the ear. The impact spun him into the pressed-steel-and-aluminum wall of the factory as the weapon clattered to the floor, sprung from deadened fingers.

McCarter took the next one with a 3-round burst to the chest. The bullets shredded chest muscle and tissue, cracking a rib or two along their routes of passage, and the man's lungs imploded with the force. They exited the gunman's back and he slid to the floor as he let out a long rasp of death.

The remaining shooters, four in all, noticed that they were taking fire now and were distracted from their murderous assault against the Moroccan police in favor of self-preservation. Unlike most of the types against which

Phoenix Force pitted themselves, this particular lot didn't seem to include a lot of fanatics. In fact, they seemed to operate on a somewhat different premise than the typical Islamic zealot or conventional terrorist.

Rafael Encizo made note of the fact, although that didn't change his fashion of dealing with these scumbags. They were murderous thugs who had just shot up a bunch of cops—cops not really able to defend themselves—from high ground with automatic weapons, in addition to the fact they had set up an ambush. Maybe it had been an ambush to destroy Phoenix Force and the cops just got in the way, but that didn't really matter to the Cuban.

Either way, these goons were going down.

Encizo locked the butt of his MP-5 against his shoulder, brought his first target into sight acquisition and squeezed the trigger. The SMG, set to 3-round-burst mode, stuttered with a distinct report in the lull of firing. At such close range it lifted the guy off his feet and slammed him against the window with enough force to shatter it. The guy's body didn't topple out, instead collapsing to the polished floor, but the next one to fall under Encizo's marksmanship didn't end up so lucky. The 9 mm Parabellums hammered the guy in the chest and neck, and spun him straight through the opening. The man triggered a few reflexive rounds into the floor before his body flew back and disappeared from view.

Hawkins got the other pair with a rise-and-sweep pattern with his M-16A3, which he held tight and low against his right hip. A maelstrom of 5.56 × 45 mm NATO rounds stitched ugly patterns across the upper torsos of the pair of Khalidi's hard guys, ripping flesh from their bodies and causing them to dance like puppets. They eventually slammed into one another and dropped to the floor in a rapidly forming puddle of blood.

"Put some heat on!" McCarter ordered Encizo and Hawkins.

The two slung their weapons and immediately detached AN-M14 TH3 incendiary grenades hanging from their LBE suspenders. Weighing a mere thirty-two ounces each, the AN-M14s were filled with thermate—an improved version of its thermite predecessor—that burned at 4,000 degrees Fahrenheit. Able to fuse the metal parts of any objects it touched made it the ideal choice for destruction, and all the field teams had put the grenades to good use as the need arose.

They withdrew the pins, nodded a ready status to each other and then let the grenades fly. McCarter and James were quite familiar with the effects and had already moved out of the danger zone, with Hawkins and Encizo on their heels. As they reached the far stairwell the grenades ignited, primed by only a very small charge, and began to burn hotter than just about any other ordnance of that size in existence. Within minutes that entire side of the factory, with its carpeted offices and wooden desks for fuel, would be fully engulfed.

"Now, let's see if we can find a bloody way out of here," McCarter told his team.

GARY MANNING HAD learned his trade while serving on the antiterrorist unit of the Royal Canadian Mounted Police. The big Canadian had never been much for close-quarters battle, finding it more preferable to eradicate the enemy with forethought and tactical planning. Besides his expertise in explosives, Manning boasted vast knowledge of the vital statistics of many of the world's terror groups, something that had come in handy on more than one occasion.

But if Manning knew anything, if there had been just one claim to fame, it was his ability to bring down a struc-

ture with some well-placed explosives. Even as he prepared
the first of a few charges, he could hear the firefight ensue
above him. He'd also have to find a way out of this place
for him and his friends, a way that would allow them to
avoid any conflict with the police. Manning couldn't be
sure but he thought he'd spotted a massive door on the
back side during his and McCarter's initial reconnaissance.
Manning knew he didn't have much time remaining but
he was fairly confident he'd have enough time to find the
door. It had looked like a large garage door, the kind that
perhaps led onto a loading dock, so it wouldn't be difficult to find.

Manning located his first choice to rig with some of
the C-4 he carried, a massive stack of oil drums that upon
closer inspection appeared to be filled with diesel fuel.
That didn't make a lot of sense. Oil for the packing machines he could see, but what the hell would Khalidi's people need with diesel and especially this much of it? Well, it
didn't matter right now so Manning decided to file it away
for later reference. The warrior withdrew four 1.25-pound
sticks of C-4 from his demo bag and tied each one with
detonator cord. He secured them to the central area of the
drums with a massive piece of electrical tape.

Manning moved on to the next area and arrived at some
of the machinery just as an explosion rocked the floor
above. He looked out one of the front windows and saw
the flickering of flames, and then grinned. McCarter and
friends were making short work of the upstairs with the
AN-M14s Encizo had brought back. All of them had seen
what the thermate grenades could do to human flesh and
they had developed a healthy respect. Their use signaled
that in all likelihood they had dispatched their enemies
and were already on the way down.

Manning had just finished rigging the machines that,

coincidentally, sat butted against a couple of support columns on that side of the warehouse, when McCarter's voice sounded in his ears.

"Sigma One to Sigma Three."

"Go," Manning replied.

"Where away?"

"Southeast corner," Manning said. He looked around in the gloom and soon spotted the garage door he'd remembered. "Think I've found a back way out."

"Stand fast. We're on our way."

"Wilco, out," Manning acknowledged.

Manning double-checked his work and then secured his equipment and headed for the large metal garage-style door. He wouldn't activate it until he saw the whites of his teammates' eyes, since opening it too soon would simply give the police a potential way in, or even expose Phoenix Force before absolutely necessary. He didn't figure the Moroccan police had tried to cover the back since Khalidi's men had kept them occupied on the west side. Manning reached the door, located the control and then crouched in the dark with weapon at the ready. Another minute passed and he checked the luminous hands of his watch.

Blast it! Where the hell were they?

The seconds ticked by at an agonizing pace and then Manning heard the shuffle of footfalls. He raised the muzzle of his weapon, but lowered it as soon as the unmistakable form of Hawkins came into view. Manning hissed—the sound seemed deafening in the tomblike silence of the plant—to draw Hawkins's attention. The big Texan joined him and several moments passed as the remaining members fell on his position.

"Status?"

Manning jabbed his thumb at the controls. "Looks like

this operates the door. Only two buttons so I figure one stops it and one starts it."

"Which means if we raise it then we're committed," Encizo said as he eyed the buttons, one red, one green.

"No way to reverse direction," James agreed.

"How about we raise it enough just to roll under," Hawkins suggested.

McCarter shook his head. "Too risky. It'd leave us vulnerable with no cover."

A clang of metal and the sound of shouts outside reminded the team it wasn't time for a discussion. They would have to act fast if they wanted to get out of this alive.

"Even if we can get out of here before the cops find us, how do we get back to our vehicle?" James asked.

"We'll just have to make it up as we go, mates," McCarter replied as he reached out and stabbed the green button.

"I hate improvisation," Hawkins muttered.

As soon as the door had cleared enough space from the floor they could duck under, they emerged at the corner, moving one man at a time and keeping plenty of distance between each other. Encizo went first, followed by James and then McCarter. Those three swept the area with their muzzles on the move, while Hawkins and finally Manning made their egress. They were surprised to find the door opened onto an interior loading dock. The external door at the far end was wide open, which probably meant somebody had heard the commotion and made their escape out the back. A ramp descended down either side of the dock enclosure and in the central loading area—wide enough only for one truck or car—there sat a small van.

James grinned. "Lucky us."

"Rafe, check for keys," McCarter ordered.

Encizo complied and after about a thirty-second search

he held up his hand with a pair of keys dangling from a long keychain made of what looked like a leather strap.

"All aboard who're going aboard!" McCarter exclaimed with glee.

The Phoenix Force warriors piled into the cramped van as Encizo cranked the starter, revved the engine and then popped it into second. They rolled through the doorway and emerged on the tarmac. Encizo purposely kept the lights out as he eased on the accelerator. They had made it maybe fifty yards from the factory when the blinking blue of police lights flashed in the passenger-side mirror. A squad had rounded the corner of the building.

"Bloody bugger it!" McCarter grimaced and added, "Of course they'd be onto us. Bad guys get away scot-bloody-free, but the cops just happen onto us."

"Wait for it...." Manning said from the back of the van as he checked the action on his assault rifle.

"What do you mean?" James inquired.

He'd barely finished his statement when the factory went up, a huge explosion of flame shooting from the garage. They watched with fascination as the blast proved enough to do something to disable the police squad. A moment later, the explosives Manning had attached to the interior went and the entire southeast rear portion of the factory immediately became awash in flames.

"What the—" Hawkins began and then he looked at Manning. "What did you do?"

Manning made a show of inspecting his fingernails, blowing on them and then rubbing them against his fatigue shirt. "Dropped an extra little present just outside the van before I closed the door."

"You figured they might send a cruiser around back," James said.

"Yeah, I guess I thought it was sort of inevitable. I figured at least an explosion would cause some commotion, enough to cover our tracks if we needed it."

"Well, looks like you were right."

"Nice show, Gary," McCarter said. "Really nice show!"

"What's our next move?" Encizo said.

"Let's find ourselves the long way around the complex," McCarter said. "Circle back to the SUV and ditch this thing. Then we'll head for Mazouzi's digs."

"What do you think he's been up to while we were doing this job?" Hawkins asked.

"No telling. But I'd be willing to bet he's doing something to get himself in trouble."

And all of McCarter's teammates agreed with him in silence.

CHAPTER SEVENTEEN

Zafar Mazouzi looked at his watch one last time and then watched intently as the vehicle pulled up in front of the house he'd been staking out.

Ran Bakkum climbed from his sedan and proceeded up the walk to his house. A cold rain had begun to fall, unusual for this time of year, but Mazouzi resisted the urge to use the heater or wipers. It wasn't raining hard and the wool overcoat he wore kept him warm enough.

Mazouzi waited until Bakkum had made it about halfway to his front door before he climbed from the sedan, closed the door easily and jogged up the sidewalk to where Bakkum had parked. He stopped at a hedge and waited a moment, intent on making sure Bakkum hadn't spotted him before proceeding in step until he'd come up behind the man. Bakkum stood on the unlit porch fumbling with his keys. The dumb bastard didn't even know when to tell his wife to turn the lights on; of course, that assumed she wasn't out running around on him. This had become common knowledge about the chief of the constabulary, and he'd been the ass of many jokes both inside and outside the department, in addition to just plain being an ass.

Bakkum finally got the door open and as he pushed through it, Mazouzi threw his weight into the guy and helped him inside. Mazouzi slammed the door shut with his foot and then reached down, grabbed Bakkum by the collar of his coat and hauled him to his feet. He tossed the guy halfway through the small living room on the right, grabbed Bakkum before he could fall completely from his stumbling and then shoved him onto a small tweed couch.

It took Bakkum's eyes a moment to adjust to the gloom, but eventually a look of horror, followed by one of surprise, crossed his features. Like a snake he hissed through clenched teeth and said, "Zafar. What the fuck are you doing here?"

"Shut up," Mazouzi said. He reached into his coat and withdrew the PPK, sound suppressor still attached. "I have already killed one man tonight, and may have to kill a second. One more will not bother me either way."

"You're no killer," Bakkum said, finding a new boldness. "I've known you too long."

"I thought I knew you, too," Mazouzi said. "Until I found out you were in bed with Abbas el Khalidi."

"What? I don't even know—"

Mazouzi raised a hand to cut him off. "Spare me the denials, Ran. I've just met with one of your cronies."

"And who might that be?"

"Hasidim Trebba."

Mazouzi had considered not answering at first, unwilling to show his hand too soon, but he opted to give out the information and see where it led him. At this point in the game he really didn't have anything to lose and he figured it was worth it to try to get whatever intelligence he could for his American friends. The chances he would walk away from this mission were slim, especially now that this visit would mean the entire Casablanca police force would go on a manhunt to find him and kill him. He supposed he could've just learned what he could and then shot Ran Bakkum in the head, but that wouldn't buy him any goodwill. Besides, Bakkum had been right in one thing: Zafar Mazouzi was no murderer.

"Trebba?" Bakkum let out a scornful laugh. "I wouldn't ally myself with that son of a dog for all the pussy in paradise."

"Funny, he said the same thing about you," Mazouzi said, playing a hunch. He got the reaction he hoped for. "Did you know that Trebba tried to get Aziz Saqaf to do his dirty work for him? By the way, Saqaf will no longer pose a threat. To anyone."

"I suppose you killed him, too."

"Only because I thought he'd been sent to kill me," Mazouzi said. "Now I know it's actually Hasidim who intends to pull the trigger. Or he will tell el Khalidi, who will in turn send his own men to do the job. But I think probably Hasidim wants to do it personally. I'm sure it will mean more money than the half-million dollars he doesn't think I know about him having stashed in a Zurich bank."

"You're filled with theories of conspiracies but you bring me no proof," Bakkum said.

"Don't, Ran. Don't pretend like you actually care about being a policeman. You're not a *real* cop—you're a politician. And like most politicians you can be bought and you have been bought and el Khalidi is your master. Isn't that so?"

Bakkum shook his head. "It doesn't matter what I tell you, Zafar. I could admit to having raped and plundered every widow in the city or having done nothing at all but my job, and in any case you would not believe me."

"That is probably true. But let's suppose I'm willing to give you the chance to redeem yourself instead of simply putting a bullet in your head. What might you tell me with that chance?"

"Probably whatever you want to hear."

"Don't toy with me, Ran. I'm not in the mood. Let us instead play a little game. I'm going to give you a name and then I'm going to give you about a minute to think about that name. And when that minute's up you'll get your chance to save your life or lose it depending on what you tell me. And if you simply decide not to play the game I will kill you and then I will go upstairs and kill your family. What do you think of that?"

"I think you're puffing up," Bakkum replied.

He shifted slightly and Mazouzi watched him carefully, tightening his grip on the pistol and moving the barrel a few inches closer to Bakkum's head while still keeping out of reach.

"Ah-ah. Don't be stupid."

"Let me get my coat off, at least."

Mazouzi nodded and watched carefully for any possible tricks. Bakkum might have been a politician but he regularly was required to keep up his skills training with a gun, as well as his hand-to-hand combat expertise. Mazouzi had lived this long on the streets of Casablanca by not underestimating anyone or anything, always remaining alert in a situation for someone who might attempt to seize the advantage when he wasn't looking. What made Bakkum more dangerous was that he had the same training.

That didn't necessarily make up for experience, however, and in that department Mazouzi knew he had Bakkum hands down.

"The name is Ebi Sahaf," Mazouzi said.

Bakkum didn't take even more than a second to reply, a reply that came way too soon for Mazouzi's tastes.

"Never heard the name."

"A lie."

"Not a lie," Bakkum said.

"Then we'll just say you are mistaken, because you were the one who signed off on his visa renewal every time it came up. He's a native of India and would not be allowed to remain in the country unless approved by the constabulary, among others. As the chief of the constabulary you are required to sign off on these approvals every year."

"I sign many such approvals on practically a weekly basis," Bakkum said with an expression of disbelief. "How do you expect me to remember one name?"

"Because you're a part of el Khalidi's network to keep this man under wraps," Mazouzi replied. "Everyone knows that Ebi Sahaf is a famous figure in the technical-engineering world. And everyone knows that at one time he worked for Abbas el Khalidi. My American contacts believe that he still does and they think that Sahaf is building something for el Khalidi."

"Building what, Zafar, huh? And your American *friends?* Your friends are supposed to be your brothers on the streets." Bakkum let out a disgusted wheeze. "Listen to yourself, Zafar. You sound like a madman!"

"Maybe I am a madman," Mazouzi replied. "Or maybe I'm just very tired of having you pull my chain every time a subject like this comes up. You do understand, of course, that if you continue to deny the information that I'll simply kill you and your family. I have nothing to lose."

"Good luck killing my family," Bakkum said. "Sulame took the children and left me six months ago."

"How could anyone blame her? You were never home and when you were you were thinking about the other women with which you've had sex. The *many* women."

"Do not pretend to be so righteous that you can judge me, Zafar. You do not come from a past that is so clean you can point the finger at any of us."

"I never took a bribe and I never traded favors," Mazouzi said. "That's what makes me different from you, Ran, not necessarily better. That's something you've never been able to understand about me. The reason I identify so well with these Americans is because I've seen the fire in them.

They burn with passion for their country, yes, but they also believe in doing what is good and right."

"Bullshit! They want what is in the best interests of their country!"

"They want," Mazouzi continued without missing a beat, "what is best for all of us. Every month, Abbas el Khalidi gets stronger and richer as he pours drugs out of this country and pours in more white slaves. Did you know that he uses terrorists to operate a slaving operation out of America?"

"What evidence do you have of this?"

"Shut up and listen, Ran, I'm educating you," Mazouzi said, sneering and slightly curling his upper lip. "Did you also know that the slaves he's bringing into Morocco are young American boys and girls? Teenagers? That's right, you have a couple of children about that age, now, don't you? Could you imagine someone taking them out of the country and making them slaves in another country?"

"Abbas el Khalidi is a good man," Bakkum said but there was no real conviction in his tone. He tried to bolster confidence by adding, "An important man."

"El Khalidi is a purveyor of drugs and innocent flesh," Mazouzi countered. "And a piece of filth, and I cannot believe that you would want to even associate yourself with such an individual. Now we're back to my original question. What can you tell me about Ebi Sahaf and where can I find him?"

"I already told you—" Bakkum said but he never finished.

Something silver seemed to materialize in his hand and flashed in the streetlight coming through the large single-pane window of Bakkum's living room, where they were talking. Mazouzi squeezed the trigger but Bakkum had already moved and the 7.65 mm round punched into the backrest of the couch with a *thwap* sound. The silvery outline of whatever Bakkum had been holding spun toward Mazouzi's head and he jumped aside, but not quite fast enough.

The point of the throwing knife went through Mazouzi's overcoat and shirt and punctured the point between the chest wall and shoulder deep enough to render Mazouzi's left shoulder virtually useless. Mazouzi tried to reacquire a sight picture, but Bakkum was relatively fast for an older man, with an agility Mazouzi hadn't quite expected possible. Bakkum managed to get around the corner of the living room where it entered a combination sitting area and entertainment bar.

Mazouzi jumped over the couch back, using the seat cushion to give him lift, and managed to reach Bakkum before the guy could clear a pistol he kept behind the bar. Mazouzi kicked the pistol from his grip and pointed his own, but Bakkum slapped it aside and jammed the blade deeper into Mazouzi's shoulder. The Maroc cop let out a howl and dropped the PPK. While he'd been a veteran street fighter and had a pretty high tolerance for pain, he'd never quite felt agony like this and he danced out of reach just in time to avoid having the interior of his left shoulder turned to mush.

The knife blade came free as he pulled back suddenly but Bakkum couldn't hold on to it, the handle slick with Mazouzi's blood. The two now stood off with each other in the cramped space behind the bar. That was fine; Mazouzi would have preferred a straight fight between them where the victor was the one who could best his opponent in a fair contest of determination coupled with skill.

Mazouzi didn't worry about it, although he willed his attention not to waver for a moment. Bakkum had already proved to be a worthy and cunning opponent, and a slipup now would most certainly cost Mazouzi his life. He held no illusions about that.

"You must realize this is a fight to the death," Bakkum said, apparently trying to psych-out Mazouzi. "We can still stop this."

"If I am to die today, or any day while Abbas el Khalidi is still alive, it will definitely not be by your hand, Ran," Mazouzi said. "It will be by the hand of only an equal or my better."

"Go to hell!" came Bakkum's response and he charged.

Mazouzi danced to the left and jumped so that he sat on the bar, determined not to get hung up on the wall. He swung up both legs, the toe of one shoe catching Bakkum under the chin. The man bit his tongue and blood sprayed from the wound as Mazouzi rolled over the bar and landed catlike on his feet. His right hand he held in a defensive posture while his left dangled somewhat useless.

Mazouzi realized with horror that he'd put himself in a position where Bakkum now stood between him and the PPK, although he didn't let his expression betray his fear. Bakkum had obviously forgotten this fact—just as he'd forgotten he could've retrieved his own pistol and there wasn't anything Mazouzi could do about it—apparently more angered that Mazouzi had caught him off guard.

The man charged at Mazouzi now, his arms flailing with wild abandon as he tried to connect with a punch. The offensive proved to be neither coordinated nor with a specific intent, and thereby it was completely ineffective. With one arm disabled Mazouzi considered the real possibility Bakkum should have been able to overcome him, especially with such a decisive advantage, and yet it seemed as if the man had truly lost his own mind. He was more like a child throwing a tantrum than an experienced fighter.

Mazouzi decided not to let his opponent's wildness dissuade him and he pressed the advantage by turning his defense against Bakkum's uncoordinated attack into an offense of sorts. Mazouzi waited until the last moment and then, ducking under Bakkum's attacks, he bent at the waist and threw his defenseless left shoulder into a point just at the level of Bakkum's hips. Using his back as a pivot point, Mazouzi threw Bakkum completely over his own body and the man sailed through the air before coming down on the couch, bouncing once and landing on the coffee table. The old, weak table shattered under the impact but it was enough to somewhat break the fall and deplete the full force of the throw.

Had it been through the massive window against the wall, the fight would've been over now.

Mazouzi realized that now he was the one who had the advantage. He whirled and moved through the dark to find his former police chief's own pistol. He located it and hefted the weapon in his hand: a late-model stainless .45 ACP, Colt M1911-A1 Platinum Cup Edition. A very real pistol and, from everything Mazouzi could recall, a very expensive one. Mazouzi whipped the pistol up and had it pointed at Bakkum just as the cop regained his feet.

"Where did this come from?" Mazouzi asked. "A present from el Khalidi, perhaps? Or maybe you bought it for yourself with some of el Khalidi's blood money. Is that it?"

"You will never get away with this."

"I'm offering you one last chance to tell me about Ebi Sahaf."

"And I'm telling you that I have never heard of him."

"Too bad," Mazouzi said as he squeezed the trigger twice.

It HAD STOPPED RAINING by the time Mazouzi reached the meeting point.

Well, it wasn't really supposed to be a meeting point. It was more like where Hasidim Trebba thought he would put the problem named Zafar Mazouzi to rest. Mazouzi looked at his watch. He hoped he had timed the entire thing right. He reached to his shoulder and winced with the pain. Eventually the sharp and stabbing sensations had subsided and now it just started to ache. He would have to let the black American, the one who went by Mr. White, of all things, look at it. He'd seen the job the man had done on his comrades and deduced he was a crack medic.

Before he could think on it further, Mazouzi saw Trebba's car roll past and pull to the curb. It was too dark and the visibility too poor for Trebba to notice Mazouzi sitting in his car. He waited for a minute as Trebba climbed from his vehicle and crept around back of the dusty, abandoned office building. It wasn't a large complex and was isolated, near the waterfront; Mazouzi knew it would seem like a perfectly legitimate hiding place for his friend to take up sanctuary.

Mazouzi climbed from his sedan after waiting about three minutes and approached Trebba's car. He looked around, made sure no one was observing, and then he opened the passenger door and dropped the pistol on the passenger seat. He then climbed into the backseat and got down low so he couldn't be seen.

As he waited, Mazouzi considered his next move. He couldn't be sure that the cops would believe his story when he called to tell them but at least the call would be recorded and the entire thing would be on record. If he couldn't bring down Abbas el Khalidi's empire legally— a fact that had become quite evident to him as it never had before—then he would be forced to step outside the bounds of the law.

Trebba returned.

The dirty cop climbed into his car, closed the door and then turned and muttered, "What the—"

"Thank you," Mazouzi said as he sat up and pressed the muzzle of the PPK to Trebba's head. "I needed your fingerprints on that weapon."

"Zafar? What are you doing, my friend?"

"Isn't it obvious, my *friend?*" Mazouzi asked. "I'm doing the only thing that is left for me to do. You know, I once loved being a policeman. There was nothing unclear to me about it. The law is not a judge, Hasidim. It simply is. It is black-and-white and everything may be handled through it, at least from the perspective of cops. The law says you get arrested for this offense and we arrest that person. We let the judges and the lawyers and the juries decide the rest.

"But you have taken that away from me," Mazouzi said with real emotion. "You and Abbas el Khalidi and all of the goons on the payroll. You have turned me against the law I once held sacred and I resent you for it. And I would like to kill you for it. But instead I think I will let you live and remind you, long down the road when you are sitting in a prison cell until the flesh begins to fall off your bones, that it was *you* who turned me to these acts of desperation."

"Have you lost your fucking mind, Zafar?"

"It's funny," Mazouzi said. "You are the second one to ask me that question tonight. But first, before I leave you to whatever Fate judges as your deserving end, I have a question for you. Tell me what you know about a man named Ebi Sahaf."

CHAPTER EIGHTEEN

"Looks like some damage to the muscle and tendons," Calvin James proclaimed as he stripped off the gloves with a snap.

"Will I be able to use it again?" Mazouzi asked.

"It'll heal and you'll get use back but it will probably bother you for the rest of your life. Especially in cold weather. I suppose a surgeon's out of the question?"

"I do not know one," Mazouzi said as he began to slide gingerly into his shirt with James's assistance. "At least not one that I don't risk infection from his instruments."

"I won't even ask," James replied.

As Mazouzi completed buttoning his shirt one-handed, James departed and McCarter came into the bathroom facility at Mazouzi's headquarters, which they had converted to a makeshift medical ward, of sorts. The place was actually big enough, being it had a large open space with two urinals, as well as a full stall enclosure that contained a shower, commode and twin sinks.

"The use of space in this place never ceases to amaze me," McCarter remarked.

Mazouzi nodded, not saying anything as he continued to focus on buttoning his shirt with one hand. It would definitely take practice to get that done.

McCarter gestured at the shoulder. "How's it feeling?"

"It doesn't hurt that much but it aches."

"That's going to take a long time to shake, mate," Mc-Carter replied. "You want some pain meds?"

"Mr. White already asked and I told him no. I do not want anything that might cause me not to think clearly."

"Suit yourself."

Mazouzi rose and McCarter held the door for him. They emerged onto the main tactical area in the center of the house. The smells of food assailed their nostrils and Mazouzi remarked that it smelled good. T. J. Hawkins gestured with a spoon before turning back to the pot in front of him, and Manning nodded while he slowly carved a loaf of bread. The team members were all decent cooks in their own right and were fully capable of preparing a meal for hungry soldiers.

"Trebba proved surprisingly cooperative when I asked him about Sahaf," Mazouzi told McCarter.

They had received information before leaving for the factory that Stony Man had stumbled onto Sahaf's name, as well as their theory that he was up to something. Since he specialized in technology and technological engineering, it wasn't difficult to reach the assumption he'd been commissioned by Khalidi to build something.

"The question remains what is that something and how close is it to completion?" Encizo asked as Mazouzi and McCarter joined him at the briefing table.

Mazouzi fired up a cigarette and said, "There are two possibilities, neither of which Trebba claims he could confirm or deny since he does not know Sahaf and has never met him. In fact, he says that he only heard his name once and when he inquired about it, el Khalidi got very angry and told him never to ask about the man again. Of course, Trebba only became more curious and began to investigate everything he could find."

"So what are these two possibilities?" McCarter interjected.

"First, Sahaf could be building a processing plant for the drugs either here or in some other location."

"Has to be here," James said. "Remember what the Farm told us? Sahaf hasn't been seen for some time and he hasn't left the country."

"That we know about," Hawkins said. "A guy with Khalidi's connections could easily get Sahaf out of Morocco without batting an eyelash. It wouldn't be difficult for Sahaf to move in or out of here right under the noses of the Moroccan customs officials. That's assuming Khalidi doesn't have half of them bribed anyway. We already know that he has half the Casablanca police force on the payroll. No offense, Mazouzi."

"None taken." Mazouzi took a deep drag off his cigarette before continuing. "Even if he's building a processing facility inside of the country, it would not make much sense."

"Why's that?" McCarter asked.

"There's a very big risk to el Khalidi if he is caught manufacturing drugs in Morocco. Not only would the scandal destroy his reputation as Prince Story, it would throw the country further into economic depression. There are lots of companies out there that fall under the umbrella of Khalidi's news agency."

"In other words he employs a lot of people," Manning said.

"Yes. He is also very popular among the high-society types because of his significant work and his deep pockets. He donates regularly to a number of charitable causes and is well liked by the public, although he's rarely seen at the regular fundraising events and his travel plans are never given to anyone in advance. He will do an occasional interview but this is always in a controlled setting.

"Once, in fact, I remember a unit with one of the Rabat police force came to Casablanca to ask him questions. Except that they could not get past the army of attorneys and security officers to question him. He operates with considerable influence in my country and I don't know how easy it will be to bring him down. Even if we locate this Ebi Sahaf."

"You mentioned a second possibility," Encizo said.

Mazouzi nodded. "I think that a man of Sahaf's talents might be building a weapon."

"What sort of weapon?" McCarter asked, eyebrows furrowed.

"Of this I cannot begin to guess," he said. "I was thinking possibly a missile launcher or some other type of facility from which to launch attacks."

"Or maybe a place from which to smuggle the drugs out of the country?" Manning said.

A long silence fell on the Phoenix Force warriors and Mazouzi and they all turned, giving their full attention to the Canadian, each with a questioning look. Manning noted the shift in attention to him and figured he'd best come up with a summation of the theory he'd been working for some time.

"Just before we blew his factory, I found a whole bunch of fifty-five-gallon drums of oil. In fact, that's what I used to help accelerate the blast."

"So?" Hawkins asked. "What's so strange about oil?"

"Well, this wasn't just any oil," Manning replied quickly. "It was two-cycle oil. You know, the kind used to power up small boat engines and the like."

"Still not sure what you're getting at, mate," McCarter said.

"Well, if they had all that two-cycle stocked there for the fishing boats, don't you think it would be more convenient to store it near the moorings or marinas where they're anchored? Why have them that far inland so that you got to truck them out there every single time a boat has to refuel?"

"Those are good questions," Encizo said, and the rest nodded their heads in agreement.

"Well, if they are not using this for their fishing boats then what would they need it for?" Mazouzi asked.

"Maybe they're going to use it for whatever Sahaf's building," James said.

"I have a different theory, although it's not far off from what's already been proposed," Manning said. "We all know that the only reason Khalidi's been able to operate this long in secret is because he's careful. He has to run sex-trade operations out of other countries to finance his operations. But why so much money? He's making enough cash that he should be able to turn it into instant profit. Why risk ventures like white slavery that could get him imprisoned or killed at a moment's notice?

"So, I'm figuring there has to be something else. I think Khalidi's building some sort of secret facility from which he can stockpile and make deliveries of the drugs to ships that are already outbound from ports along the Moroccan coast. He loads the boats with the drugs, and then he bribes officials in select European countries to look the other way while the drugs are again off-loaded to small boats in international waters and smuggled in that way."

"That would explain the need for all of that marine two-cycle," James said.

"It would also be useful for getting the slave-trade children into the country," McCarter said.

"In order for him to do this," Mazouzi said, "he would have to construct such a place in secret."

"He'd also need to be very close to the water," Hawkins said. "Probably right on the coast somewhere."

"Well, that narrows down the search a bit," James said. "He's somewhere on the Moroccan coastline that's probably what…more than a thousand miles? That's an impossible search."

"For us, maybe," McCarter said.

"Uh-oh," Hawkins drawled. "He's got that look in his eye again, boys."

"I think we need to contact the Farm and see if they can't pull some strings for us," McCarter said.

"With whom are you going to try to 'pull strings,' as you say?" Mazouzi asked.

"Why, the fine folks of the U.S. Navy, of course," David McCarter replied.

South Atlantic Ocean

WHEN THE ORDERS CAME through straight from Rear Admiral M. Charles McKenzie, commander of Strike Group 8, Captain Thomas Burdette sat up and took notice.

What interested Burdette most was they were flagged "top secret" and only a handful of commanding officers were aware of the reasons. It seemed strange that Pacific Command would order such a mission for Burdette's command, Strike Fighter Squadron 143. Currently deployed aboard the U.S.S. *Dwight D. Eisenhower,* flagship of CSG-8, the "Pukin Dogs" were normally reserved to hit targets hard and fast. They had repeatedly demonstrated their talents for such missions during most of the first and second Gulf Wars, although since returning from a recent public-relations tour for U.S. Naval Academy graduation ceremonies, the Dogs hadn't seen much action.

Burdette confirmed the orders before descending to the quarters of Commander Robert Halstedter, of Carrier Air Wing 7. He rapped on the frame of the open doorway of Halstedter's office.

"Come," Halstedter said without looking up from the documents in front of him.

"Morning, sir," Burdette said. He snapped to attention in front of Halstedter and saluted.

Halstedter returned it. "Morning, Tom. What's up?"

"Sir, have you seen this directive from PACCOM?" Burdette asked as he passed the orders to his CO.

Halstedter glanced briefly at it and then nodded, handing it back to Burdette and waving him to a chair. As Burdette took a seat, Halstedter said, "Yeah, just came across my desk early this morning. I even got a call from McKenzie, woke me out of a sound sleep."

"Not that I'm going to question naval command intelligence folks even for a moment, sir, but…"

"You wonder why they'd use the Pukin Dogs for a reconnaissance mission instead of an AWACS or E3-C."

"It had occurred to me," Burdette replied. "I'm not sure this would be the wisest use of the squadron, particularly when you consider the distance we're talking."

"They don't want to use the entire squadron, Tom," Halstedter said, shaking his head and leaning back with a creak from his chair. "They just want to send a couple from the wing. Look, the boys just have to do some fly-bys at very low altitude along the Moroccan coast and take pictures. They're looking for something in particular."

"And what's that?"

"We don't know." Halstedter sighed. "Admiral Mc-

Kenzie told me personally that we probably wouldn't know until we saw it."

"And what if we find this mysterious thingamajig, sir?" Burdette said.

"You saw the orders." Halstedter waved at the paper Burdette had shown him. "We're to take the pictures, transmit them to the field intelligence unit aboard *Ike* and then wait for further instructions."

"I'm hoping those instructions will include blowing the thing to kingdom come."

"Maybe they will, maybe they won't," Halstedter said. "But until we find something to blow up it won't really do us much good to hope."

Burdette nodded and stood. "I understand, sir."

"How long?"

"Pardon me?"

"How long's it going to take for them to get airborne?"

"We can be up within the next twenty minutes. Only thing I have to do is see who's up next on the rotation." Burdette grinned. "Not that all of them wouldn't jump at the opportunity to take to the air."

Halstedter chuckled but Burdette noted the no-bullshit look in his eyes. "You only send two for now. We can't afford to attract too much attention on this one initially. Whatever it is we're looking for, SIGINT people say they think it will have a considerable heat signature."

"In Morocco?" Now Burdette seemed puzzled. "Sir, do you *really* not know what we're looking for?"

"Officially, I don't have any more of an idea than you do, Tom. Unofficially, I'd have to say there's a good chance we're searching for some sort of underwater complex. I wouldn't put it past the boys to keep the details from us. For whatever reason they don't think it's in our best interest to be forthcoming too early."

"I'm fine with that, sir, as long as we're not doing anything to endanger our pilots unnecessarily. There is an unspoken bond between a flight commander and—"

"I'm aware of the unspoken bond between commanders and their group pilots, Captain Burdette. Just as you're aware of the bond between carrier wing commanders and their squadron leaders. Are we clear?"

"Crystal, sir."

Halstedter visibly relaxed. "Then we understand each other. Carry on, Captain."

"Aye, sir. Thank you, sir."

And with that, Burdette saluted smartly and left the commander's office.

TWENTY MINUTES AFTER Burdette and Halstedter had finished speaking, a pair of F/A-18E Super Hornets shot from the deck of the Nimitz-class *Dwight D. Eisenhower,* piloted by naval aviators Lieutenant Carrie Sturm and her wingman, Lieutenant Junior Grade Jaime Mendoza. The flight took a mere twenty-eight minutes, a testament to the speed and capabilities of the near Mach 2 speed achievable by the fighters.

Sturm checked her orders against the navigational computer one last time and shook her head. Do a low-altitude maneuver up the coast of Morocco, paying particular attention to the north. Look for any large infrared heat signatures and take photographs only. Do not engage any targets or answer any hails from civilian traffic, and contact with any vessel should be avoided at all costs.

This is for the AWACS boys, Sturm thought. We're fighter pilots. We're used to making noise and lots of it.

Well, Sturm couldn't fight it too much since she loved a mission, *any* mission, to stave off the boredom of carrier life. While she loved being a naval aviator, Sturm wondered sometimes why there weren't more chances to see action. She'd begun her career with enough excitement while providing forward maritime security near Bahrain, but the Pukin Dogs hadn't seen any action since then. All the rest had been training exercises or PR and that wasn't why she'd joined the Navy.

Whatever the reason for this mission, then, Sturm was pretty certain it held some sort of critical importance and she planned to do it right. No matter how stupid it might seem to her, she'd been in the U.S. Navy long enough to know that nothing was ever really as it seemed.

"Storm Cloud to Viper," she called to her wingman. "I have the southern point of the coast marked and locked in. Two minutes."

"Roger and I confirm that, Storm Cloud," Mendoza replied immediately.

"I'm dropping to max floor," she replied.

"Roger, I've got your six."

The two planes dipped steadily and leveled off at ten thousand feet, the absolute floor of the flight ceiling. While they were still visible to radar they were moving so fast that it didn't really matter. Their mission orders were clear. Look for heavy IR and *no* communications with anyone but each other, it didn't matter what they heard. They had been ordered not even to respond to potential hails from *Ike* unless they received the code word that signaled they were to immediately abort the mission.

For the first twenty minutes of their flight up the coast they didn't see anything unusual. At minute twenty-one, just shy of the nine-hundred-mile mark along the thousand-mile stretch of Moroccan coast, something pinged on Sturm's instrument panel. She'd set her thermal imaging system, the same one they used for hitting surface targets with ASMs.

"Hold on here a second, Viper," Sturm said. "I think we've got something."

"Roger that, Storm Cloud. I see it, too."

The fighters cut a sharp angle and swung around for another pass. They would only be able to do this once since they had to conserve enough fuel so they could return from their mission. They had a limited range as fighter jets, not designed to travel long distances but to perform close-in strike operations.

"What is it?" Mendoza finally asked.

"That's for the intel analysts to figure out," Sturm said as she depressed the button on the special camera that had been mounted to her fighter.

Their job wasn't to interpret the results, only obtain the information. The fact that some sort of military operation could be happening within the borders of Morocco intrigued Sturm, but she knew they couldn't make any such assumptions. Until they had better information and Burdette could be more forthcoming, they wouldn't probably know. In fact, the possibility existed they would never know exactly what it was they were photographing. From the looks of it, this could've been anything from a desalinization plant to a missile complex, although there weren't the typical telltale signs of the latter.

If a foreign enemy had managed to broker a deal with the government of Morocco and place a first-strike capability within the country, or even if the Moroccan government had opted to implement their own offensive initiatives, it would certainly pose a threat to U.S. forces operating in the region. Not to mention a missile complex or other similar installation could potentially launch against targets in South America. That was coming a little too close to home, not to mention the potential threat to Seventh Fleet operations that cruised through that region on a regular basis.

Finally, the mission completed, Sturm pulled out and called for Mendoza to follow.

"Looks like we found our hidden treasure," Mendoza said.

"Looks like, Viper," Lieutenant Carrie Sturm replied.

CHAPTER NINETEEN

Volusia County, Florida

It took Stony Man time to narrow down possible locations for Genseric Biinadaz to hide and operate a terrorist force but eventually the wait paid off.

After poring through many hours of data and whittling it down to only a couple of choices, Barbara Price thought she had a pretty good handle on the situation. There were a number of places Biinadaz *could* be operating, but most of those locations weren't probable because they really had no connection to Biinadaz or the late Congressman Acres.

One, however, seemed perfect for the needs of someone like Biinadaz, and by the time she'd finished pulling the intelligence together, Price was all but convinced she'd found the Red Brood's area of operations. After phoning Brognola at home and running it by him, Price made contact with Able Team and gave them the details. Within an hour they had left their hotel room and were now making their way toward the swampland preserve.

"Two members of the FDLE will meet you there," Price had told them.

"We don't really need anybody to tag along, Barb," Lyons had told her.

"You'll want these guys," she said. "They're experts in the terrain you'll be faced with, and unless all of you are swampland experts it won't hurt to have them along."

"We're still FBI?"

"Yes, but from what they know you're part of a special task force," Price told him. "They have strict orders to cooperate fully with you, supply whatever you need and follow orders. For all intents and purposes they've been attached to you as a part of a special cooperative venture between Homeland Security and the governor's new special initiative for the prevention of illegal immigration and terrorism. You say jump and they ask 'how high, sir,' without questions."

"Let's hope so," Lyons said. "We don't have time to babysit."

As they discussed possible scenarios on the trip out to the special conservation area that had been put together through the handiwork of Acres's office, Lyons considered this new predicament.

"We can't be completely sure that Biinadaz or his people are operating there," Lyons said. "This is Barb's best guess so we're taking somewhat of a risk."

"The Farm's intelligence has always been solid in the past, Ironman," Blancanales replied. "I'm not sure why you're so skittish."

"Yeah, really," Schwarz added. "It's not like we don't know what to expect."

"Well, in fact we really don't know what to expect," Lyons insisted. "We weren't expecting to run into as much trouble as we did back there in town."

"At least we found the kids and were able to return them safely to their parents."

Yeah. There was that and Lyons had to admit the experience had left him feeling as if it was all worth the sweat and blood. What Khalidi and Biinadaz had done here was violate one of the most sacred of all American treasures: its children. These maniacs had gone after innocent teenagers for nothing more than greed. In Able Team's book that would never stand and all three had sworn to put down Khalidi's operation in America no matter where they had to go or what they had to do.

It wasn't the first time the Able Team warriors had been given control of the ball and told to run the game however they saw fit. So far this had proved to be one of those missions and while the rules of the game might change based on the enemy's plan, Able Team could only return the same result. Complete and utter destruction of the enemy at any cost—including their own lives. Of course, Carl "Ironman" Lyons had no immediate plans for such an outcome.

Able Team would be on the offensive until either they were dead or the mission objectives were satisfied.

"So did Barb give you any ideas as to what we can expect?" Schwarz asked.

Lyons shrugged. "There is any number of possibilities. If this land is being used by Biinadaz's little homegrown terrorist club, you can be pretty sure we'll see more of the same thing we saw back in the city. She did say that our contacts with FDLE are some of the best and most experienced operating in this kind of territory."

"It's unusual for them to let the cops in on this," Blancanales remarked.

"I mentioned that but it seemed like the Farm didn't get much say on the subject," Lyons replied.

"I guess because the Oval Office is involved we have to play nice-nice," Schwarz said.

Lyons shook his head. "I don't care what the politics are here and neither should you two. The fact is we have a job to do and if these guys are everything the Farm promised then we should be okay. First time they step on it or fail to obey an order and we bounce them out of the op, plain and simple. Agreed?"

"Agreed!" his friends answered simultaneously.

They arrived at the wetlands preserve ten minutes later and found an unmarked, late-model Jeep waiting for them with two men aboard. The first had dark, slicked-back hair and the whitest teeth they'd ever seen, and he introduced himself as Santiago Armenteros. He told them, "But everyone just calls me Chago." He introduced the other guy, a lanky Caucasian, as Jeff Montrose. The guy tipped his ball cap at them but said nothing.

Lyons introduced each of them by their cover names and then said, "You've been briefed on what we're looking for?"

When they nodded Lyons continued. "Okay, let's cut right to the chase. We're not really from the FBI and although I'm not technically supposed to tell you that I figure you're putting your necks on the line same as us, so you deserve the truth. So let me give you the 411. We're after a guy named Genseric Biinadaz, a former Taliban fighter who's been in the United States for some time and operating a white-slavery ring. They've been grabbing up hundreds of teenagers around the country and pimping them to big-time buyers overseas to finance the operations of a drug lord in Morocco. So we're not really here to take anybody into custody. You catch my drift?"

Something went very hard in the two faces of the cops when they heard Lyons mention a child-slavery ring. Almost no man who had even an ounce of morals would take kindly to that, and their reaction was exactly what the Able Team leader had been hoping for.

"Here's what my friend's trying to say," Blancanales said. "We have one mission and one mission only. Find Biinadaz and his terrorist friends and kill them. Simple. If you decide to join us then you might as well consider anything you learned in police academy out the window.

These are terrorists and as far as we're concerned they are enemy hostiles. There won't be any reading of the Miranda and there won't be any handcuffing or taking of prisoners."

"So from here out, it's war," Lyons concluded. "You guys understand that?"

They nodded.

"Any problem with anything we just said?"

They shook their heads, again in unison.

Lyons smiled. "Good. I can see your superiors were right about you two. You've been around. Now, tell me what we're up against."

Armenteros, who reminded Lyons a lot of Rafael Encizo, gestured for them to join him at the hood of the Jeep. He laid a large topographic map across it and pointed to a sizable area marked in green and circled with a red grease pencil.

"This area here is where we think it's most probable you could hide a force of men," Armenteros said.

Montrose, who had a deep Southern accent that sounded as if it might be right out of the heart of Georgia, picked it up at that point. "These maps were drawn from satellite photographs taken as recently as a month ago. There's a structure there now."

"One that wasn't there before," Armenteros added.

"It's definitely constructed similar to what you'd expect in a barracks," Montrose continued. "Single story and very long, rectangular in shape, dimensions are about twenty feet by one hundred feet."

Schwarz let out a whistle. "That could comfortably house fifty men. Maybe more."

Lyons nodded and Blancanales asked, "Anything else interesting about the area?"

"Quite a bit," Armenteros replied. "We know there's been some sort of human activity in there and we found that really strange considering it's supposed to be protected wetlands. We weren't even allowed to go in there unless absolutely necessary. Bunch of bleeding-heart liberals out of Congressman Acres's office shouting about preserving the place, not disturbing anything, yada yada yada."

"A ruse," Lyons replied.

"Biinadaz was the one who actually set the whole thing up while working as personal assistant to Acres," Blancanales explained. "The SOB's been using it to hold the kids until they can pipeline them out, as well as a training base. Chances are good we're going to meet considerable resistance on this trip."

"Last chance to back out," Schwarz said.

"Not on your life, sir," Montrose replied.

THEY PROCEEDED INTO the wetlands area by an access road in the Jeep, Able Team following them in the SUV. Eventually they reached a shallow river and had to pile out and climb into a shallow-water boat designed for fording just that type of terrain. The boat differed from the standard ones in that its engine didn't contain any propellers or rely on any moving parts. Instead, it was run by a large compressor that ran the length of the craft. A sealed gas motor ran the compressor, circulating a combination of air and water through a complex intake-and-output system that propelled the boat.

While it didn't move that fast it was highly efficient in the swampy, murky waters and it didn't prove anywhere as noisy as the standard airboats. Constructed from brushed aircraft aluminum and boasting a pressed-steel frame overlaid with a plastic-and-fiberglass composite panel system, the boat could travel better than thirty miles per hour over the water fully loaded with its capacity of eight men.

"Nice ride," Schwarz observed as Montrose steered the boat down the waterway.

"How long to target?" Lyons asked.

Armenteros, who was on point, watching for any potential snares that could hang them up—no boat was completely safe from being entangled in the murky waters of the Florida Everglades—checked his watch. "Five minutes, tops."

Lyons nodded and gestured to his teammates, who went into action.

They'd brought a select complement of weapons in a sealed, waterproof case that now rode in the center of the boat. Within the case was a pair of FNCs, selected unanimously by Able Team for their ruggedness and reliability. They had also acquired a dozen Diehl DM51s. Manufactured in Germany, the Diehl had proved a reliable addition to Stony Man Farm's armory. It consisted of a prism-shaped body packed with PETN high explosive. A removable, watertight plastic sheath—filled with hundreds of steel balls 2 mm in size—surrounded the body and provided a considerable advantage when used in the antipersonnel role. Finally, they had the M-16A4 with M-203, a satchel of 40 mm HE grenades and an M-60A2 machine gun provided courtesy of Armenteros and Montrose, who had additionally brought MP-5 A-2s that were now slung across their backs.

"Where did you get all the hardware?" Lyons asked.

"Checked out from the Florida Army National Guard."

"Very thoughtful of them," Schwarz replied.

"We thought so," Montrose said.

As it turned out, Montrose was from Atlanta originally and possessed a sense of humor similar to that of Able Team's electronics wizard. Lyons wasn't sure he'd be able to take them together very long but for the moment he'd have to make do. Such were the horrors and sacrifice of war, he told himself. Besides, Stony Man did have psychologists ready to perform critical stress debriefing on a moment's notice so that he didn't ultimately kill his friend when the desire arose.

"We're close," Armenteros said.

"Kill the engine," Lyons ordered.

Montrose complied and Lyons nodded with satisfaction. The two men appeared to be keeping their agreement to follow orders without question and Lyons had begun to recant his reservations about letting them tag along. Not that there hadn't been something completely different about this pair. They were obviously experienced cops—it wasn't that anyway. No, something about these two made Lyons think this wasn't the first time they'd been selected for a "special" mission here in Florida, and Lyons silently thanked Barbara Price for her foresight in finding guides who weren't afraid to show some initiative.

Lyons imagined Blancanales's suggestion to just shoot straight with the pair had contributed a lot to their conciliatory manner.

For a long time—it seemed like forever but was really only a couple of minutes—the five men sat and listened. At first they could only hear the gentle laps of water against the boat, the sounds of the wetlands around them, the calls of strange birds and the croak of bullfrogs. The occasional slither of a water snake past the boat and somewhere in the near distance, the unmistakable noise of a crocodile or two splashing about.

Finally Lyons asked Armenteros, "You hear that?"

The cop nodded and looked inquiringly at him. "Underground generator?"

"Probably," Lyons said. He turned to the rest of them

and twirled his finger, then made a couple of hand gestures.

Blancanales and Schwarz immediately went into action, Schwarz taking up the over-and-under and priming it with a grenade while Blancanales loaded and put into battery the two FNCs. He handed one to Lyons, who took it, and then they passed out the grenades, two to each man with Lyons taking charge of the spare. Ready for action, Blancanales and Schwarz took up short paddles mounted to the inside rim of the boat and began to slowly move them toward the steady thrum while Montrose steered with the shallow rudder. Lyons and Armenteros knelt parallel to each other toward the front of the boat, eyes flicking in all directions and looking for any threats. They didn't intend to get the lot of them killed by assuming that Biinadaz's people weren't prepared for them; they would be on high alert after the events in Daytona Beach.

Lyons's caution to all of them that they should be careful paid off because it was Armenteros who actually turned, snatched the paddle from Schwarz's grip and jammed it into the water in front of them. The move nearly tossed Lyons out of the boat but the Able Team leader suppressed the curse forming on his lips as Armenteros put his finger to his lips and then pointed.

At first Lyons saw nothing but then the sun flickered off something just ahead of the boat. A thin, silvery wire maybe a yard in length ran taut across their path, tied off at what appeared to be reeds protruding from the water. Instead what they turned out to be were cleverly disguised triggers, probably attached to underwater mines of some kind.

Lyons looked at Armenteros with utter surprise on his face and then clapped a firm hand on the guy's shoulder and nodded. Armenteros nodded in return and then returned the paddle to Schwarz. Lyons gestured at the wire and then indicated they should slowly ease out of the marshy pocket they occupied. They continued up the river for about fifty yards and attempted access once more, this time reaching solid footing unmolested and without blowing their team to smithereens.

Armenteros and Lyons cleared the boat first, checking the immediate area for any more booby traps before they returned to pull the boat aground. The remaining trio bailed out then and they fanned out to put distance between one another. On a hand signal from Lyons, the group began to walk a sort of skirmish line, jagged as it was, using the thrum as their focus point. As they got closer they remained alert for trip wires and other pitfalls that might be in place, but to everyone's surprise they didn't encounter any.

Eventually, Lyons called a halt and signaled they should form on him.

"We're close," he whispered to the others.

"Something doesn't feel right, Ironman," Schwarz replied.

"What do you mean?"

"They bothered to rig the shoreline but not the ground side of the perimeter?"

Blancanales shook his head. "Doesn't make sense to me, either, but we have to consider the fact they thought they'd be alone. That trip wire was probably placed there because they figured any approach would have to be made from the water."

Lyons nodded in agreement. "That would explain it."

Schwarz asked Armenteros, "How the hell did you spot that thing?"

"Gents, you're looking at a former Navy SWCC," Montrose said, pronouncing it *swick* as the mnemonic for a Special Warfare Combatant-craft Crewman.

"I knew it," Lyons said. "I knew there was something different about you guys."

Blancanales looked at Montrose. "What about you, Montrose? Any special training?"

"Guilty as charged," he replied with a smile. "I was a combat controller in the United States Air Force."

The men of Able Team nodded. These two weren't at all what they had appeared to be and that came as a surprise to them, although now they understood fully why they'd been selected. Armenteros knew boats like nobody else's business and that training was probably how he'd spotted the booby trap. And Montrose? Hell, the guy belonged to an elite group of individuals that ranked among some of the most highly trained combat operators in the world. Very little had been publicized or romanticized about the USAF's Special Operations Force, but that didn't mean they weren't out there kicking ass and taking names all the same.

"Okay, listen up, then," Lyons said. "We're going to hit this place full on. We'll start off with some fireworks to shake them up and keep them off balance, then we go in and surgically take down any stragglers. No prisoners and nobody leaves alive, and *everybody* on this team had best walk out in one piece. We clear?"

They nodded and Lyons pointed to Montrose. "You'll take point. Once Mr. Black here starts the fireworks—" he gestured at Schwarz with a thumb "—you and I will commence into the perimeter as fire team one. Chago, you and Mr. Rose here will follow up as fire team two. Black will stay on the perimeter and give us covering fire."

Armenteros nodded and then looked at Schwarz. "Just do me a favor and make sure of your targets."

Schwarz favored his Cuban ally with a wan smile. "No offense, Armenteros, but I was probably doing this before you were out of diapers."

Armenteros looked at Schwarz a moment and then nodded. "Sorry."

"Forget it."

"Okay," Lyons whispered with a taut expression, "if you two are done socializing could we please get this show on the road?"

"What's your hurry, Ironman?" Schwarz said as he cracked the breech of the M-203 and loaded a 40 mm shell. "You got a hot date when this is over?"

"I might," Lyons said with a wicked grin before he turned and prepared to move out. "Light 'em up, Gadgets."

"Music to my ears," Schwarz replied.

The warrior locked the buttstock of the M-16A4/M-203 to his shoulder, aimed down the leaf sight of the grenade launcher and squeezed the trigger.

CHAPTER TWENTY

Lyons and Armenteros were in motion before Schwarz's first 40 mm grenade landed.

They kept low, weapons held at the ready. While Lyons wouldn't have selected an MP-5 for this particular kind of mission, he understood Armenteros's decision. As a former SWCC, the cop would be very comfortable with the MP-5 to make no mention of the fact he'd probably qualified regularly with the weapon to keep up his skills. Lyons hoped those two factors would be enough for the guy to survive this one. Armenteros also appeared to be in pretty good shape. He moved with the grace of a professional combatant. Lyons reaffirmed in his own mind that Stony Man's choices had been sound and he actually found himself eager to see how this pair performed under heat. Able Team had been known to keep the more competent allies on the proverbial speed dial in case a mission brought them to a point where they needed the services of such again.

Lyons and Armenteros crashed through the dense swamp foliage, jumping over the aboveground snarl of tree roots or ducking under the broad, canopy-style leaves indigenous to the Florida wetlands.

Watery muck sucked at their boots as they breached the perimeter of the encampment and entered the clearing where the terrorists had built the barracks-style structure. It seemed almost surreal to Lyons to think that Islamic terrorists could actually build such a camp this deep in U.S.

territory without anyone being the wiser. Just a few miles away he knew that Floridians had slept snug in their beds while murderous, child-stealing thugs were training to kill those very same citizens.

Well, Carl Lyons aimed to make sure it never came to fruition.

The grenade blast didn't come anywhere close to hitting the structure, but it did do a lot to throw the several clusters of terrorists outside their structure into a panic. Good—Lyons had hoped for the element of surprise and the bet had paid off. He paused, crouched and keyed up the microphone of his mobile combat headset.

"Gadgets, adjust elevation by forty mikes and try again."

"Roger."

Lyons then turned and shouted to Armenteros, swiping his hand downward as a gesture that he could engage the enemy at will. The guy tossed a thumbs-up. He knelt alongside an outcropping of a thick gnarly vine, shouldered the MP-5 and squeezed off two 3-round bursts. Lyons grabbed cover and took up a similar firing position. He aimed the muzzle at the closest knot of terrorists, who were still getting in each other's way trying to avoid the very thing that happened next.

Lyons caught the first one with a corkscrew pattern across the midsection and chest, tearing flesh and puncturing vital organs. The next one caught a part of the sustained autofire to the jaw. The impact of the 5.56 mm rounds decimated bone and crunched through the roof of his mouth to render more damage to the skull.

The staccato of reports from Lyons and Armenteros were joined by the shotgunlike pop from Schwarz's M-203. This 40 mm HE shell struck the side of the wood-frame-and-panel structure. It blew out the side of the building in a bright orange ball of superheated gases and rained chunks of splintered coals on the terrorists. Despite the initial ferocity of the attack the terrorists got their act together quickly and the squad leaders started shouting orders. Most of the terrorists were readily armed and they fanned out to attempt to repel the assault.

They didn't make much headway.

BLANCANALES AND Montrose had now joined the fight. Blancanales had suggested they swing around to the right side in a flanking maneuver. The tactic proved effective as the terrorists were so intently focused on Lyons and Armenteros ahead they were caught unprepared by a two-pronged assault.

Blancanales found cover, leveled his FN-FNC and began taking down targets at random. One terrorist stepped back from a rocky protrusion, an odd feature given this terrain, and stepped right into the Able Team commando's line of fire. The 5.56 × 45 mm NATO rounds cut an ugly pattern up the terrorist's left side and flipped him onto his back. A second terrorist whirled and swept the area with autofire from an AK-47 assault rifle but the rounds were much too high. Blancanales cut him down with a short burst to the chest.

Montrose did plenty well from his own vantage point sprawled in the tall, reedy grasses. He had the MP-5 held in front of him, his left hand braced against a tree root, and was taking his time to acquire targets with a skill that indicated his training as a USAF combat controller. The first terrorist he got with a clean head shot, the 9 mm Parabellum entering the forehead and punching out some of the back of the man's skull. He stiffened and then toppled to the mucky floor of the wetlands. A second terrorist met a similar fate—bullets crunched through his breastbone and exploded his lungs.

Schwarz dropped another grenade on the party at that point, and that's when the pitch of battle really increased.

The terrorists were now getting organized and from the looks of it they had plenty of bodies equal to the task. Still, the surprise attack had done significant damage on both the physical and psychological scales, tipping the odds in the favor of the offense. Blancanales knew, as did all the members of their team, that they would have to press this until they got them all. Lyons had said no survivors and he'd meant it, and Blancanales, for one, planned to execute that battle plan to his last round.

Determined to keep the heat on, Blancanales signaled for Montrose to cover him and then jumped to his feet and burst from cover. He sprinted across the open, slippery ground as fast as he could without taking a dive and when he got within distance of the rear of the compound he snatched one of the Diehl DM51s from his harness and thumbed away the pin one-handed. Blancanales didn't bother to remove the sleeve. While he had no intention of using the grenade in a defensive posture he already had his target in sight.

Three drums of diesel fuel probably used to power vehicles or boats—perhaps even the generators—were aligned across the back of the barracks. Schwarz's handiwork had created plenty of psychological impact but it hadn't done much real damage. Blancanales knew blowing diesel fuel this close to the building would immediately engulf it in flames. Where there was fire there was smoke, and where there was smoke there was confusion. Blancanales reached the target unmolested, released the spoon and tossed the grenade underhanded.

Blancanales kept going even as he counted off the seconds in his head. He had eight at most, probably more like five. It came down on six when the grenade went, immediately blowing the drums apart and sending scorching hot diesel fuel across the back of the barracks structure. While diesel fumes weren't ignitable, it did take on a gel-like consistency when exposed to the air and heat simultaneously. This made it toxic and caused it to burn hot, which worked as a perfect accelerant for the wood building.

A wall of flame followed the fuel and within moments it began to burn with fervor. Black smoke immediately belched from the window that had been shattered in the blast, and flame had obviously ignited whatever contents it may have reached inside—most probably bed linens or wood-and-canvas furniture.

Blancanales had nearly reached the tree line on the back side of the building when he encountered a trio of terrorists rounding the back on the far side. Blancanales threw himself flat as the three leveled their varying SMGs and opened fire. Blancanales rolled left until he got up against an as-yet-unburned part of the exterior wall. He triggered the FNC, sweeping the muzzle from side to side like a fire hose and chopping holes into his enemies. The bullets scored, ripping ribbon patterns in the three terrorists. Blancanales was on his feet and headed for cover in the dense foliage even before the last body had hit the ground.

As soon as Hermann Schwarz lit off the third grenade, he shouldered the over-and-under and grabbed the M-60E3 by its carrying handle.

In his other hand he held an ammo can filled with what Montrose had told him contained two hundred rounds of 7.62×39 mm ammo interspersed with tracers every fifth round. Even as he neared the perimeter of the encampment, Schwarz could detect the heavy exchange of small-arms fire, among the many reports being the distinctive sound of Kalashnikov rifles. So, the child-stealing sons of bitches had Russian-made weapons; it seemed almost apropos.

Schwarz found a good vantage point, snapped out the bipod of the M-60E3 and went prone. He flipped open the lid of the ammo can, withdrew the belt of ammunition and loaded it. After a quick adjustment of the sights to an average of twenty-meter target range, he tipped the ammo can gently on its side with the open end facing the feed side, jacked the charging handle to the rear and swung the muzzle into target acquisition. He would have to make sure of the location of his targets, something that got more difficult when an explosion toward the back produced some of the blackest smoke he'd ever seen.

One of his comrades had been up to their usual shenanigans, and Schwarz's chest swelled with pride even as he locked the buttstock to his shoulder and opened up the ceremonies on the terrorists. The weapon reported with all its fury, a sound that was really music to his ears. Probably best never to admit something like that to the Stony Man shrinks. The warrior began to hammer a metal storm of destruction on his enemies, chopping their ranks to shreds with the heavy-caliber fire.

The M-60E3 had two barrel styles, a longer and heavier barrel for fire and a shorter and more lightweight profile for squad missions. This one was equipped with the heavier barrel, so the sustained output wouldn't be too much of a problem. Unlike its predecessor, which had a tendency to get hot enough that it could run away, the E3 variant performed with better efficiency as well as unerring accuracy.

It was just what the doctor ordered and Schwarz put it to good use, dropping four terrorists in under five seconds and adding to the confusion. They had been taken completely off guard and while they were regrouping and attempting to act with the proficiency for which they'd been trained, it was quite apparent they hadn't expected Able Team to come knocking on their door, such as it was. Schwarz eased off the trigger a minute, allowing the M-60E3 to cool as he tried to judge the position of his teammates. If they were doing their jobs, and he had no reason to think otherwise, they would be on the move. Somebody had already blown something on the back side of the building—a move that smelled strongly of Blancanales's handiwork—and that had done a lot to shake the terrorists' collective resolve.

Schwarz spotted a new group of a half-dozen terrorists attempting to retreat *toward* his position, apparently oblivious to the fact the machine-gun fire had been coming from that direction. Schwarz waited until they were practically on top of him before he opened up, sure of the targets and that he didn't risk hitting anything but more terrorists on the back side. The enemy combatants danced under the continuous hail of bullets, the heavy-caliber slugs ripping flesh, cracking bone and generally tearing the terrorists to shreds. They piled onto each other in front of Schwarz's position, resembling marionettes abandoned by their puppeteers.

Let whatever terrorist goons might still be alive think on that sight, he thought.

As soon as Carl Lyons heard the machine gun open up and watched the terrorists' numbers reduced by even more, he grinned with a self-assured nod.

They were kicking ass—screw the name-taking. The steady, droning report from the M-60E3 sounded as if it were actually causing the ground to rumble. Lyons had also seen Blancanales take off, dashing from cover to disappear behind the building. At first, the Able Team leader had considered scolding his friend for taking that kind of chance when they were still considerably outnumbered, but he recanted the decision when the grenade exploded a minute later.

An idea then flashed through his mind and Lyons keyed up his radio. "Gadgets, keep them pinned down. The rest of you prep all the grenades you have. We're going to try a ditch digger."

While he didn't have any actual military-service experience, Lyons had been trained in military tactics by those of his friends who had—most of the other Stony Man operators—along with the soldier of soldiers, Mack Bolan. Lyons figured that all of the team members would know the reference. A ditch digger was, in fact, a tactic whereby a small-arms emplacement would pin an enemy into the corner and then the remaining team members would flood that point with explosive ordnance. In effect, it was a brutal and utterly unethical way to fight—one of the dirtiest of tactics, really—but Carl Lyons didn't really give a damn about that. They had sworn to put down the Red Brood operation here and now and that was exactly what he planned to see through.

Lyons waited until he'd received a confirmation from every man and then they all ceased firing, save for Schwarz. The terrorists didn't show themselves immediately, but after a few testing and probing volleys from the M-60E3 they got the message and decided to break cover and head for the southwest corner of the clearing. There couldn't have been more than a dozen and Schwarz kept them busy by driving his fire just to the rear of them, forcing them toward the neutral corner.

Lyons waited until they were bunched as close together as he thought they would get, most of them ducking and dodging to avoid the pseudo-attempts by Schwarz to shoot them down, and then armed two of the Diehl DM51s. He waited, counted off a few more seconds and then gave the go signal. As the M-60E3 died out and the terrorists turned and looked back to determine why they were no longer being fired upon, seven grenades sailed high and wide and landed around them almost simultaneously. Complete panic erupted and the last thing Lyons would remember was the look of complete shock and horror on the faces of his enemies. The grenades blew in almost concurrent order, maybe a couple coming a bit late, but the bulk of them rendered such a horrific shock wave that some of the terrorists found their limbs separated from their torsos. The blasts of hot gas and thousands of searing pellets pummeled their bodies. Most were killed instantaneously but a few didn't die immediately.

Blancanales and Lyons finished those survivors with well-placed mercy rounds.

Montrose and Armenteros joined them a moment later, and if they were shocked to see the pair not hesitate to pump lead into the ones still alive they didn't say anything. Schwarz joined them a minute later, maintaining his vantage point to ensure there were no stragglers before he broke cover. The building was really starting to burn now, and Lyons suggested they check the interior for any intelligence before it became fully engulfed.

The men spread out and performed a quick search, ultimately coming away with a treasure trove of documents, maps and some email printouts with Arabic characters they would need to have translated. Blancanales and Montrose then went about the task of piling beds against another wall and lighting them up while Lyons, Schwarz and Armenteros walked the perimeter one last time to make sure none of the terrorists had managed to escape and were hiding.

They found only one but he was deceased with severe burns over more than half his body—probably caught in the splash of diesel fuel, and he'd been running around trying to find water to put it out.

"Crispy critter," Armenteros remarked and he spit on the body. When Lyons and Schwarz looked at him in mild surprise, he said, "What? I don't like terrorists, man."

The Able Team pair simply looked at each other and shrugged.

AS SOON AS they had returned to their vehicles, the Able Team warriors shook hands all around and then departed for Daytona Beach.

During the trip, Lyons contacted Stony Man Farm. "We'll be sending this information as soon as we get to the hotel."

"Did you get Biinadaz?" Brognola asked, the tension obvious in his voice.

"No dice, Hal. Sorry."

The head Fed sighed. "Not your fault. When he heard you recovered the two kids he probably got the hell out of there."

"It's a little odd that he'd run away," Price said. "His profile suggests he's a crazy bastard and that he'd put up a fight before running. Religious radicals like Biinadaz may be a dime a dozen but this guy's a little bit more... well, let's just say unique."

"I don't think he ran because he was afraid," Lyons said.

"No?"

Blancanales was behind the wheel but he directed his voice toward the speaker, as Lyons had his phone plugged into the auxiliary jack of the late-model SUV, which was designed to permit hands-free talk. "Most of the intelligence we retrieved was printed in Arabic, but there were a couple of maps of Florida, as well as one with rather detailed markings of Seattle."

"Seattle," Price echoed. "Why Seattle?"

"We're not sure but we think maybe this has something to do with Khalidi's pipeline."

"Why?" Brognola asked.

"Why not?" Lyons replied. "It's a coastal city so there's plenty of ways for this Red Brood to get the teenagers out of the country. It's far enough detached from the Florida operation so that if one got compromised the other could continue to operate independently."

"It would also provide a place for Biinadaz to smuggle his private little army *in,* don't forget," Schwarz said.

"I think I'm beginning to see the big picture now," Price said in a slow, deliberate tone.

"You believe Biinadaz has gone to Seattle?" Brognola asked.

"I'd bet cash money on it," Lyons said. "And seeing as how you say the Man wanted a full-court press on this thing, I'd have to say it's not over yet until we go there and finish what we started."

"What do you need?" Price asked.

"I want the works for this one," Lyons said. "Complete resupply of weapons, first-class passage to Seattle and Black Betty waiting for us when we get there."

"Done."

"What about Jack? He available?"

"He is and we can have him down there in short order," Brognola said.

"As McCarter would say," Schwarz said, switching to his best impression of the Briton's Cockney accent, "Make it so, guv'na."

"I'm going to tell him you were poking fun at his accent," Blancanales said.

Schwarz stuck his tongue out.

"Oh, and one other thing, Hal," Lyons snapped.

"Sure."

"Can I trade these two for newer models?"

CHAPTER TWENTY-ONE

Stony Man Farm, Virginia

Hal Brognola and Barbara Price sat in the Operations Center of the Annex as the first real-time images streamed into view on the massive digital screen.

"These were taken approximately three hours ago," Kurtzman said, as he tapped at the keys to cycle through the images. "They were downloaded from a reconnaissance mission performed by the 143rd Fighter Squadron, Air Wing 7, currently deployed aboard the *Ike*."

Brognola nodded. "Any idea what we're looking at, Bear?"

"Carmen hasn't finished her evaluation, but I'd say it's some sort of underwater complex. Some of the thermal-heat images were too regular in shape to be natural spring formations. Their distinct circular patterns here and here—" he indicated them with a laser pointer "—present strong evidence this is a large man-made structure."

"How large?" Price asked.

Kurtzman sucked his breath through his teeth, referred to some separate data on a terminal screen and replied, "I'd say around two hundred square yards. That's just height by width—no telling how deep it goes."

Brognola let out a low whistle and Price looked at him with concern. "That's a sizable complex."

"At least now we know why Khalidi recruited Ebi Sahaf," he replied.

"This would be right up his alley," Kurtzman added.

"Not to mention a radical like Sahaf would jump at the opportunity to construct something like this given he probably had almost unlimited funding."

Kurtzman produced a hum and said, "Seems to me that if Able Team can shut down the human-trafficking pipeline here in the States, that would do significant damage to Khalidi's fiscal resources."

Price shook her head. "Yes, but would it be enough to shut down this operation is the real question at hand. And if this facility is complete or even close to completion, whatever Khalidi has planned for its use will probably begin soon. Phoenix Force and their contact, Mazouzi, have actually come up with a pretty good theory.

"The fish-packing plant they hit in Safi was storing marine oil and a lot of it. They think Khalidi may be shipping this to other locations and using it to power boats that rendezvous with shipping freighters, upload the drugs after the freighters leave Morocco, then off-load them again to his distribution points in foreign countries."

"Before the ships enter customs," Brognola interjected.

Price nodded. "Exactly."

"I wonder if Interpol already had some idea it was going on," Brognola said. "There are no agencies established exclusively to handle drug trafficking outside the boundaries of sovereign countries. It's typically mandated by international maritime laws and rules, which falls under the jurisdiction of the UN General Assembly."

"Just as piracy," Price added.

Brognola nodded. "It's almost a form of mutual aid. Now if American civilian ships are pirated we have the full jurisdiction to take care of our own, naturally. However, there are agreements with our allies that if an American naval vessel cannot intercept within a reasonable time, the ships of NATO countries may do so on our behalf."

"Okay," Kurtzman said, waving at the screen, "but these turkeys are operating all over the map. Even if we can figure out where they're going, how do we choose who to notify and what control do we have over the actions they take?"

"We don't," Price said. She looked at Brognola. "Which means the only choice left to us is destroy Khalidi's facility before he can implement his plans."

"Right," Brognola replied. "Bear, did the Navy provide any geographical photos, particularly close-in shots?"

"Yeah, I believe so." Kurtzman tapped at the keys and a moment later two large photographs were displayed side by side. "The first one was taken directly from above. It looks like the complex is built right into the rock of a natural cove approximately two miles north of Rabat. The second one is more of a head-on shot, or at least as best as the aviators could get for us from ten thousand feet."

Price shook her head. "That looks like a pretty treacherous approach. I don't know, Hal."

"We'll have to let Phoenix Force make the call ultimately, but I would have to agree with you. And judging from these photographs, even if they were able to breach that side of the facility there's no guarantee they'd have an entry point."

"Not necessarily, Hal," Price said, arching an eyebrow as she stared at the photograph. "Bear, do you see that rectangular protrusion there in the corner?"

"Uh?" Kurtzman squinted and then nodded. "Yes…yes, I do. Nice catch, Barb."

She smiled sweetly. "Thank you. Now let's enhance it and see if we can figure out what it is."

After about a minute of finagling with the image, Kurtzman sat back with a forlorn sigh. "That's about the best resolution I'm going to be able to get."

"It's enough," Price replied. "I know exactly what that is because I've seen it before in other photographs. It's a surf guide."

"A what?" Brognola inquired.

"It's called a surf guide. Coastal cliffs like the one there are notorious for having very choppy waters. When you are launching or receiving small submarines, you build surf guides so that when the tides are rough, the watercraft can be safely towed in and not subsequently get smashed against the rocks or run aground. Usually they are then lowered beneath the water and towed into a dock or maintenance facility."

"Wow," Kurtzman said. "That's high-tech."

"Exactly," Brognola replied, "and just another reason that Khalidi would need a man like Sahaf to help him construct it."

"That would definitely explain the two-cycle marine oil, too," Price said. "It's for their private fleet of submarines used to transport the drugs to the freighters. They're not seen leaving and they're not seen returning, and that's how Khalidi has managed to keep his construction project a secret all this time."

Brognola nodded. "It's a good theory. Let's get Phoenix Force on the horn. Pronto."

"Submarines, eh?" T. J. Hawkins said in response to McCarter's brief, scratching at his five-o'clock shadow. "Well, I'll be calf-roped and horse-dragged."

"Careful, pard-ner," James teased. "You might end up hornswoggled, too."

"The question I have is could he actually do it," Manning said. He looked to Mazouzi, who nodded with a grave expression.

"Amazing he's gotten this far without drawing attention," McCarter said.

"It is as I've already told you," Mazouzi said. "This man is quite the celebrity in my country. Nobody questions him, mostly because his political donations are substantial, and because nobody wants their name dragged through all of the *Abd-el-Aziz* affiliations in other countries. They do not call him Prince Story for nothing. He is all at once a popular and dangerous man."

"He's obviously had his claws deep into the Casablanca police community," Encizo replied.

Mazouzi's nod dripped with regret and sadness. "I am ashamed of what has happened in that regard."

"Do you think setting up Trebba will pull attention away from searching for you?"

"I am hopeful," Mazouzi said. "As soon as I drove away there were three units around him. I've not heard any news of his arrest, but between leaving Chief Bakkum's weapon in his possession and then placing the anonymous call to them saying I'd witnessed a man matching his description leaving the chief's residence, I am sure it will be some time before he is released."

"All I can say is I'm sure as hell glad a devious bloke like you is on *our* side," McCarter replied.

"Do not mistake my intentions," Mazouzi said. "I am not proud of what I have done. But I am sworn to uphold the law and sometimes…well—"

"Sometimes you have to step outside of it to protect the common good," Manning finished. "I was a cop once. I can understand that. And I can also understand you didn't do it for us."

"This is correct," Mazouzi said. "But all of you have

earned my respect this day. And that is something from where I come. And I hope you will not exclude me from whatever your plans may be regarding el Khalidi's facility."

"Not this time," McCarter assured him. "We're going to definitely need your expertise this time around. We have no idea of the odds we'll face or the type of terrain we have to breach."

Encizo said, "Our people tell us that if there's a secret entrance to this facility that it wasn't visible in any of the intelligence they received from their military analysts. It's obviously well hidden, then, and most probably the security will be such we couldn't get within a mile of the place before they'd blow us all to kingdom come."

"That means we have to find another way in," McCarter said. "The only way we can see to approach this place is via the coast. What are the tides currently like at this time of year?"

"They will be strong, particularly at night," Mazouzi replied immediately. "Although not particularly shallow, which means you have a strong chance of reaching the shore without being smashed into rocks. There are other hazards you must consider, however."

James's eyebrows rose. "Such as?"

"Sharks," Mazouzi said. "We will also have to be on the lookout for pirates. They are known to operate in those waters, and any vessel we take in would be a potential target, especially since we will have to operate without any communications."

"Which brings us to our next problem," McCarter said. "Assuming no pirates and no dangers from marine life, and we can get our bloody arses close enough to breach the coastal side of this facility, *and* assuming we can get inside once we're ashore, what about transportation? Can you help us with that?"

"What kind will you need?"

"Well…" McCarter looked to his teammates for assistance.

After some silence, Manning said, "For one, we'll need some type of boat to get in. I'd say probably something small and fast, maybe even a couple of them so we can split up our efforts. We'll have to assume there will be resistance."

"Yeah," Encizo agreed. "If one team gets hit we'll at least have a contingency."

Mazouzi appeared thoughtful. "There is a man I know who can perhaps help us. He owes me a debt and I have not yet had a need to collect. But I do know he could only provide us with one boat."

"What about a helicopter?" Hawkins asked.

"This might be possible."

"What do you have in mind, mate?" McCarter asked him.

"I was just thinking that if we wanted to split up our teams, we might consider half could approach by watercraft and the other half via an air-assault drop. Fly in low altitude, drop onto the promontory and then rappel down and see if we can find an alternative entrance. I mean, there have to be airshafts or something down there."

"No heat signatures according to the photographs," Manning countered, waving at the pictures Stony Man had transmitted.

"Might be obscured by overhanging rocks," Hawkins said easily. "Might even be pressurized and just beneath the surface of the water. Sahaf's supposed to be some kind of construction genius, right? Who knows what's down there until we take a look?"

"Seems to me we would actually benefit from sending the rappel team in first," McCarter offered. "Volunteers?"

"I'm definitely in," Hawkins said. "My idea and besides, I had a lot of experience with this kind of thing while in the Army."

McCarter nodded. "Then by that account, I'm probably the next most qualified."

Manning looked at first like he might argue but then clammed up. While he had significant experience operating over similar terrain while with the Royal Canadian Mounted Police, McCarter had come from a tour of duty on Her Majesty's Special Air Service. He and Hawkins really were the two most experienced with air-assault tactics, then, so it made sense they should be the ones to use for this leg of the mission.

"It's decided, then," McCarter said. He looked at Mazouzi. "You start working on getting our transportation and we'll get geared up."

As ABBAS EL KHALIDI descended into the bowels of his underwater superstructure, he seethed at the sheer incompetence of some of his men.

The Mazouzi bastard had managed to expose the corruption inside the Casablanca police by murdering Ran Bakkum and then setting up Hasidim Trebba to take the fall. As soon as Trebba had encountered trouble he had contacted Khalidi, a call that had been surely recorded if not set up by Trebba to save his own worthless skin. Khalidi had managed to deflect Trebba's calls and then immediately put out a termination order. The man's life would be snuffed within twenty-four hours.

So his personal assassination squad had assured him.

Mazouzi had also murdered one of Sahib's best men, and Khalidi had to wonder why he'd bothered to trust the man to begin with. Sahib had ended up hooked on his own stuff and after he'd been released by the police—a release that Khalidi had arranged at some personal risk—he'd apparently gone into hiding and was last seen sucking up enough opium to anesthetize a small elephant.

To top it off, Khalidi had just learned of the destruction of his plant in Safi and hundreds of thousands of dollars' worth of equipment. That equipment had been vital to completing the construction of parts of his underwater complex, as well as a good part of their fuel reserves. Now he would have to find his stockpile of fuel somewhere else. Thankfully, Ebi Sahaf had been thinking ahead and counseled Khalidi sometime back to move part of his reserves to the complex.

They would have enough to begin the operation.

But it was the recent news Sahaf had sent a courier to deliver personally that most concerned Khalidi. Something had gone very wrong with his operation in the United States. No…not very wrong, it had become a complete disaster. There had been a number of engagements between American special operatives and the private army that Genseric Biinadaz had apparently been building right under his nose. They had lost more than a half-million dollars, funds that he urgently needed to complete all of his plans for his distribution empire. And according to his spies, Biinadaz wasn't finished.

As soon as Sahaf heard that Khalidi was there, he met him in the private office that adjoined Khalidi's quarters. Khalidi tried not to show how badly his nerves were even as the decanter of liquor clinked like the chain of a ghost against the snifter. Khalidi finished pouring and corked the expensive German cognac. He took a long pull and then sat in his office chair, propped his feet on his desk and rubbed his eyes.

"I take it you will remain here for some time?" Sahaf said as he dropped into a stuffed chair made from calfskin.

"I will remain here indefinitely," Khalidi said. He took another drink and added, "It's no longer safe for me to be seen in public."

"Does this have something to do with Zafar Mazouzi?" Khalidi looked sharply at his friend in surprise.

Sahaf merely smiled and shrugged. "His name has been all over the news, and I've heard you talk of him randomly in the past. It would seem he is almost your arch enemy. In fact, I have it on good authority that he's been running around Casablanca asking questions of anyone who will listen to him, and I've heard that he's even dropped my name."

"How would he know about you?"

Sahaf shook his head and sighed, removing his glasses and withdrawing a microfiber cloth to clean them. "I'm sure he got the information from the Americans. It is of no consequence, however. They still would know nothing of this facility."

"What about the destruction of our reserve equipment in Safi?" Khalidi asked. "Will this impact our schedule?"

"Not by any critical factor." Sahaf replaced his glasses, then sighed and folded his arms. He studied his longtime associate and finally said, "You should not worry, Abbas. There is no danger to our operations."

"You are certain of this?"

"I'm staking my life on it," Sahaf said. "And even if they knew about this place they wouldn't have any reason to tie it back to you or me. For all intents and purposes, we are virtually invulnerable. No team of American commandos, no matter how good, can penetrate our defenses. The most viable entrance is guarded and more secure than bank vaults. The coastal approach is too treacherous for assault by ships of any consequence. I've even accounted for an air strike."

Khalidi nodded. "I have complete faith in you, my friend."

"I know this. It is faith in yourself that you lack most."

"You were right about Genseric," Khalidi said. "I should have let you move on him when you first asked me."

"I am only sorry that I could not determine sooner what he was up to," Sahaf replied with a measure of genuine regret in his expression. "I have failed you."

"Hardly," Khalidi said with a snort. "I should've listened to you when you warned me before but I was too stubborn…too confident. My ego has cost me and I've definitely paid a price."

"What is it you intend to do?"

"I understand that he has something planned in Seattle. I cannot imagine what it is but I have already taken steps to see that his plans come to nothing. If these American agents that attacked his operation in Florida are as fierce as I am led to understand, Genseric will not be long for this life. He is on a path to seeing his precious Allah much sooner than he might believe."

"And what if they are unsuccessful? These Americans?"

"My men already have instructions to ensure that the job gets done, either way. If it appears that he might attempt to move forward with his operation before the Americans can stop him, they have orders to eliminate him and his entire team. Permanently."

"And what if the Americans get in the way?"

Khalidi's reply was cold, quiet and even. "Then they will burn in hell along with him."

CHAPTER TWENTY-TWO

Everett, Washington

A steady rain hammered the streets of the city.

Genseric Biinadaz had chartered a private plane to take him from Daytona Beach to Paine Field, a small airport north of Seattle. This particular airport saw quite a bit of activity, including increased tourism in recent years due to a new tour program and museum sponsored by Boeing. Additionally, Boeing had a factory there for production of many of its 700 series aircraft, so heavy traffic wasn't out of the ordinary. In fact, Biinadaz had selected it for that very reason—nobody would remember him. He'd paid cash for the ticket, not wanting to charge it to Acres's account. They would've been able to track him that way. By paying cash for the charter and giving a false name, he could avoid any undesired attention.

It wasn't the Americans that worried him as much as Abbas el Khalidi. The fool actually thought he could outwit Biinadaz. The problem was that el Khalidi—like the cerebral and tight-assed Sahaf with whom he associated—didn't understand the cause. The man had been brought up in luxury, or at least he'd possessed enough wealth for long enough that he no longer understood what is was like to have to fight for everything: food, clothing, shelter and even women. The despicable luxury with which he'd surrounded himself had made el Khalidi soft. Biinadaz despised soft men. And he despised incompetent men, which was why it didn't really bother him that much about the destruction of the force secreted in the wetlands. They had let the Americans outwit them at every turn, and Biinadaz simply didn't need that kind of trouble right now. He had too many important things to do, like terrorize an American city.

Their plans were set and he still had enough men to accomplish the job, despite their losses in Florida. The thing he couldn't let bother him now was the thought they might be able to follow his trail; he'd been careful and planned all of it to the last detail for just such a contingency. That kind of planning and foresight was what truly separated him from men like the one he worked for, no...*had* worked for. Biinadaz had resigned if only in his own mind.

He took a bus for the thirty-mile trip into the city, and then caught a taxi to the waterfront district. The small business office on the wharf they had leased had been a steal. The lease company had only been too happy to sign them up for a six-month term. Commercial property sales and rentals weren't a terribly profitable venture at the moment given the economic decline of the Great Satan, a natural evolution for a country filled with greedy, capitalist infidels who cared for nothing but their palatial houses and fancy automobiles.

Biinadaz didn't hate money as most might have assumed. That was another lie about Islam that the Westerners had let be perpetrated among their social cliques. In reality, most of what Biinadaz had done had been about money, although not so much money for his personal use as much as to contribute to his cause. Money bought weapons and information and loyalty; that's why it was so effective in the political arena and why it took so much to get ahead. The Americans had become victims of their own system, allowing European and Asian countries to do all of their manufacturing and service provision for them. It had all been for the purpose of destroying the American economy. Biinadaz had to admit that those like the Red Chinese, while he didn't care for their religious or social views, had done a very good job of ensuring that very thing.

When all of it was said and done, Biinadaz knew that his private army of only twenty-five men couldn't do much. But they could do something, and so far they had proceeded with their meticulous plans unmolested. Not even the FBI or CIA had managed to find out what they were up to. Biinadaz had ensured that the Red Brood's activities were public enough to throw the American police off the real intent of their presence. They were busy chasing those who they thought were interested in stealing teenagers and kids, when in fact Biinadaz and his men had been planning something else all this time.

Even el Khalidi had fallen for the ruse!

Biinadaz entered the office to find his friend and fellow Taliban fighter waiting for him. The man was a giant, with the muscular chest, shoulders and arms to back it up. He stood about six and a half feet tall with black, curly hair and a beard. His eyes were nearly as dark as those of Biinadaz. A thin, jagged scar ran the length of his forehead, the result of being struck by a rock dislodged from the ground after a missile exploded near his position one night while fighting in the mountains of Afghanistan against American forces.

Biinadaz hugged the giant man and they greeted each other with a ceremonial exchange of kisses.

Biinadaz stepped back and smiled, his eyes beaming with a mix of pride and relief. "Sardar, my friend, it is so good to see you again."

Sardar Mojaddi nodded and clapped a meaty hand on

his friend's shoulder. "And you, my brother. The men were very anxious for your arrival after I told them you were coming."

"I would have preferred to surprise them," Biinadaz replied, although he was cautious not to sound upset. "A spot inspection tends to improve their skills and maintains order."

"There is no cause for concern. I have followed your instructions to the letter." Mojaddi lowered his voice and looked around them before adding, "New intelligence suggests that el Khalidi has ordered your assassination. I feared for your safety every minute I knew you were traveling here."

"There's no reason to ever worry about me, brother." Biinadaz thumped his chest. "In me beats the heart of a warrior for Allah. As long as there is the jihad then my spirit lives on with it."

When Mojaddi nodded emphatically, Biinadaz couldn't resist a smile.

"You think me mad, perhaps."

"Not at all."

"You do," Biinadaz said and he slapped his friend's arm. "But that is okay, I take no offense in it. In fact, I consider it somewhat of a compliment. What do we know of the Americans who attacked our encampment in Florida?"

"They have surely tracked us here. One of our men managed to hide until they had left."

"Hide? A filthy coward!"

Mojaddi shook his head. "Not fair, Genseric. The man was on patrol and returned to the perimeter too late. He was outnumbered and he felt it better to watch the Americans. They collected many of the maps and some of the documents from the camp. He advised that they looked like some of the operational briefings you had given the trainers when you last visited the site."

"Those fools!" Biinadaz pounded his fist on the table. "That was more than a month ago. I ordered them to study the plans and then destroy them immediately. Allah's wrath take them all!"

After Biinadaz had released a few more curses and appeared calm again, Mojaddi said, "Whether they know of our location or not, they could not know of our plans."

"No. I brought nothing that gave them specific details."

Mojaddi nodded. "Then it is of no concern. They will probably do nothing more than notify the police in this city. Besides, they only know of you and you will be running the operation from here. As long as you were careful in coming here…"

Mojaddi didn't finish the statement because he didn't want to make it sound as if he was insulting the volition of his friend. Biinadaz would have taken great care to ensure that he wasn't followed, and if he'd at all suspected that was the case he wouldn't have come here to their operational headquarters.

For the longest time when they were planning this operation, Biinadaz had resisted leading the operation from the sidelines. He'd always been a working leader, never asking any of his men to do something he was not prepared and able to do better and faster than any of the men he led. But Mojaddi had finally convinced him that without his leadership they wouldn't be as organized, and if he died in the field the entire thing could go bad. After much prodding and coaxing from Mojaddi, Biinadaz had finally given in and promised he would not attempt to lead the operation in person.

"I will instead reserve that privilege for you," Biinadaz had told Mojaddi at the time.

Biinadaz looked at his watch. "We only have twelve hours before the operation begins. Are you certain that all of our plans are in place?"

"We've been drilling steadily for two months," Mojaddi replied. He took a seat behind the plain wooden desk left there by the previous occupants. Its surface was marred by age and abuse, and the only thing atop it was an ashtray filled nearly to overflowing.

Mojaddi lit a Turkish cigarette and said, "They have become quite devoted and it is obvious that most are excited about the plan. Nothing like this has ever been done before in the history of the jihad. This strike will be unlike any that has come before and perhaps will ever come again."

Biinadaz nodded. "We will most definitely send a clear message to our enemies with this strike. And they won't have any way to respond immediately to our assault, which means we will have time to make our escape."

"And perhaps to strike again somewhere else," Mojaddi said through the cloud of smoke.

Biinadaz raised a finger. "Let's not get ahead of our own plans, brother. While this operation will send an unprecedented message for our cause and yes, it will shake the Americans to the depths of their souls, this will also cause an embittered and passionate response from many. We will be hunted down and destroyed, which means that once we have completed this mission we will have to leave."

"Leave?" Mojaddi expressed surprise.

"Now before you rebuff me, let me explain this in another way that you can understand my concern. The Americans have never been known to respond to these kinds of attacks with insanity. After our victory against New York and Washington, they responded with great military force and invaded several of our allies' nations. As well as our own home, let us never forget the blood spilled. It is that one act from which much outrage was generated, and many who were ill-prepared died for the glory of the cause.

"The response will be no less brutal this time around. They will become angry and they will drop many bombs on our brothers and sisters wherever they might be hiding. We will not come out of this unscathed, if we come out of it at all, and for the bravery of our men I wish to give them at least the chance to survive."

"They are prepared to die for this, Genseric."

"I know, brother, but dead men do not fight. Live men fight. That is the way of our world and it is as unchangeable as our god. If we can complete our mission and survive, and we are granted the mercy of Allah for our escape plan, then we may have another chance to fight for our cause at some later time."

"Do you really think they will respond with such heated vengeance?"

Biinadaz shook his head and tendered a frown. "It is in their nature—it is who they are. We can know nothing for certain until it happens. And tomorrow at dawn, your question will finally be answered."

ONCE JACK GRIMALDI had reached Daytona Beach and picked up Able Team, it took a mere five hours—including one fuel stop—for Stony Man's Gulfstream G280 to reach Seattle. Still in its prototype phase, the G280 had been under rigorous testing by the teams for the past few months and they were impressed with its speed and comfort. Grimaldi had put the thing through its paces on his own, first, to be sure. He had also let U.S. Navy and DARPA engineers equip it with all of the extra bells and whistles that came in handy on missions like those of Phoenix Force and Able Team.

They had actually replaced the C-21As they'd been

using for a long time, and the Oval Office had managed to broker a special deal with the manufacturer so that they could keep the prototype for a small charge. Also under the agreement, they would order a second one when it actually went into full production. Brognola had gone for the deal after getting the nod from Grimaldi. That time was approaching soon and Grimaldi had hardly been able to talk about much else since it was first announced they'd be switching the planes out.

"I love this new bird," he'd told Able Team as they were loading up in Daytona Beach.

Now they had clearance and were soon taxied to a special section of Sea-Tac reserved for government charters. Through the port window, Gadgets Schwarz spotted a USAF C-17 Globemaster III parked not fifty yards from their plane. He watched even as the ramp started to lower. The twinkle in his eye told it all, and Blancanales and Lyons began to chuckle as they watched him watch the action. From the ramp descended the sleek, unmistakable lines of Able Team's adopted sister.

Black Betty.

She was no ordinary woman. They'd waxed her from bumper to bumper, probably unaware that lining her gleaming exterior was a Kevlar material capable of shielding her occupants from rounds from most .50-caliber machine guns. Her windshield was bulletproof and her tires self-sealing; she boasted surveillance and counter electronic security features that could put some modern aircraft to shame; she could reach speeds exceeding 120 miles per hour. Most beloved was her portable armory.

"Come to poppa, you sweet beast!" Schwarz cried.

This brought outright laughter from his friends but Schwarz didn't care. That was his baby and he loved her like one of his own.

The three men left Grimaldi with their thanks and headed for the van.

Lyons took the wheel for the trip to police headquarters while Blancanales and Schwarz went to work in back. They had magazines to load, weapons to inspect and equipment to check. They would wait to check in with Stony Man Farm after they had made their rounds with the chief of police and the head of SPD's tactical-response-unit leader. The entire meet had been arranged by Stony Man, and while Lyons had objected to wasting their time he knew gaining the cooperation of local law enforcement could ultimately make their jobs easier.

"Not to mention it's plain damn courtesy, so just do it," Brognola had told Lyons.

Out of the blue on their trip to the police HQ, almost as if reading Lyons's mind, Schwarz popped off with one of his usual quips. "Anybody notice Hal getting grumpier these days?"

"Maybe he's getting old," Blancanales said.

"What, Hal?" Schwarz shook his head. "No way. I don't think Hal's ever going to get old."

"Maybe it's just senility," Lyons muttered.

"You think we're senile, too?" Schwarz cracked. He looked at Blancanales. "Look at this guy, our fearless leader. He thinks age and senility go hand in hand. That's kind of prejudiced."

"Naw, I don't think he's prejudiced," Blancanales said in his easy and good-natured way. "I just think he's still upset at Hal for barking up his trousers."

"Well, this is stupid!" Lyons snapped, letting his hands come off and back onto the steering wheel. "We're wasting our time talking to the cops instead of getting out among the real world and finding these terrorists."

"Oh, I get it," Schwarz said. "He's like a man of the people."

"Exactly," Blancanales said.

"Impossible," Lyons growled. "Completely impossible."

After making a quick stop at a department store for some off-the-rack suits, the three proceeded to the headquarters building located in downtown Seattle on Fifth Avenue. Lyons pulled around back to the parking area and into an empty spot labeled R. Castanucci, Deputy Chief—Operations. He climbed out, went around back and opened the rear doors. Blancanales handed him a plate with U.S. government tags that he affixed to the rear door with magnets. He then returned to the front and stuck a blue-and-white tag on the driver's-side window that read: FBI, Official Business Only, U.S. Government. That would prevent anyone from towing them.

The trio proceeded around the corner to the main entrance that faced Fifth between James and Cherry Streets. Squads were parked along the street directly opposite the building and the one-way road was very busy, crammed mostly with rush-hour traffic as it was past 1600 hours. Once inside they announced themselves to the desk officer. He called upstairs to administration, and someone was sent to escort the three men to the chief's office in the Justice Center.

Chief Michael R. Taksten greeted the three amiably enough, shaking their hands in turn, and then offered seats and coffee. They accepted both. They made small talk while waiting for the other missing party to the meeting, who ended up being almost ten minutes late. The guy who entered was tall with blond-white hair, almost Nordic-looking, with broad shoulders and a bushy mustache. His eyes were deep blue and he carried himself with the air of a man in great authority.

"Gentlemen, please meet Dan Kline, my assistant chief of special operations," Taksten said.

Kline apologized for being late and forsook handshakes in favor of a curt wave after Taksten had introduced each man in turn by his alias.

After they were reseated, Taksten kicked it off. "Dan, this meeting was requested by representatives at the U.S. Department of Justice. The FBI has come into some information and it's pretty disturbing. I've only heard just a small bit of it so far since I wanted to wait on you before getting more details."

Kline nodded and Taksten explained to Able Team, "As head of special operations, Dan's the best qualified to hear what you have to say."

Lyons nodded and sized up Kline for a moment before he began. "I don't think we have much time so I'll get right to the point. You have a cache of Islamic terrorists operating in this city and they've been here for some time. We think they're about to pull off a major strike right here in Seattle. What we don't know is where or when."

Kline nodded, his face stern. "We've been hearing some chatter on the streets about this. A few of our sources have recently come forward and told us there's a buzz going on, something about Arab types turning up in strange places and asking strange questions. We were about to contact DHS in Washington when we got the call from the Justice Department."

"You said they've been turning up in strange places?" Blancanales retorted.

"Yes."

"Tell us where," Carl Lyons replied.

CHAPTER TWENTY-THREE

Dressed in urban camouflage and black combat boots, Able Team sat in their van parked across from Dinky's Place, a rave club known for its large Arab clientele.

In another place and time Kline's intelligence people might have been accused of racial profiling, but right now it appeared to have paid off. Among those who spent time in the club on a regular basis were two undercover officers who belonged to the CI squad. Criminal intelligence remained the most important area of operations in Kline's division, which was something the big cop had been candid about. Better than ninety percent of the information that came out of the division formed the basis for how he'd developed their protocols and operating procedures.

According to a quick background check conducted by Kurtzman, Kline was a smart cop with a distinguished career and experience in multiple arenas of tactical policing. He'd served as a SWAT officer, later promoted to sergeant. Courses at night college earned him his criminal-justice degree and a position as a lieutenant for the metro response unit. Kline finally transferred out of that field and did a stint as assistant to SPD's director of professional oversight, a civilian post, and then returned to full active duty right after 9/11 as deputy chief. He'd been an assistant chief for two years.

The Able Team warriors had admitted to one another they were impressed with Kline, not only because of his no-bullshit manner but also because of his understanding of antiterrorist tactics. He'd apparently undergone training at Quantico and FLETC, and had even participated in a number of joint task-force exercises at the DOE's National Training Center at Kirtland Air Force Base in New Mexico.

Kline had tried to disabuse them of the notion they could run the show, though whether out of a sense of territorialism or simply a taste for action remained to be seen. Not that Lyons had let him get far with that one. They ultimately decided to let Kline and his men participate in the operation but only as observers and to keep any civilians safe if things went hard. Brognola had issued a special order that Able Team not step on any toes if it could be helped and Lyons acquiesced.

"I bet Phoenix Force doesn't have to put up with that kind of bullshit," Lyons said as he hung up the phone and pocketed it. "We have to worry about everybody's civil rights these days, don't you know. McCarter and crew get to hobnob in the war-torn countries and kill all the terrorists they please."

"Go easy, Ironman," Blancanales replied in his usual congenial tone. "Hal's never been a political guy, at least not with us. You know that by now."

Lyons nodded and grumbled, "Yeah."

"Shape it up, you two," Schwarz said. "I think we've got our guy."

Indeed, the guy did match the description that the intelligence boys had passed on to Kline. He sauntered down the sidewalk, moving past the line waiting to get in and ignoring everybody and everything. He wore an almost intent expression, as if he were on some sort of important mission. The mark's name was Alzabir and he had a sheet filled with a litany of politically based offenses touting the sovereignty of Islam. Although he'd been active and had a police record, ultimately making him a person of interest for the SPD, he'd never demonstrated any violent tendencies. This seemed both odd and interesting to Able Team and they had immediately pegged him as a likely suspect. If anybody knew where the Red Brood might be operating in Seattle and what they had planned, it would be Alzabir.

"Maybe this will be easier than I thought," Lyons said. "I didn't think we'd be so quick to find him."

"This is his regular hangout," Schwarz said. "Shouldn't be tough to take him quickly and quietly if we play our cards right."

"Then again, maybe not," Blancanales replied. "Look."

Through the observation cameras mounted to the small, circular window toward the back of the van that was about the size of a cruise ship porthole, two men appeared about a half block up from Alzabir's position. They looked determined to intercept the mark before he entered the club and their intentions weren't likely friendly.

"Hold position," Lyons told his partners and he was out of the van before either man could reply.

Lyons crossed the street at a flat run and intercepted Alzabir just as the two swarthy types reached him. One of the pair managed to get a hand wrapped around the unsuspecting Alzabir's wrist but Lyons broke that with a Shotokan karate chop to the forearm where bone met nerve. The blow caused the man to release his grip. Lyons followed with a low kick to the shin, running the side of his boot down the inside of the leg. It wasn't debilitating but it proved plenty painful.

As the guy bent over to grab his throbbing shin, Lyons pivoted into the man's partner and kneed his groin. The man bent at the waist and twisted, and Lyons helped him along by an upward palm strike to the chin while simultaneously grabbing the back of his head and twisting down and around. The man's body slammed to the pavement.

Lyons grabbed Alzabir by the collar and half dragged him toward the van. He was midway across the street—ignoring the cacophony of screeching tires and cursing drivers—when more trouble materialized. Three men on a far street corner saw the commotion and began sprinting up the sidewalk in Lyons's direction. They toted machine pistols and that made their intentions abundantly clear.

Lyons maintained a hold on Alzabir's collar as he shoved him out in front and made a beeline for the cover of a late-model Cadillac parked at the curb. He withdrew his Colt Anaconda on the move. Without slowing, he leveled the pistol, sighted down the slide and squeezed the trigger. A .44 Magnum slug rocketed toward the point guy as the weapon boomed with a report that reverberated down the street, traveling between the taller buildings like wind through a canyon. Bystanders and concealed SWAT members alike beheld Lyons's marksmanship as the bullet punched through the man's chest and lodged in his heart, not penetrating due to foresight in loading special frangible rounds developed by Kissinger.

The other two gunners realized they were under fire as their comrade fell and they split to grab cover. Lyons cursed that their hand had been forced, but he was grateful for the reprieve because it bought enough time for him to get Alzabir some modicum of protection. This man was their only lead, whatever his sins, and it would not bode well for Able Team if Alzabir got killed before they had a chance to interrogate him.

Blancanales and Schwarz came to the rescue, exiting the rear of the van and moving up the side facing the street. Blancanales had his SIG-Sauer P-229 but Schwarz had emerged with a Beretta ARX-160. Designed as a replace-

ment for the Italian army's AR-70/90, this new assault rifle
chambered the same 5.56 mm NATO rounds as its predecessor but was two pounds lighter and capable of mount-
ing its specially designed GLX-160 grenade launcher. It
also had a folding stock but this one doubled with a tele-
scoping butt.

Blancanales barely slowed down as he grabbed Alzabir
and hauled him toward the tactical truck that just rounded
the corner. Inside the truck were six members of the most
experienced MRU teams available, and they were proving
it right at that moment. Blancanales continued with Alzabir in tow, moving toward the truck even before it had
skidded to a stop in front of the club.

Lyons shook his head, incredulous that the team leader
had enough foresight to get the truck between the people
at the club, reducing the risk of them getting hit while
also giving the Able Team warriors a chance to retreat
to safety. Too bad they weren't going to have any of the
pie today, because there were still two terrorists out there
and neither Schwarz nor Lyons intended to let them walk
away from this one.

Schwarz had laid the rifle on the hood of the Cadillac
and was now searching for a target. One of the terrorists
popped up and let off a shot but he wasn't up long enough
for Schwarz to risk firing on him.

"I can't get a clean shot," Schwarz told Lyons. "And I
can't risk openly firing. The rounds might hit somebody
in one of those buildings."

"Let's see if we can't get something else to draw their
attention," Lyons replied.

The Able Team warrior keyed up his microphone after
switching to the SWAT team frequency. "Irons to MRU
team leader."

"This is MRU leader," came back the voice of Sergeant Jerry Stepakonous. "Go, Irons."

"We need a distraction. Soon as you've got our men aboard, proceed down the street and see if you can't draw the attention of the other two."

"Roger, wilco."

Forty seconds elapsed and the truck went into motion, a signal to Schwarz and Lyons they should move. The pair moved back up to Able Team's van, and Lyons jumped behind the wheel while Schwarz got in back. Lyons cranked the engine, turned the wheel hard left and roared out of the parking spot, barely missing the bumper of the car in front of him. There were more honking and cursing drivers, but Lyons ignored their protests once more.

"Working here!" he shouted at one old lady who gave him the finger.

The van fishtailed and then straightened. Schwarz had popped the driver's-side top hatch and jumped onto the armory case. He let the Beretta lead him as he maneuvered head and shoulders through the hatch that was just wide enough for one man. He now had a high-ground view of the situation, which would be all he needed. The electronics wizard swung the Beretta into target acquisition on the pair who were now busy taking potshots at the retreating SWAT truck.

Glad that thing's armor-plated, Schwarz thought.

The terrorists didn't stand a chance between their preoccupation with the truck and their realization they were sorely outgunned. Schwarz took the first one with a short burst to the chest that shredded flesh, cracked bone and did a generally decent job of turning his lungs and heart to mush. The second terrorist snapped a hasty shot but then realized the futility and turned to depart. Schwarz cut him down by firing at his legs first, and then following up with a well-placed double-tap into his torso after he hit the sidewalk face-first.

"We're clear!" he shouted to Lyons.

And with that, Able Team beat a hasty retreat from the scene.

"AWFUL LOT OF YELLING going on in there," Schwarz said to his colleagues.

Neither Lyons nor Blancanales deigned to reply as they sat outside Chief Taksten's office. They had been listening to him bawl out Kline for the past ten minutes, the assistant chief even firing back with a few barbs of his own. Lyons checked his watch and shook his head. The longer they waited to talk to Alzabir, the more likely the chance the guy would simply shut up and demand a lawyer. They couldn't do anything about it, at least not here, since they had to maintain their cover as FBI special agents.

"We're wasting time," Lyons said. "Enough of this."

Lyons got on his feet and pushed through the door of the chief's office without knocking. Both men stopped shouting and looked at him in surprise. Kline seemed mildly surprised and a bit on the speechless side, but Taksten was clearly incensed, his face red, veins bulging out everywhere on his forehead. The look in his eyes said the intrusion had only done more to infuriate him. How dare this federal boob invade on his inner sanctum.

"Get out!" he told Lyons.

While the Able Team leader would have reached out to throttle the man under other circumstances, he knew he had to play the role here. He had enough troubles without having to get Brognola to bail them out of some political jam, and he knew they'd lock him up if he did what he really wanted to do at this point, which was to knock Taksten's perfect white teeth out of his skull.

Lyons took a menacing step closer and in a quiet voice said, "With all due respect, Chief Taksten, shut your pie-hole. Now I don't know just exactly what you think is going on here and I don't really give a shit. Your men went to some personal risk to protect our hides and that of our witness, although the guy hardly deserves it."

Taksten was speechless.

Lyons jerked a thumb at Kline. "And I think it takes real balls for a police chief to tell his man to cooperate fully, then turn around and stick a knife in his back for following orders. So let's be clear on something. We're operating on orders straight from that big white house with the pillars in front. You know what I mean? And on this day, or any other really, I'd say the man in that house outranks you. So here's what you're going to do. You're going to let this one go and you're going to let us talk to our witness. And then we'll be out of your hair and go spend our time on the things that really matter. Like saving your city from a bunch of bloodthirsty fanatics."

"And your job, too," Schwarz added with a helpful grin.

Blancanales simply sighed, obviously glad that Lyons had opted not to reach out and beat the chief of the SPD black and blue.

"This isn't over," Taksten finally blurted.

"Yes…it is," Lyons said.

With that, the three Able Team warriors left. They headed for the elevator that would take them down to Fifth Avenue, where they'd left the van parked. Lyons knew he'd have to call in some favors and get them access to King County jail, where they were holding Alzabir. It was entirely possible his little encounter with Taksten might have created more problems than it solved but he didn't have time to worry about that.

"Irons, wait up!" called Kline as the elevator doors were closing.

Blancanales managed to get a forearm wedged between them and the safety bars engaged and caused them to open. Kline charged in and nodded a thanks to Blancanales before turning his attention to Lyons. "Listen, I'm sorry about all of that. I know you guys are only trying to help."

"Look, Kline, I appreciate your empathy but that's not going to help us. We need to get to Alzabir before he engages a lawyer or worse. If we get to him before an attorney, I can guarantee we can get him to talk to us."

"I know," Kline replied. "That's what I'm trying to tell you guys. I don't give two shits what Mike says. Not much they can do to me that hasn't already been done. And if I'm out of a job, I'm out of a job. Maybe I'll retire early and go fishing."

"Tell you what," Blancanales interjected, "if you help us, I can guarantee you a job until you're ready to retire."

Lyons gave Blancanales a sour look but his friend ignored it.

Kline nodded. "Deal."

THE KING COUNTY Correctional Facility adjoined the Justice Center and offices of police headquarters along with the district courts. Most defendants who had been sentenced were either transferred to Snohomish County or to another, more remote location for long-term incarcerations. Maximum-security inmates were also farmed out to state penitentiaries, leaving the remaining facilities to deal with the less serious offenders. This didn't make Alzabir's detainment at KCCF seem all that strange.

However, the assistant chief of special operations accompanied by three men identifying themselves as FBI agents would have been somewhat unusual. Able Team decided to play it cool by sending Sergeant Stepakonous with Blancanales to interrogate Alzabir. They could get the information they needed while Schwarz and Lyons worked with Kline on other angles. The idea was to get the maximum work output in the minimum amount of time.

"Time is something we don't have," Lyons had told the group and they all agreed.

Blancanales and Stepakonous got into the facility without even so much as a second look and in a few minutes they were in a holding room with Alzabir. The man was still in his civilian clothes with hands fettered by a set of wrist manacles with a long chain. Blancanales ordered the restraints removed and only after a nod from Stepakonous did the detention officer comply.

When they were alone, Blancanales took a seat across from Alzabir. He studied the man for a while, saying nothing, looking into the dark eyes of a fanatic. He'd seen that look many times before. Blancanales had stared into faces just like this more times than he dared count, although usually those encounters ended in violence and bloodshed on the side of the enemy. But Alzabir's expression lacked one thing present in so many other faces: hatred. Alzabir possessed an intensity, a fervor, but he didn't give off the aura of a killer and that struck Blancanales with profound curiosity.

"You're Alzabir?"

"I am," the man replied, his eyes flicking briefly to Stepakonous, who stood with arms folded in the corner of the cell. "But then you know that."

"I'm Special Agent Rose. Your English is excellent," Blancanales remarked.

"It should be. I'm an American."

"You're an American who hates this country?"

"No. I'm an American who hates the way those who follow Islam are treated in this country."

"Muslims aren't treated any differently," Blancanales said.

Alzabir took on a new level of frostiness. "The Muslims in this country are treated very differently. As are the Jews and the other non-Catholics. I am doing all that I can to change that fact."

"By protesting in the streets and throwing dog shit at politicians and police officers? By promoting political discord and civil disobedience to achieve your aims? That sort of sounds like it borders on terrorism."

"If it's terrorism for me to devote myself to Allah, to practice my beliefs and pray five times a day and listen to the Koran, then I guess under that definition I'm a terrorist. But what you people seem to forget—"

"Look," Blancanales interrupted with a thump of his fist on the table, "I'm not concerned with your religion and I'm not interested in debating politics. I need some very specific information and I think you can give it to me. Now's your chance to prove you're an American, that you're nonviolent. And if the information pays off, you'll be released with no questions asked."

Alzabir sat back and folded his arms. "What do you want to know?"

"Have you ever heard of a man named Genseric Biinadaz?"

Blancanales got his answer even before Alzabir voiced it, the look on the man's face showing some measure of panic. "Now *he* is a terrorist. A bad man. And yes, I know him."

"Well, maybe what you don't know is that he's been working for a drug runner overseas. A drug runner who recently engaged in the kidnapping of two children and the murder of their fathers. You have any kids?"

"No." He shook his head and lowered it. "But I'm sorry to hear this. I don't believe in violent means to achieve the goals of Islam."

"I sensed that in you," Blancanales replied. "But you should know that Biinadaz is now here in Seattle and according to our information he's planning another large-scale terrorist attack. You know where he is? Any idea where he operates from?"

"I don't know. I don't know where he stays or what he has planned. But I can tell you about a man who would."

And Blancanales listened intently as Alzabir told him about the man named Sardar Mojaddi.

CHAPTER TWENTY-FOUR

"We found Alzabir," Lyons told Price and Brognola over the speaker in Black Betty. "We're on our way to the waterfront district now."

"Did Alzabir have any idea what the Red Brood has planned?" Price asked.

Lyons looked at Blancanales behind the wheel and tapped his shoulder.

"The head of the unit is actually a man named Sardar Mojaddi," Blancanales replied, his eyes never leaving the street ahead. "According to Alzabir, Mojaddi's been training the Islam fighters being smuggled in by Biinadaz through Khalidi's human-trafficking network. By the way, it's probably not that important but he also gave me some insight into this organization's name. Apparently it's taken from the red stripe on the Afghani flag, which represents the blood sacrifice for Islam and liberty. The brood is translated from an Arabic word I won't even try to pronounce, but it is essentially the pure definition of the term related to when a mare's used for breeding."

"Hmm, interesting," Brognola replied. "So essentially it is new warriors born out of the blood sacrifice of the Afghan people."

"The only reason Pol brings it up is because we don't think it was ever really part of Khalidi's operation," Lyons interjected. "It sounds more like some christening that Biinadaz gave to the group."

"Which solidifies our theory that Biinadaz hijacked Khalidi's operation," Price concluded. "That's not good, men. It definitely helped us because Biinadaz's actions exposed the group and put us onto their trail after they botched the kidnappings of Natalie Maser and John Jay Acres. But it also spells trouble because if Khalidi finds out he'll retaliate against Biinadaz with whatever allies he still has here."

"I think he already knows," Blancanales said evenly.

"Because..." Brognola prompted.

"The five men who tried to kill him in front of the club. You see, Alzabir knows Mojaddi pretty well, even though he says he's not involved with the Red Brood. I tend to believe him and so does Kline."

"Yeah," Lyons added. "And by the way, he's a different topic of conversation we'll need to have when all of this is over."

"Trouble?" Price asked.

"Not anything you guys can't handle," Lyons said.

"It's not important right now," Blancanales reminded them. "The important thing is that Alzabir didn't recognize any of the men who tried to kill him. Granted it was getting dark and granted they were some distance away. But Alzabir swore he didn't know either of the two men Ironman floored in front of the club, and he was pretty certain they weren't Mojaddi's men."

"So we think they were working for Khalidi, and they just happened to try to get Biinadaz through Alzabir the same as we were," Lyons said.

Price replied, "If Khalidi's people reach Biinadaz or Mojaddi before you do, we could have a full-scale terrorist war right there on the streets of Seattle. We need to do everything we can to prevent that from happening."

"Any suggestions for a tactical plan?" Brognola asked.

"Kline's running down the Khalidi angle by checking into the three deceased from the shoot-out at the club," Lyons said, "as well as one of the two alive they managed to arrest. The other guy escaped before uniforms could take him into custody, but Kline thinks they can get the guy they have to talk. We, uh, advised him that threats of GTMO were usually effective in these circumstances."

"Good call," Price replied. "It's true that Khalidi's people aren't likely fanatical Muslims like Biinadaz's terrorist fighters. They tend to be more cooperative in those cases."

"We may be hedging our bets a little, letting Kline and his people handle the Khalidi side of this," Lyons said. "But the fact is that Mojaddi is the more solid lead. If we can take out him and the Red Brood terrorists before Khalidi's people get to them, we can buy ourselves some time."

"And if you don't find Mojaddi or Biinadaz in time?" Price asked.

"No disrespect, love, but I don't want to get into what-ifs," Lyons replied as gently as possible. "We have a lead and we're pursuing that lead. We'll worry about retreat and a defensive posture if it comes to it."

"Fair enough."

"All right, then," Brognola said. "You know how to contact us if you need anything."

"Hey, Hal," Schwarz said from the back, "any word from Phoenix Force?"

"We think we've pinpointed Khalidi's secret project site," Brognola said. "They're getting ready to move on it now. Appears he's running some type of complex designed to act as a gateway for getting drugs out to designated freighters bound for Europe and other areas. Most likely he has something similar set up here for his child-trafficking ring, so if you come upon anything that appears to be like that, shut it down. Permanently."

"We'll do everything we can to keep you informed of their progress as we hear of it," Price said.

"Wish them Godspeed for us, Barb," Blancanales said.

"Will do."

"And the same to you, men," Brognola added.

A CHILL, DENSE MIST blanketed the commercial wharf that looked upon Puget Sound.

The location Alzabir had pointed them to sat adjacent to the Vigor shipyards on Seattle's south side. The lights of the Seattle-Bremerton ferry *Hyak* twinkled in the distance as it made its hour-long journey across the sound from the central waterfront terminal to Bremerton, Washington— a route it had been taking since the early fifties. As Able Team sat watch on the target site and occasionally glanced across the water at the sights and sounds of night, the silence weighed heavy.

"What do you think?" Schwarz finally asked, unable to take any more of the intense quiet.

"Looks awfully dead," Blancanales replied.

"All the more reason to think we've got the right place," Lyons said.

"There isn't much we're going to be able to do until we see something make a move," Schwarz said. "Unless we try a soft probe."

Lyons shook his head. "No way. I don't want to risk exposing us before we absolutely have to. We're better off just watching and waiting, see what happens."

"You know, we haven't considered the possibility that Alzabir's just taking us all for a ride and he's actually working for this Mojaddi. That could be why Khalidi's people tried to get to him and not simply because they were operating off the same intelligence we are."

Blancanales shook his head. "Not true. I had already considered that possibility and dismissed it."

"On what grounds?"

"If Alzabir were actually in on this deal with Mojaddi and Biinadaz, why would he risk exposing himself so close to their operation? And he definitely seemed as surprised as the rest of us that they would try to snatch him."

Lyons nodded. "I agree with you, Pol. Let's not forget that those clowns back at that club didn't try to actually gun us down until we intercepted the two who'd latched onto Alzabir. I was right there and I can tell you that they didn't intend to kill him. They were going to grab him and escort him away, and that tells me they thought he'd be a useful source of information."

"Of course, I didn't let him think that," Blancanales said. "I made it quite apparent that they had tried to assassinate him. It was amazing how cooperative and forthcoming he became when he learned that the Red Brood was out to murder him. And his outrage that Biinadaz's people had been murdering politicians and kidnapping young people was genuine. I got no vibes he was deceiving us in the information he provided."

"Looks like you're right," Schwarz said, eyes focused on the wharf office. He nodded toward it and said, "Check it out."

Two shadowy figures emerged from a car that had pulled up with its headlights extinguished. At first, the three men of Able Team were all thinking the exact same thing: these men were working for Abbas el Khalidi. But they quickly dismissed those thoughts when the pair didn't produce any weapons and didn't appear to approach the office in a covert fashion. No, they were entirely comfortable in this environment; that much was obvious.

Lyons reached into the pouch behind his seat and came

up with a pair of Yukon Digital Ranger Pro 5 × 42 night-vision binoculars. He flipped down the lens covers, engaged the power switch and lifted them to his eyes. A moment passed before a gray-green haze replaced the blackness of the viewfinder. The return through this NVB was phenomenal, providing Lyons with a clear view of the two men. He didn't recognize the one but the other was unquestionably Genseric Biinadaz.

Lyons passed the binoculars to Schwarz. "That's our guy."

"Sure is," Schwarz agreed, giving the binocs to Blancanales.

As Blancanales put them to his eyes, the two men were entering the office and the light they flipped on provided an even clearer image. "And I'm betting that's Mojaddi with him."

"That would be a pretty good bet," Schwarz replied.

Before they could discuss their options, the phone on Lyons's belt buzzed for attention. He checked the screen and said, "It's Kline."

"Where are you at?" Kline asked.

"Waterfront district," he replied. "Harbor Island, to be specific. Near the shipyards."

"You may want to get out of there," Kline said. "Our prisoner here squealed like a pig. He ratted out the whole operation. Your idea of threatening to send him to Guantanamo Bay did the trick."

"Not my idea but glad it helped," Lyons replied. "Why do we need to get out of here? We just got eyes on Biinadaz a minute ago. He's with another guy we think is Mojaddi."

"Yeah, well, apparently Khalidi's people have their eyes on them, too. They've been getting their information from more than one source. Sounds like there may be a mole inside Biinadaz's outfit and he's been busy."

"How do you know?"

"Just learned it through our intelligence people," Kline said. "Apparently they didn't know where Biinadaz had been operating before now because their mole hadn't been able to get word out to him. But now they have and there's apparently an entire killing team on its way to that location. We're sending an MRU out to you now, and a second one to the location where Khalidi's men are holed up."

The sudden squeal of tires and flash of lights drew Able Team's attention as three sedans pulled into the parking area in front of the wharf office.

"Might want to send them both our way," Lyons replied. He hung up and said, "Those are Khalidi's people. Let's do it."

BLANCANALES NODDED, cranked the van engine and put it in gear. He depressed the accelerator in a smooth fashion and the powerful, twin-valve, turbo-charged engine propelled them across the massive open parking lot adjacent to the office parking area.

The wharf office was a long, single-story building with a vaulted center structure for small truck deliveries surrounded on either side by office space. It was one of the more modern structures in the area and designed to withstand the potentially rough seaside weather of the northwest U.S. What it hadn't been designed to do was defend against trained terrorist assassins with fully automatic small arms.

Black Betty crossed the deserted parking lot in a minute-thirty flat, arriving at the office parking separated from the open lot by tall concrete curbs and an eight-foot-high chain-link fence. Blancanales swung the van so it was stopped parallel with the office, her armored body facing broadside to the enemy on the driver's side. He put it in Park and then ducked into the back as Lyons went EVA with an FNC clutched in his hands. He whirled to receive the AA-12 combat shotgun Schwarz passed to him and then sprinted from the cover of the van and toward the open gate that would allow him to get into flanking position without being detected.

Schwarz and Blancanales remained in back. Schwarz was putting all of the electronic-warfare systems into play while Blancanales worked on more practical matters. Included in Black Betty's arsenal of tricks was a fully functional HK-GR9 machine gun that recessed into the roof on a manual, hydraulic hinge. While extremely rare with few ever having been manufactured by Heckler & Koch, the GR9 chambered 5.56×45 mm NATO with an affixed belt box and a permanent optical sight with IR and laser capabilities. With a rugged build, cyclic rate of 750 rounds per minute and a muzzle velocity of nearly 1,000 mps, the GR9 served as Black Betty's primary weapon in both the offensive and defensive role.

In this case, Blancanales didn't see any reason to be discerning about how he'd use it here. Terrorists were terrorists and he wasn't going to waste time picking sides. Neither of these parties was concerned with how their actions affected American citizens and Blancanales figured all was fair. They stood little chance of having to worry about bystanders getting in the way in this remote part of the city and at this late hour. If they had to draw a line then Blancanales figured now was the time and place.

Blancanales released the clamps holding the roof plate in place and with a tug the machine gun came up on its hydraulic hinges and locked into place on its swiveling pod. Blancanales jacked the charging handle on the GR9 to put the weapon in battery and sighted on the three sedans that had seemed to vomit a plethora of Khalidi's terrorist assassins. Blancanales flipped out the optical sight, keyed in on the rear quarter panel of the closest vehicle and opened up with a steady salvo.

The GR9 belched flame as Blancanales poured on the heat. In this case it turned out to be the literal truth because the bullets penetrated the rear fiberglass panel of one of the sedans and continued on to the gas tank. Gas began to spill from the puncture but the terrorists, completely oblivious to the real intent, were more concerned that Blancanales was aiming for them. The men scrambled and did their best to avoid being ventilated by the high-velocity rounds even though Blancanales was actually coming nowhere near them.

Able Team had other ideas.

Once convinced he'd perforated the tank adequately, Blancanales then swung the machine-gun muzzle up and began to sweep across the building, punching out windows and shattering the exterior facade. He wasn't intent on trying to take the place down with the gunfire, knowing he'd need many thousands and thousands of rounds to even do real damage. In this case, he was using it as a delaying action to keep heads down and prevent having to fight on two fronts in case the occupants got the idea they wanted to engage Able Team with Khalidi's men in a concerted effort.

It was amazing how terrorists would band together when they had a common enemy to fight.

Blancanales smiled with satisfaction when he saw the blast from Lyons's AA-12. Schwarz had also provided Lyons with a 6-round belt of shells filled with gunpowder and a small charge designed to blow on impact. While it couldn't do much more than provide a flash-in-the-pan effect, it was wicked when delivered to an accelerant—like gasoline, for example. When the shell hit, it immediately

caught the pool of gasoline and immediately expanded into
flame with enough force to lift the sedan off the ground
and melt the inside walls of the rear tires.

The shock knocked the concealed terrorists off their
feet, but it had the added effect of casting considerable
light on their position while the Able Team warriors remained safely cloaked by the misty darkness.

Blancanales took up a new firing solution now with
fresh vigor, flipping the selector to 3-round-burst mode,
another enhancement of the GR9 over its HK23E predecessor, and taking the targets in a more selective fashion.
He triggered the first volley and caught a terrorist full in
the chest, ripping flesh and vital organs and lifting the man
off his feet. He hit the pavement on his back with bone-
crunching impact.

SCHWARZ HAD THE terrorists not visible from Blancanales's
position pegged using IR technology and was giving Lyons
rough estimates on their positions.

Lyons lay prone on the pavement, his weapon steadied
against a concrete parking block, and sighted down the infrared scope. He watched carefully all of the action, taking in the scene from a safe distance, and whenever the
opportunity presented itself he would zero in on a target
and take it out. Between his sniping the more difficult and
elusive terrorists and Blancanales raining down a hailstorm of 5.56 mm hell, Lyons knew it wouldn't take long
to eradicate the enemy terrorists.

Lyons caught sight of another terrorist through the scope,
took a deep breath and let half out, and then squeezed the
trigger. The scope filled with an image of the man's head
exploding when the high-speed bullet crashed through the
side of his head and splattered his brains and skull all over
the rear of one of the sedans where he'd taken cover, trying

to get a fresh angle of attack on Blancanales. He continued to sweep the area with the FN-FNC, but either their enemies were keeping their heads down or Blancanales had been dispatching them with the thoroughness he'd come to expect from his colleague.

Schwarz gave him his next target, indicating a terrorist was trying to retreat for the cover of the building. Lyons tried leading the man first but then thought better of it and swung in on the front door and waited. Sure enough, the terrorist showed up exactly where expected and a moment later he took two rounds—one through the chest and the other in the neck—for his troubles.

"Nice shooting, Ironman!" Schwarz called through the headset.

"I know," he replied with a wicked grin.

"WHAT THE HELL is going on out there, Sardar?" Biinadaz demanded of his friend.

"I don't know!" he replied. "Somehow el Khalidi has discovered this location."

"There is only one way," Biinadaz said, fighting to be heard over the thunderous din of combat going on right outside the wharf office. "You have a spy among the team."

Something changed in Mojaddi's expression and for the longest moment Biinadaz tried to determine what that something was. It then dawned on him even as Sardar Mojaddi reached beneath his coat and came away with a Russian-made PSM. Similar in size and construction to the Walther PP, the PSM fired an unusual 5.45 mm cartridge. The rarity of such a personal sidearm belied the strange and unwieldy personality of its owner.

"What the fuck are you doing?" Biinadaz demanded.

"I can no longer pretend, my brother," Mojaddi said. "It was I who gave Abbas el Khalidi this information."

"You *dare* to call me a brother?" Spittle rocketed from Biinadaz's mouth as he shouted, "You're a traitor to everything, Sardar! You're a traitor to Allah and a traitor to me! And if I live through this I will most definitely hunt you down and kill you."

"I am afraid not. You see, while you offered me a chance to gain revenge on the Americans for their crimes against our people in Afghanistan, Abbas actually offered me more. He offered me that chance and money. And I decided to accept his more-than-generous offer."

Biinadaz's voice was a growl as he asked, "When?"

"A few hours before you arrived. I spoke with him personally and we had quite an interesting conversation. His offer was much, much too appealing for me to say no."

"So you sold out for money!" Biinadaz waved at the explosive battle going on outside the walls of the office, the flames casting a haunting light against his face. "Like the Westerners."

"I'm sorry, brother."

"So am I," Biinadaz replied, his eyes ablaze with fanatical fervor.

And then a single shot rang out and Mojaddi's eyes burst wide open with shock. He never heard the bullet that crashed through the base of his neck because it severed his spinal cord. His body stiffened a long moment as trickles of blood formed at the corner of his lips, produced by the bullet lodging in his sinus cavity and cracking the soft palate in the roof of his mouth. Then his body toppled prone to the cheap linoleum floor.

From the shadows emerged the shooter and when Biinadaz met his gaze he nodded with profound respect.

"I knew I could rely on you. Thank you."

"Make no mention of it," Alzabir replied. "You will repay me one day."

"Your plan to bring them here worked perfectly. How did you know?"

"Simple," he said. "Who else could've told el Khalidi's assassins where I would be? It wasn't until the Americans foolishly stepped in to save me that I realized Mojaddi had betrayed our cause. It was easy to manipulate them into doing exactly what I wanted them to."

A fresh explosion sounded outside, flames erupting into the air like a red-orange fountain.

"And now I think it is time we leave," Alzabir replied.

"Leave? We cannot leave!" Biinadaz countered. "We must complete our operation."

"And so we shall," Alzabir said. "I just gave the signal for the operation to commence a few minutes ago. Even as we speak our men are moving into position. But we must go. I've told the captain to prepare for our arrival."

"Run? You mean you do not wish to join the men in their final triumph?"

"And so we shall, Genseric." Alzabir holstered his pistol. "But you must come with me now. We can escape through the tunnel to my car. I'll explain all of it to you on the way."

And with that, the two men escaped the inevitable encounter with the American commandos.

CHAPTER TWENTY-FIVE

"Gone? What do you mean gone?"

"Just like I said," Lyons replied to Kline's inquiry. "We took out Khalidi's men but we couldn't find Biinadaz. Only thing we found inside was Mojaddi's body. He'd been shot in the back of the head."

"Biinadaz?"

"Maybe," Lyons replied. "Though it doesn't make a lot of sense."

"No, it doesn't." A long pause ensued over the line. Then Kline said, "Alzabir?"

"You just read my mind."

"You think he's been behind all of this?"

"He's the common denominator," Lyons said. "Look at it this way. He's loyal and devoted to the Islamic cause but he's never been in any real trouble to speak of. That allows him to fly under the radar but it also makes him a poster child against racial profiling by the police. Every time you guys picked him up you had to tread carefully so everyone from the Arab League to the ACLU didn't come crawling up your ass."

"And then we get this magical information practically handed to our intelligence agents inside the Arab community at the most opportune time," Kline replied. "What are the chances of that?"

"Slim to none," Lyons said. "I don't know Alzabir set up the assassination attempt but I'm betting he or one of his associates let Khalidi's people on to the fact he'd be at that place and time."

"And Khalidi's people took the bait."

"Right," Lyons replied. With an edge to his voice he added, "And so did we. Hook, line and sinker. Damn it!"

"Don't beat yourself up," Kline said. "Alzabir played my people, too. Maybe I should've listened to the chief after all."

"No. He's an idiot."

"But what the hell does it all mean? They've gone to an awful lot of trouble to prevent us from discovering the truth of whatever it is they're up to. Double crosses and false leads. They've killed a number of their own people to keep a lid on their operations and risked their lives to defy the one man who's been providing all the cash for their operations. I just can't put my finger on what their real target might be."

"That *is* the million-dollar question," Lyons said. "If you—"

"Holy Christ!" Kline shouted.

Lyons heard it, too, the whip-crack sound followed by a low rumble coming through the cellular connection. "What was that?"

"Not sure but I think maybe I know what they're up to! Irons, I have to go. I have to go now!"

"Kline, don't you hang up," Lyons countered. "Don't hang up!"

But only dead air greeted his ear.

Lyons cursed as he slammed the cover closed on his cellular phone and clipped it to his belt.

"What happened?" Schwarz asked.

"I don't know," Lyons replied. "But we need to get downtown to the Justice Center."

"Okay?" Blancanales retorted with an askance gaze.

"I think the SPD headquarters just came under attack," Lyons said.

BY THE TIME Able Team had turned onto Fifth Avenue, the air was filled with black smoke.

The sidewalks and streets were devoid of people, thankfully—probably due to the fact it was still early morning—and they didn't see the bodies of any bystanders lying about. That didn't make the scene before them any less horrific. This part of the block looked like a gutted section of downtown Fallujah. Three police cruisers that had been parked directly across from the entrance to headquarters were fully engulfed in flames, the charred remains of a police officer half out of one vehicle, his upper torso sprawled across the hood.

White-hot rage cut through Lyons's gut.

As a former sergeant with the LAPD, seeing a dead cop still bothered him to a great degree—especially when he could have potentially done something to prevent it. It didn't matter or even occur to him that this wasn't his fault. He couldn't read minds and he didn't have a crystal ball to see what the plans of the enemy were. But that didn't make him take it any less personally, and to a guy like Lyons it was as much a factor of duty and professional responsibility as it was his stony pride.

But sometimes even Able Team couldn't always get there in time.

"¡Madre de Dios!" Blancanales said, crossing himself.

"Get in there," Lyons said, his voice calm and cold, his expression like a mask of chiseled granite. "Get as close to the headquarters building as you can."

As soon as Blancanales did as ordered, the three got clear of the van and were immediately engaged by a half-

dozen terrorists waiting in the lobby. The Able trio spread
out even as the glass entryway was shattered under the
impact of dozens of rounds. A horde of bullets passed
over their heads like red-hot angry wasps, but none of the
Able Team warriors seemed intent on their near escape
from death.

It was all about killing terrorists now.

Lyons rolled to a kneeling position, coming up with his
shoulder propped against the building frame where it met the
glass windows—or what remained of them. Through one
of the jagged openings in the glass he sighted the FNC and
triggered a sustained, rising burst. A maelstrom of 5.56 mm
rounds rushed through the terrorist positions, cutting a
couple down immediately while grazing or completely
missing others.

Blancanales joined Lyons a moment later, opening up
with the Beretta ARX-160. A fresh torrent of 5.56 × 45 mm
NATO slugs pinned the terrorists in a cross fire, the heavy
fire zone ripping up splinters of metal and wood where they
didn't actually contact flesh. Schwarz was the last one to
join his comrades but he'd selected an M-16A4/M-203. He
delivered his own series of short bursts and then shouted
at Blancanales to join him in a coordinated clearing tactic.

Blancanales nodded and moved his hand from the rifle
trigger to that of the GLX-160 grenade launcher while
Schwarz followed suit with the M-203. At a nod, the pair
squeezed the triggers on the launchers simultaneously
and delivered a pair of 40 mm HE grenades into the back
wall of the reception area. All three lowered their heads
and clapped their hands over their ears as the grenades
exploded. Plaster, wood, debris and metal whooshed
through the interior, shredding the flesh off the terrorists who weren't killed by being in the immediate shock
wave of the blast.

Able Team scrambled to get into the building even before the remnants of dust and chunks of plaster had finished falling. The ceiling tiles were scorched from the heat and only one terrorist who'd somehow managed to survive foolishly tried to repel the invaders. He took rounds from Schwarz and Lyons at the same moment, the impact slamming him into the gaping, smoking hole left by the grenades. His body came to settle among the flaming, charred refuse of what little remained of that wall.

"Elevators?" Schwarz asked.

Lyons shook his head. "They'll expect that. Let's go through the stairs."

"Wait," Blancanales said, his face brightening some. "Before we do that, I have an idea."

OF ALL THE MAYBE half-dozen times he could remember being in a firefight, Daniel Kline had never recalled anything quite this bad.

Whether for better or worse, he hadn't seen something like this coming. These terrorists had proved themselves as fanatical and fearless as any Kline had hoped not to encounter. One thing was for certain—the three men who claimed to be in the FBI weren't anything of the sort. Kline knew antiterrorists when he met them and whether they were DHS, Delta Force or a page that wasn't in the book, Kline was happy as hell to have them on his side.

Kline entered the Tac-Ops room on the ninth floor of the SPD headquarters where Stepakonous and his team were looking over the building plans.

"Sit-rep," Kline snapped.

Stepakonous shook his head. "It's shit, sir, that's what. We never even remotely considered something like this could happen. I mean, assaulting police headquarters?"

"I don't give a good goddamn what we considered,

Jerry. This is what we're faced with and it's our duty to defend this facility. We aren't going to give up and we're not going to just stand idly by while our fellow officers get massacred. So tell me something or I'll get somebody who can."

Stepakonous nodded and shook himself out of it. He was a hell of a tactical sergeant, one of the best Kline had ever known. A veteran of the Iraq war and one of the best-trained men Kline had ever mentored, the cops of SPD couldn't have asked for a better man to lead their defense.

Stepakonous recited mechanically, "The sixth floor is the office staff and HR and we know that's clear. Same with PR on the eighth floor. That leaves detective squads, vice and nighttime robbery. According to stats, most of the detectives were out when the terrorists hit. Office personnel are also gone, including all of the deputy chiefs."

"What about civilians?" Kline asked. "Janitorial staff or legal reps?"

Stepakonous shook his head. "Can't be sure, Chief. There's a good chance they might be trapped on the second floor. But until we get a unit down there we won't know."

"Well, we can't spend any more time dicking around here. Let's get suited up and gather everything we can from the armory. Any way we can get to the basement?"

"Um, we've looked at that, sir," said one of the weapons specialists. "Somehow they've managed to gain control of the rear elevator and they've locked it to the first floor. We'd have to take the stairwells."

Kline nodded. "Suggestions?"

"I was thinking a small team," Stepakonous replied immediately. "Maybe two men to attempt a recon down the north stairwell. It's a risk since if we get in a firefight in those narrow confines and we're outnumbered, things could go very badly."

"No choice," Kline replied. "Do I have any volunteers?"

Every man in the room raised his hand, including Stepakonous, and Kline couldn't remember a time he'd been prouder. These were the crème de la crème of the department. Hell, they were the best cops in the whole state, as far as Kline was concerned, and he was privileged to be their chief.

"Okay, Slater and Guerra, take a spare magazine each and get moving. North stairwell and try to get to the basement. You can then get out there and go for reinforcements." They saluted even though it wasn't really a formal courtesy, and Kline returned their salute smartly. This was a time to remain strong and show respect. He turned to Stepakonous again. "Jerry, what's the situation with the phones?"

"Dead. And our radio signals are being jammed."

"What about the dispatch center?"

"That was the explosion you heard, sir," another officer replied, his forehead creased with worry lines.

"God help us all," Kline whispered.

HAD IT NOT BEEN for the three men of Able Team, neither Slater nor Guerra would've ever made it to his destination.

The pair was on the landing between the third and fourth floors when they encountered a cluster of terrorists racing up the steps. The men leveled their AR-15s but the sudden chatter of automatic weapons sent them scrambling for the safety of the stairs from which they'd just descended. The terrorists leapfrogged up the steps and were just getting within range when a new enemy appeared in the form of the three fatigue-clad warriors toting heavy assault weapons and full load-bearing combat gear.

The terrorists turned and were met with a fusillade of 5.56 mm rounds. Lyons caught one with a burst that entered under the terrorist's chin and blew off the top of his head, showering his three companions in gore. The other three tried to get up the stairs for cover but realized they would meet resistance from the police. They instead panicked and tripped over one another, ultimately two of them shoving a third man in front to avoid being ventilated with autofire.

It didn't work.

Instead of avoiding death, the terrorists were forced to embrace it while their poor companion, whom they had used as a sacrificial lamb, actually fell below the fire field and tumbled down the steps. The other two were pummeled with rounds from all three assault rifles, bullets tearing and ripping their bodies without mercy. They collapsed in a bloody, pulpy mess as the smell of spent cordite and gray smoke from assault-rifle barrels twirled toward the ceiling.

The terrorist who'd been shoved into Able Team's laps had lost his weapon but he was no less ferocious for it. Frightened at suddenly being placed in such proximity with his enemies, the terrorist jumped to his feet and immediately began to flail at Blancanales with his fists. The attack so surprised Blancanales he barely knew how to respond and a full-on, full-contact brawl in such cramped quarters was hardly practical.

Schwarz ended up dropping to one knee and ramming the buttstock of his weapon into the side of the terrorist's thigh. It wasn't debilitating but it caused enough pain to distract the man from his assault on Blancanales. Now free of the terrorist's flailing, Blancanales responded with a rock-hard punch that connected with his opponent's chin. The terrorist fell back, landing hard on the stairs, and Blancanales fired a side kick that drove his heel into the man's larynx. Bone and cartilage crunched together into a blob and the terrorist began to choke on the pieces.

Lyons finished it with a mercy round to the head.

"You, boys!" Blancanales called. "Identify yourselves and your unit."

They didn't show themselves but one of them called, "Why don't you tell us who the hell you are first?"

That voice tried to sound tough but all it sounded was scared. "Special agents with the FBI!" Blancanales responded. "We've been working with Assistant Chief Kline to bring down this terrorist group."

"Oh, yeah?" the voice answered. "Well, if you know Kline then tell us who heads up MRU One?"

"You mean the team leader?" Lyons barked. "It's Sergeant Jerry Stepakonous!"

That immediately brought the men into view. They had their weapons held at the ready, but pointed down and away enough not to pose a threat to Able Team. The men smiled and the members of Able Team smiled in return, and then the two sides started shaking hands. The two officers introduced themselves and explained they were headed for an exit in the basement.

"Are we glad to see you guys!" Slater finally said.

"Likewise," Schwarz replied.

"What's your situation?" Lyons asked.

Slater scratched his head beneath his tactical helmet. "I'm still not sure myself. It started with this, like, huge explosion in the communications center. Then we just heard a lot of commotion and shooting and who the hell knows what else."

"You're under a full-scale terrorist attack," Lyons replied.

"That much we know," Guerra replied. "What we don't know is why."

"Or what they want," Slater added.

"What do terrorists ever want?" Schwarz said. "To terrorize."

"There's a chance they could be after something, though," Blancanales said. "Just because they're terrorists doesn't mean they don't have an agenda. Can you guys think of anything of value they might want to get their hands on here? Weapons or explosives maybe."

"We have an armory but it's guarded at night, has a key-coded access and is practically blast-proof. They'd need a couple of acetylene torches and about an hour to cut their way in."

"No, it wouldn't be weapons," Schwarz said with a vigorous shake of his head. "Too easy for them to get those by other means."

"What about a person?" Guerra replied. "Maybe they planned to kidnap the chief or something."

"At 4:00 a.m.?" Blancanales replied easily. "Doubtful."

"Oh, shit," Slater mumbled.

"What's 'oh, shit'?"

Slater looked at Guerra and said, "The new chopper!"

"Chopper?" Lyons said with a cock of his head.

"Yeah, we just got it. It's an Apache Blackhawk. Army donated it to the department. It's been disarmed and all, missile tubes rendered inert, but the thing is sweet! Been completely refitted and with just a bit of help they could easily convert it back into a combat copter. Maybe they're planning to do that."

Blancanales nodded. "It would be a worthwhile target."

"You two continue on mission, just like Kline ordered. We'll take care of securing the helicopter," Lyons said.

They said their farewells and Able Team continued up the stairs as a unit, hustling as fast as their legs could carry them. They couldn't figure why the terrorists would want an old chopper, even one that had been refitted. As they advanced, they tossed the idea among themselves.

"Maybe they just want to use it to escape," Blancanales replied. "They could've just attacked the squad cars, blown the dispatch and beat feet. Instead they posted guards at the entrance."

"No doubts about that," Lyons said. When they reached the ninth floor he said, "Pol, your stop's here. Find Kline and the rest of the MRU Team One and tell them what's happening. Gadgets and I will continue toward the roof."

"Is separating such a good idea?"

"Good idea or not, we don't have time to discuss it in committee," Lyons said. "So just nut up and do it."

Blancanales nodded and tossed his partners a farewell salute as they pushed on to the top floor.

They hit trouble as soon as they emerged on the hallway. A gaggle of terrorists were waiting at the far end of a long narrow corridor. Beyond them, Lyons and Schwarz saw a glass door that emerged onto a ramp that went up to the roof. Even in the narrow confines of the hallway they could hear the steady thrum of the rotors as the chopper blades were already in motion.

The half-dozen terrorists were holding their ground, firing on Lyons and Schwarz's position with near-deadly accuracy. The warriors ate carpet and Schwarz managed to actually find a potted plant to provide some measure of security, but the terrorists had them outgunned and pinned down.

"These aren't favorable conditions!" Lyons shouted at his friend as they opened fire on the terrorists.

The rounds from terrorist SMGs that ranged from Uzis to AKSUs chewed up the hallway walls and floors. A particularly nasty line came too close to Lyons, one of them even nicking his side as he rolled up against the wall to avoid getting stitched to the floor where he lay. Then there was a fresh component of autofire, but it wasn't coming from the terrorists, and when Lyons and Schwarz looked up they saw the terrorists twitching and flopping around like drunken hula dancers.

The pair of Able Team warriors then turned to look to their flanks and saw Blancanales charging up the hallway toward them, an army of MRU officers on his heels, weapons blazing as they cut the terrorists down like a scythe through tall grass. The pair then joined the others, and the terrorists, with nowhere to go, simply collapsed one atop the other in a stinking pile of dust, heat and blood.

"The chopper!" Kline shouted. "It's going airborne!"

"Come on, boys!" Lyons said. "Let's get back to Black Betty."

"You can track them from there?" Kline asked disbelievingly.

Schwarz grinned. "You'd be surprised what we can do from her."

"I'm coming with," he said even as the trio rushed for the stairwell. He whirled on Stepakonous. "Sergeant, secure this building. Kill any terrorists that you encounter. No prisoners, understood?"

"Yes, sir!"

Kline turned and then followed on the heels of his new friends.

ONCE THEY WERE IN Black Betty and moving up the street, Blancanales flipped on the aerial reconnaissance systems.

"First thing we have to do is get its transponder codes."

"Like they'd turn them on?" Kline asked.

Schwarz eyed the assistant chief. "They don't have any choice. It's automatic. They assumed, wrongly of course, that by blowing the communications center that nobody could track them."

"They just forgot one tiny detail," Lyons said.

Kline looked confused. "What's that?"

"Us."

"There, that's them!" Schwarz said, jabbing a finger at a bright blue blip. He turned his attention to Blancanales in the driver's seat. "Pol, looks like they're heading back to the shipyards."

"Shipyards?" Kline asked. "What the hell would they be going back there for? Their base is toast."

"Yeah," Lyons retorted, "but not their boat."

"They have a boat?"

Lyons nodded. "It makes sense. They had to be getting their private little army into the country somehow. They were using their connections through Alzabir to get terrorists into the country. I noticed earlier when looking over Alzabir's arrest records that every time you hit that guy it was down on the docks among a gaggle of Arabs."

"Yeah?"

"So who goes and checks the ID of every Arab in the crowd? Who has time?" Kline looked sheepish and Lyons waved it away. "Look, Kline, I was a cop once myself. I know how it goes. There was no way you could've known they'd insert our terrorists right into those crowds. So their leader gets hauled in, they break it up peacefully and everybody's happy."

"Except the people in dispatch," he said. "And maybe some very good officers."

"Quit feeling sorry for yourself." Lyons's voice took on a hard edge. "We got a chance to make this right and we're going to do it. Here and now."

They reached the docks in twenty minutes, no mean feat even with the nonexistent traffic. Dawn had just broken and the light wasn't that great yet, but the chopper had stopped and Schwarz's equipment had a strong fix on it.

"Too bad we don't have somebody we could call on to just put a missile right down on top of them," Kline said.

"Nope," Lyons replied. "We'll have to do this the old-fashioned way."

They parked the van and Able Team went EVA.

Lyons ordered Kline to stay behind and watch the van but the older man immediately started arguing with him. It was actually Blancanales who intervened at that point, warning Kline if he was going to get a position within the Justice Department that he'd have to learn to follow orders. Kline at least nodded and lowered his head.

Satisfied Kline would stay put, the three warriors advanced on the ship moored in dock number two. They couldn't see the chopper anymore. It had probably been concealed by the terrorists, but they knew they had the right boat all the same. That became obvious when they started taking fire as soon as they boarded.

Terrorists directly above on the bridge deck were firing down on them, maybe a half dozen in all, with automatic weapons. The three fanned out and found decent cover on deck. Schwarz and Blancanales both loaded their grenade launchers, aimed on the deck and fired at almost the same time. The twin blasts from the HE grenades tore through the terrorists like it was nobody's business, strong enough to blow a couple over the railing while shrapnel was sent whistling through the remainder.

Schwarz loaded a second grenade and fired again for good measure.

The three started taking fire from the right but these shots were sporadic. That's because they were coming from Biinadaz and Alzabir, neither of whom had the common sense to arm himself adequately against the Able Team veterans. It made no difference to Lyons, Blancanales and Schwarz. These two villains had been responsible for the deaths of a lot of good people and the blatant, disgusting exploitation of innocent teens.

And without reservation, Able Team ended their reign of terror in a firestorm of high-velocity justice. With Bii-nadaz and Alzabir neutralized, mop-up was a mere formality. The pilot of the helicopter and the ship's crew were quick to surrender once their leaders were no longer a factor.

Lyons summoned Kline from the Able Team van. "Trade you one ship and one chopper for one van."

The assistant chief nodded and smiled with relief as he surveyed the ship's deck.

"Done," he said.

CHAPTER TWENTY-SIX

Rabat, Morocco

"Sigma One to Sigma Team, we're heading down now."

David McCarter switched his headset over to hands free and with a nod at Hawkins the pair went over the side of the cliff.

Waves crashed below them, terminating against the jagged rocks in white foam. The seas were choppy that day, true to Mazouzi's word, and it would prove quite a challenge to the other men of Phoenix Force when they actually made their assault in the boat.

The boat! It was hardly deserving of the term. That was another thing that nagged McCarter, a constant worry in the back of his mind. The old wreck that Mazouzi's friend had given them hadn't even looked to be seaworthy. From the outside it appeared to be an old fishing trawler, if a bit small, but it was beat-up and ugly. The assurances from the owner didn't do much to make McCarter feel better, but Mazouzi assured them the craft was sound. Apparently he'd used it a few other times for some cases, so McCarter approved it for the mission. Besides, he wouldn't be the one who actually had to approach the stronghold in it, so he couldn't really make the call with an easy conscience. Enciso, Manning and James had mutually agreed to go with it, and that had pretty much settled the issue.

It wasn't as if they had much of a choice; the numbers were ticking off and this was what they had available.

The plan was for Mazouzi to pilot the craft and the three Phoenix Force warriors with him would do any heavy lifting from the combat side of things. They would wait far enough offshore to not look suspicious. Hawkins and McCarter were assigned to rappel down the cliffs and attempt to locate any sort of surface entrance. Once they found it, the boat would make its approach and together the five would penetrate the fortress in a unified assault against whatever they found.

Barring that, Stony Man had arranged to put the United States Navy on the proverbial speed dial. If they could not destroy, or better yet, secure the facility in a timely manner without risking harm to bystanders or themselves, then they were to send a signal and the Navy would do the rest. It would likely cause an international incident and perhaps even create hostilities between the Moroccan and U.S. governments, but that just couldn't be helped. Phoenix Force was going to do whatever was necessary to defend America against predators like Abbas el Khalidi.

McCarter and Hawkins descended in short, steady rhythm—maintaining distance and speed to stay abreast of each other but offset just enough that one could cover the other as they progressed. No point in getting shot in the back unnecessarily. Chances were fifty-fifty Sahaf had equipped the external cliff with infrared sensors or other intrusion-detection systems, but they'd decided it was a calculated risk worth exploiting.

As they stopped midway down and began to inspect the cliff face on both sides, Hawkins shouted to be heard over the noisy waves slamming the rocks below. "I don't think we'll be detected."

"Why?" McCarter asked.

Hawkins shook his head and pointed at his ear.

McCarter put his hand to his mouth and repeated, "Why?"

"It's too much of a risk for someone to attempt approaching from this side. Look at these rocks. They're slippery and sharp, covered with moss!"

McCarter had to admit his friend was correct about that. He hoped even the brand-new rappelling ropes they were using didn't succumb to the jagged protrusions of the rock, pitted and honed by hundreds if not thousands of years of blasting saltwater spray and stiff, angry winds. They'd known it would be a risk to descend such a natural obstacle but they'd not seen any other choice. And to simply attack the place with missiles before verifying its occupants was neither logical nor moral.

"Let's keep going," McCarter called back. "Maybe we'll find something farther down."

Hawkins nodded and the two continued to descend, slowly and meticulously, double-checking their equipment with each pause. An exceptionally treacherous gust of wind materialized, slamming McCarter and Hawkins against the rock. The Briton felt a sharp piece of rock bite into his left knee and he knew it had probably been strong enough to penetrate the skin.

Nothing more than a flesh wound, mate, he told himself. Bugger up and stay hard.

The pair continued, eight to ten yards between each drop. They were perhaps forty-five yards or so above the water when McCarter spotted what they'd been looking for. It was about three yards across by two yards high and covered with a thick metal grate. It had been so close to him, in fact, that the Phoenix Force leader had nearly missed the thing entirely—a sort of forest-for-the-trees scenario.

Luckily he'd been paying attention, and if their luck paid off this might just provide a way inside the facility.

"Stand fast," McCarter told Hawkins.

"Not much more I can do!" Hawkins shouted back.

McCarter nodded and then kicked out from the rock. Keeping his hand behind him, he threw his body to the left so he could get his feet onto the natural ledge formed from the shaft. The grate was recessed into the rock about a yard, maybe slightly less. McCarter steadied his legs on the ledge and then reached down. He felt his hand almost pulled to the grating. An air intake vent. That meant it would have to lead to the interior.

"I think we found our way in," McCarter said, clamping off his belay line and securing the carabiner with a brake so he could work with both hands. While McCarter set about the task of figuring out how to remove the grate, Hawkins keyed up his radio and signaled the other members they'd possibly hit the jackpot.

Manning acknowledged the transmission and then they returned to full radio silence.

"Give me a hand, will you?" McCarter asked Hawkins.

Hawkins readjusted his position and then slowly, gently made his way over to McCarter. He'd actually found a ledge walkway, the shelf just wide enough to accommodate a pair of feet. He remarked on this point to McCarter, who nodded in understanding. Whoever had installed the grate probably also took the time to make the ledge so he could service it if necessary.

The grate had been bolted into place but a quick inspection revealed that the bolts had also been secured with a small spot weld.

"We'll have to break the weld to get them off," Hawkins said after inspecting the grate. "Probably faster to cut through it."

McCarter shook his head. "There's not time, mate. But I have an alternative."

The Briton reached into a pouch on his load-bearing belt and withdrew a small, thin roll of green plastic. He unrolled about a foot, cut it with wire snips and handed it to Hawkins. He then cut a second one before returning the materials to his belt. McCarter withdrew a long, thin wire and inserted it into one of the rolled plastic tubes, then followed suit with a second one before affixing both to the plate by pulling away a sticky film that covered adhesive tape.

McCarter gestured for Hawkins to move to one side of the grate while he took the other, and then withdrew a small manual detonator. He attached the two wires to the box, closed his eyes and turned his face away, and then flipped a switch on the detonator and pressed the red button. There was a pop and sizzle, and then a flash of small white flame. The cutting cord, a special type of ordnance designed to go right through up to three inches of metal, neatly removed the plate entirely from the frame.

McCarter looked back into the recess, nodded with satisfaction and then carefully grabbed the grate at the center, yanked once and pulled it free. He flung it out toward the water below and then shone a flashlight into the murky black beyond. The shaft ran for about thirty yards and then dropped off.

"Good, we're in business," McCarter said. He keyed up his microphone. "Sigma One to Sigma Team. We found a way in. Go."

As soon as Encizo, Manning and Hawkins heard McCarter's signal they ordered Mazouzi to start the boat engine and head in.

"Full speed," Encizo told Mazouzi. "We don't know what kind of resistance we'll meet."

"And the slower we go the better chance we die before ever reaching shore," Manning added.

Mazouzi nodded. "Now you shall all see why I chose my friend's boat."

The Phoenix Force trio initially expected him to put the craft in gear and slowly they would gain speed. Instead, following the rumble-chug start of the main engine, the deck beneath their feet began to vibrate and a steady hum seemed to roll through the entire hull. Without warning, the three were nearly thrown off their feet as the boat lurched into action. The speed the battered craft traveled was so intense, in fact, it lifted the nose out of the water at a considerable tilt.

"Holy—" James began. "This motha be *fast!*"

Encizo began to laugh and Manning just shook his head.

Mazouzi had surprised them once more. His friend had rigged the boat to look like a harmless fishing trawler while all the time she had an engine in her bowels that made those on some professional speedboats look pathetic. Mazouzi shouted some other interesting facts at them, jabbering about its reinforced hull and extended fuel range, not to mention its superb maneuverability via a computer-controlled steering linkage.

To demonstrate, he moved the steering wheel back and forth just slightly and the boat responded immediately, slicing through the water like a skier over a fresh, powdery snowfall. The Phoenix Force team members nodded at each other with approval and then went about preparing for their arrival at ground zero. In some ways, Encizo wondered as the cliff face drew steadily nearer if this wasn't much how the Allies might have felt approaching the beaches of Normandy on D-Day. To be sure, they'd done this kind of assault a good many times before. It wasn't new but it felt new every time they did it.

But what are the unknown variables? Encizo thought.

As if the enemy had known his worst thoughts and fears, the air around them came alive with tracer rounds. They could see some of the rounds hit the water and on a couple of occasions bullets scarred the surface of the boat. They were under fire! Encizo snatched at the binoculars he'd been wearing around his neck and while maintaining cover behind the boat's conning tower he scanned the cliffs. It took him only a moment to find what he was looking for. Muzzle-flashes emanated from two separate locations on either side, apparently able to cross each other, and provided interlocking fields of fire.

Manning keyed the radio, putting it close to his mouth so he could be heard. "Sigma Three to Sigma One. Do you copy?"

"I copy."

"We got big problems here, Sigma One. There are defenses in that cliff wall. Machine guns! Can you assist, over?"

"Stand by."

THEY WERE THIRTY yards into the shaft when the call came in. McCarter was ahead of Hawkins and their passage was too confined to turn around. He glanced behind him and said, "The other team's got trouble."

"I'm on it," Hawkins replied.

He wiggled his body backward, moving slowly but steadily toward the shaft opening. He reached it in thirty seconds, finally got enough of his body out that he could reattach the rope to his harness and stepped into the open air. The brake engaged and stopped him from falling to his death.

Hawkins clung to the rocks and listened carefully for a moment. Satisfied he'd located the source of the gunfire, he reached to his LBE harness and came away with an M-67 frag grenade. He pushed from the cliff face, swung into open air and looked in the direction of the machine-gun reports. What he saw approximately ten yards below and to his left made him do a double take. The source of the fire turned out to be a Gryazev-Shipunov GSh-6-30 close-in weapon system. Manufactured by the Soviets and still in use by many Russian military ships and planes, the GSh-6-30 was a 30 mm cannon similar to the Phalanx CIWS. It could fire three to four thousand, fourteen-ounce projectiles per minute. In concert with a second weapon of identical make, being radar-controlled, the team in the boat would be cut to ribbons if Hawkins didn't act now.

The former Delta Force commando got directly over the gun and then descended until his legs straddled the recessed gun mount. The GSh-6-30 continued to blast away at the approaching boat, which zigzagged to avoid being chopped apart, and Hawkins's ears began to ring. Hawkins was surprised to see how close the boat was getting but he put it from his mind, as there was no time to worry about his discomfort. Hawkins yanked the pin on the grenade, tossed it gently into the recess and then began to scramble up the rope as fast as he could.

Hawkins got a good distance in the six seconds it took for the M-67 to blow. The explosion cracked rock and spouted flame from the opening, but the cliff structure actually did much to protect Hawkins from being hurt. The GSh-6-30 wasn't so lucky. The gun immediately fell silent as pieces from what remained of it rocketed to the water below amid rock, dust and bits of flaming wreckage.

Hawkins keyed up his microphone. "Sigma Team, the

other gun's too far away. Go hard port side and approach from starboard. That should keep you in the clear."

"Roger, Sigma Five. Appreciate the hand," Encizo replied.

"Nice work, Sigma Five," McCarter said. "Now quit your bloody dillydallying and get back into position."

Hawkins shook his head but grinned as he muttered, "No good deed goes unpunished."

"WHAT THE HELL IS GOING ON?" Abbas el Khalidi demanded of the technicians monitoring the computer systems as soon as he and Ebi Sahaf entered the control room.

Alarms resounded throughout the complex and red lights were flashing. One of the technicians, not taking his eyes from the three monitors arrayed before him, replied, "Unknown hostiles, sir. Approaching by boat."

"Shut that damn thing off!" he told them of the buzzing alarm. "I can't hear myself think."

Sahaf stepped past him and stabbed a switch. The alarm went silent, the red lights winked out and the red hue that had bathed the room returned to a more passive, cool blue. "Where did it come from?"

"It's been out there for some time, Master Sahaf."

"What do you mean it's been out there for some time?" he demanded of the technician. "Why didn't you inform me sooner?"

"It looked like a fishing trawler," the technician explained.

"In those waters?" Khalidi asked with incredulity. "Look at the size of those waves. What fishing boat would be out in this weather? You…idiot!"

"What happened to our right-quadrant gun?" Sahaf said, clicking a switch up and down.

"It just stopped functioning, sir. Just a minute ago."

Sahaf's expression became unreadable for a time. He stroked his beard thoughtfully, looked through the underwater port at the swimming fish and then turned to Khalidi. "We could have been discovered."

"So what? I thought you said it was of no concern."

"I thought that it would not be of concern," he replied. "But now I believe there is a possible threat to this facility."

Khalidi's face tightened, his skin taking a dangerous hue, and for a moment Sahaf thought he might explode. His chest started rising and falling faster, but then his posture returned to a state of passivity and control. When he'd finally calmed some, Khalidi said, "Options."

"Either we abandon this place and destroy it, or we activate the guards, bring them inside and shut off the eastern gate."

"Close the eastern gate," Khalidi said, "and cut off our only means of escape should we be overrun."

"We have more than fifty men guarding this facility, Abbas," Sahaf reminded him. "I don't think a few men in a boat pose any significant risk."

"And what if this is a full military assault? What then? What if it's the United States Navy or worse, the military of our own people? Do you not think there will be a reckoning?"

"Our own people don't know about this place," Sahaf said. "And I would remind you, with respect, the American military wouldn't dare attack this facility. This is the sovereign territory of Morocco. Any such attack against her shores would doubtless be viewed by the government and the United Nations as an act of war. The Americans would never risk that."

"I am not so sure, Ebi," Khalidi said.

"What do you wish to do? The decision is entirely yours."

Khalidi drew a long sigh and finally replied, "We have worked too hard and come too far to be defeated now. Lock us down." He stabbed his finger at the screen and added, "And destroy them. Immediately!"

WHEN T. J. HAWKINS reentered the air shaft, he'd chosen to do so feetfirst as an afterthought.

He realized with McCarter going headfirst that if they encountered issues it would be good for him to have something against which to brace his feet. He'd also convinced the Briton they needed to tie off to one another in the event they ran out of room and had to make their way back to the cliff.

Their journey proved more treacherous and difficult than either had originally thought it would be. Despite the cool air that rushed through, the howl increasing as they ventured deeper into the labyrinthine maze of air tunnels, they were sweating due to the heavy gear they wore, coupled with the exertion. This was not an ideal situation, to be certain, but neither of the men complained as they continued their grueling journey. At one point, the descent through the initial shaft extended almost thirty yards. They were both relieved when they finally reached bottom, especially in light of the fact the ropes extended that far.

"Well," McCarter said, "if we hit a dead end, at least we'll be able to climb our way out of this bloody hellhole."

"That's good," Hawkins replied. "I'd hate to die in these shafts like a rat."

"You and me both, bloke."

Eventually they found their saving grace, a metal grate similar to the one they'd encountered at the entrance to the complex. McCarter gave the grate a shove but it wouldn't budge. Bloody damn, this wasn't what he'd counted on.

Had he been facing the same direction as Hawkins, feet-first, he could have probably kicked the thing out.

"Suggestions?"

"Too cramped to squeeze by me," Hawkins said.

"Yeah, and the last cross section we passed has to be at least one hundred and fifty yards back."

"Only one choice," Hawkins said.

"Yeah," McCarter replied. The Briton reached to the Browning Hi-Power at his waist and managed to clear it from the hip holster. He backed away as far as he could, put the muzzle of the Browning close to the corner of the grate. "Plug your ears, mate."

Four shots later another push dislodged the grate.

McCarter shimmied forward until his body was half out and then turned on a flashlight and shone it into the room. A huge boiler sat in the center but the rest of the place was empty. Assuming nobody had heard the shots and would come running, the chances were good they had managed to penetrate the complex undetected. McCarter grinned when he looked down and saw the floor only a few feet below him. Silently thanking whatever deities might be listening, McCarter rolled out of the space and tumbled to the ground. He executed a perfect shoulder roll and came to his feet.

McCarter returned to the shaft and assisted Hawkins out of the confines. Once they were upright, they did a quick weapons check and then went in search of a doorway. They located it in under a minute. McCarter opened it a crack and peered out. Quiet.

"Looks like a supply room," he whispered. "Lots of boxes. I'll take point."

Hawkins nodded and then McCarter emerged into the dimly lit room. Sure enough, the place looked like nothing but storage with stacks of cardboard and wooden boxes.

As they crossed through the maze and into an open area of the room, Hawkins spotted a stack two layers deep of fifty-five-gallon drums filled with more of the two-cycle marine oil. He tapped McCarter on the shoulder and gestured toward the drums.

The Phoenix Force leader took it in and then gave his friend a thumbs-up and a smile.

The pair found another door, and when McCarter looked through a crack in this one he was rewarded with the sight of a massive array of computer screens and desks occupied by technicians. Their backs were to the pair and they seemed otherwise preoccupied. A tall, bearded man with close-cropped hair and wearing a white brimless cap was barking orders to them in Arabic.

"Sahaf?" Hawkins whispered.

McCarter nodded. "Could be."

"Well, whoever he is, he and his cronies there are most likely up to no good."

"Agreed."

"What's the plan?"

McCarter turned to his friend and with a wicked grin he replied, "Tallyho."

CHAPTER TWENTY-SEVEN

The boat came in hot.

So hot that Manning, Encizo and James thought Mazouzi was going to smash right into the side of the cliff. At the last moment, he cut power, stalled the engine, then started it again and threw the gearshift into Reverse. His technique proved flawless and the boat eased into the natural cove without problems. The waves carried them ever closer to the shore and Encizo checked his watch.

"Eight minutes," he said.

"Come on, boys," James muttered under his breath.

"They'll do it," Manning said. "They'll do it. Let's just stay optimistic."

They waited another minute. The coral and sharp, jagged protrusions of the rocks looked menacing in the falling light. They had maybe an hour before nightfall would consume them. They were now close enough to see the red, orange and amethyst of the sunset glinting off the metal frames of the surf guides, the device that would save them if Hawkins and McCarter could get it activated before they hit the rocks.

"If we don't make it, it has been a privilege to serve with you," Mazouzi said.

"Hey, we're not there yet," Encizo said.

"Yeah, Zafar," James added. "Don't jinx it."

THE MEN IN THE control room were taken by complete surprise when McCarter and Hawkins emerged with MP-5s in their hands. The man who'd been giving the orders seemed the least shaken by their sudden appearance, which was probably to be expected since he was the leader. He'd have to remain unshakable, keep up appearances so his men could draw inspiration and strength from his example.

None of them appeared to be armed so McCarter and Hawkins immediately began to shout at them and ordered them out of their seats. They were just in the process of getting them corralled into one corner of the room when a half-dozen terrorist guards suddenly emerged from a wide-open doorway toting a variety of machine pistols and SMGs.

McCarter and Hawkins went prone and rolled just as the security team opened fire. The fusillade of autofire ended up killing several of the technicians before the terrorists could adjust their aim and reacquire their enemy targets. Unfortunately for them, McCarter and Hawkins were already in motion and working to launch their own offensive.

McCarter cut a swathing burst across the enemy lines, taking out two of the six terrorists with shots to the guts and chests. Impacts from the 9 mm Parabellums slammed the pair into a metal framework, part of the support structure of the complex, and their corpses crunched against the unyielding steel frame. Hawkins came to one knee, snap-aimed his MP-5 and fired upward from the hip. The 9 mm stingers cut across two more terrorists and decimated them with several rounds to their heads. Blood and brain matter exploded under the impact and they tumbled to the highly polished floor.

McCarter removed the odds entirely when he lobbed an M-67 grenade across the room. The hand bomb hit the floor, bounced, skittered a few more feet and then stopped in the midst of the dead or dying terrorist horde. Those still on their feet got strange looks as they watched the grenade perform a wobbly spin. It was the last thing they saw. A brilliant flash was followed milliseconds later by a deafening explosion as the PETN-filled grenade did its grisly work. The shock blew them apart, separating appendages and shredding flesh with hundreds of superheated metal shards.

McCarter turned in time to see Sahaf sprint from the room. He turned to Hawkins and ordered him to get one of the surviving technicians to deploy the surf guide, then whirled and dashed after his quarry.

Hawkins turned on the remaining technicians, prodded them until one admitted he spoke English, then grabbed that man by the collar and sat him in the chair. The technician's hands danced over the keyboard as, every so often, he'd look over his shoulder to see Hawkins standing there with the MP-5 leveled at his face. Hawkins told him to pay attention to what he was doing, gesturing with the MP-5 in a way that suggested the consequences of failure.

The technician was as careful as he'd ever been in his life not to make a mistake.

THE SURF GUIDE ROSE from the water and the men of Phoenix Force shouted with relief. They began to high-five each other and then turned to the task of getting safely docked. The guide rose until it was just above the waterline and then locked in place. A moment later a clamp attached to a large rope launched through the air and landed on the deck of the boat.

Mazouzi moved immediately forward and locked the clamp against the towing ring mounted to the center of the bow. Without any other action required, the winch on the surf guide immediately began to reel the boat into dock like a fisherman hauling in a whopper. Within a minute they were docked and safe upon the shore of the cove. A circular tube came up and around to enclose them, then drew them under the massive cavern that eventually led to the internal docking area.

When the cylinder cover retracted, the quartet found Hawkins standing at the rim of a massive, pool-like structure grinning from ear to ear. "Welcome to SeaWorld, boys and girls."

"Cute," Manning said as the four quickly debarked from the boat and set foot once more on dry ground.

"Where's Mr. Brown?" Mazouzi inquired.

"This way," Hawkins said, jerking his head. "According to those technicians, this place is going to be locked down tight in a few minutes and if we're still inside when it does, we'll be trapped here."

The four immediately fell into a flat run behind their teammate as Hawkins led them out of the sub room and into the cavernous underwater complex. The five men rushed through the control room—now empty as Hawkins had advised the technicians to get the hell out—eventually winding up in an open, circular area with a ramp. They began the steady, leg-challenging trek up the ramp. All of the Phoenix Force commandos were okay, but Mazouzi was having a hard time of it.

At last, Manning and Encizo stopped long enough to get his arms around their shoulders. They picked him up and started carrying him in a flat run. They made it to the top of the ramp in less than a minute, dropped Mazouzi onto his feet and then turned to address the very grave issue at hand. McCarter was proceeding down a steep stairwell made of metal, a hail of bullets passing just over his head.

"Can't go that way, mates!" he said. "Must be thirty terrorists or more."

All four of his teammates put their weapons in battery and Mazouzi drew his pistol.

"We've faced worse odds," Encizo said.

McCarter shook his head. "Not in narrow confines like these. I've already called for the Navy fliers to do their thing."

"How long?" Manning asked.

"Five minutes. Tops."

"What about Sahaf and Khalidi?"

"I took care of Sahaf," McCarter replied.

"Follow me," Mazouzi said. "We must get back to the boat!"

"There's no time!" James protested.

"No, there's no time to argue!"

Mazouzi whirled and headed back down the ramp.

The five warriors stared a moment at each other, heard a fresh torrent of autofire and decided to heed their ally's advice. They rushed to catch up with Mazouzi, but as they approached the bottom of the ramp the cop's body stiffened and then jerked spasmodically. The staccato of weapons fire followed a heartbeat later, echoing through the cavernous complex. The men of Phoenix Force turned to see Abbas el Khalidi rushing toward them, a Micro-Uzi SMG in his hands. He swept the muzzle to and fro, his mouth wide open, eyes and face red with fury as he poured all of his vengeance out on the cop who had been instrumental in helping bring down his empire.

And in saving the lives of the five Phoenix Force warriors.

What Khalidi forgot in those next few seconds was that the Micro-Uzi was a veritable bullet hose. In his fanatical rush to take vengeance, he miscalculated the cyclic rate of fire and expended his entire 20-round magazine on Mazouzi. As the bolt locked back and Khalidi realized he was out of rounds, a look of horror and shock spread across his face. The look transformed into terror as he turned to see five hardened faces staring at him from behind five assault rifles, all leveled in his direction.

Abbas el Khalidi died the death of Zafar Mazouzi five times over.

THE PAIR OF F/A-18E Super Hornets screamed across the sky. Emblazoned across one of them was the symbol of the Pukin Dogs and stenciled letters that read C. Sturm, Lt.

Eighteen thousand feet beneath the fighters the ocean spread wide and deep blue. Carrie Sturm looked through the forward viewport of her strike fighter at the rapidly approaching Moroccan coast. While she was nervous as hell thinking about firing live weapons against the coasts of a supposed ally, Sturm had learned one thing and that was to follow orders.

No questions asked.

Secretly, Sturm was more than excited about the mission. While she hadn't been informed about the exact nature of the target she didn't doubt for a moment the veracity of Naval Intelligence. If they said the target was a hostile and threat to America and her allies, that was just fine and dandy.

Sturm already had the coordinates of the target area fed into her computer systems. When she was within ten miles she brought up the HUD display that communicated with the Raytheon AN/ASQ-228 targeting pod mounted beneath her aircraft. There wouldn't be any ground laser guiding for this one so she would have to get in close enough for her own target systems to get the job done. She would also have to remain to confirm target engagement and destruction.

The familiar display came into view and once she had

acquisition she keyed up her secure frequency transmitter that would communicate with Mendoza, as well as record everything she said. The big dogs would be listening to every word, according to Burdette, so Sturm made sure she enunciated every word perfectly.

"Storm Cloud to Viper."

"Viper copy."

"Storm Cloud to Viper, thirty seconds to target lock."

"Roger, Storm Cloud. I concur—thirty seconds to tone."

Thirty seconds took what seemed like a lifetime, each second on the chronometer ticking off. Sturm half expected to get an abort order but it never came. "Storm Cloud to Viper, I have tone."

"Viper copies, Storm Cloud. You call the ball."

"Storm Cloud, fox one!"

There was a hiss and pop, the only real sound to indicate the AGM-84H had left its underside dock. As soon as the targeting interface sounded that the weapon was released and on target, Sturm flipped, verified the firing solution for missile two and called up her wingman one more time.

"Storm Cloud to Viper, I have tone on number two."

"Viper copies, Storm Cloud, you call the ball."

"Storm Cloud...fox two!"

Again, the familiar pop and hiss as her second AGM-84H missile left the aircraft.

When she'd completed her delivery, her wingman took over and fired two more behind hers.

"It's away," Lieutenant Carrie Sturm whispered after muting her microphone. She thought of her family, her parents and brother, wondering if what she'd just done was really for their protection. Yeah. It was. She could feel it in her gut and she said, "This one's for you, family."

FROM THE BOAT, Phoenix Force watched as more than two million dollars' worth of air-to-surface missiles struck the cliff base and decimated the underwater complex. The Destex exploded in a fantastic, daytime glare of U.S. Navy might. Each missile weighed three-quarters of a ton and delivered nearly five hundred pounds of penetrating explosives. The resulting explosions were like music to the ears of the five Phoenix Force warriors as they sped from the cliffs at all the speed their craft could muster.

Hawkins turned to his comrades and said, "That was better than the Fourth of July fireworks."

James chuckled and said, "I thought so."

Encizo ran his hands along the boat as Manning powered it through the water. He actually looked as if he was admiring the thing and McCarter noticed it.

"I'm not sure I like that gleam in your eyes," the Briton said. "You have something mischievous on your mind, bloke. I just know it."

"Not really." Encizo proffered an enigmatic smile. "I was just thinking about how nice it would be to have a few fishing poles right now."

"Fishing poles?" James said.

"Yeah, you know. A little R and R."

"Getting caught fishing off the coast of Morocco after the Navy just pumped four missiles into their shoreline probably wouldn't buy us much goodwill," Manning said.

"Forget the fishing poles," Hawkins interjected. "We could roast hot dogs."

All eyes turned toward their friend questioningly.

"What?" he said. "That thing's going to burn for days."

Then they all looked at each other and burst into laughter.

"Home, James," McCarter finally told Manning.

Manning laid the point of a thumb to his chest and then said, "I'm Manning. *He's* James."

"Forget the hot dogs, too," McCarter said with a catty grin. "Which of you blokes is up for some Canadian bacon?"

* * * * *

TAKE 'EM FREE

2 action-packed novels plus a mystery bonus

NO RISK
NO OBLIGATION TO BUY